*To Sharon —
my lifelong love, no
2020*

ABOUT
MISS RUTH

Cheryle Coapstick

Several churches, missions, schools, and business entities in About Miss Ruth are historical and may still exist. They are used in a fictional way in this novel. Some historical figures are also mentioned, and they are also used in a fictional way. All other characters, except those based on certain family members, are entirely fictional and any resemblance to known persons, living or dead, is unintentional.

First paperback edition November 2021

Paperback: ISBN 978-1-7366706-9-9
eBook: ISBN 978-1-7366706-6-8

Cover design and interior formatting by Andy Towler
www.aplusscreative.com

Published by Biorka Books
chercoaps@gmail.com

For
Jo Hamilton

Who wanted to have a Miss Ruth
in her life and wanted to be a
Miss Ruth to others.

Acknowledgments

My deepest gratitude to Vicki Karlsson, Patty Huey, and Maureen Harlan, extraordinary women, incredible encouragers, and great editors. A special thank you to Doug Peterson for his careful corrections.

To the Members of My Mama's Mama Facebook Group: You have been supportive and enthused as you have taken this journey with me. You have inspired and strengthened me along the way. Thank you.

"Let your Dream Fade
and
your Destiny Shine."

—John Merritt

PROLOGUE
Texas, 1870

Robert saw her chipped nails and calluses, the hands of an old woman. She wasn't old but certainly worn out. Face, sun-chapped with furrowed lines etched deep as wagon ruts. Stoop-shouldered, burdened. Not yet thirty and hair as dull as chickweed, streaked with grey. He had done this to her; Emma, the only woman he had ever loved.

He had subjected her to this dusty, dried-up homestead. He turned away and headed to the run-down shed he called a barn.

Robert's father owned the largest ranch in the state of Texas and ran the most cattle. Robert had grown up with Emma, the foreman's pretty daughter, and thought her strong, unlike his mother, a delicate lady from the east.

His fearful gaze rested on his wife. Would she die young as his mother had? He shook his head, rubbed his chest, and stomped into the shed. His feelings followed. The new place would be better, not like these withered acres. For him. For her. He threw a bag of oats and some tools into the wagon.

Emma sat on the porch of the small makeshift cabin that overlooked her parched garden and stared at the dusty hill where the boys were buried.

"We need to leave, Emma."

"How can I abandon our children?"

Robert took her hands in his, "Emma, it's just their bodies in the ground. We have to go, make a better life for the one on the way."

He placed his hands on her belly. She covered them with her own and raised her tired eyes to his. "Have you prayed this through, Robert?"

"Of course." He turned and leaned against the porch railing. He had thought about it long and hard, which was practically the same thing.

"If it's what the Lord wants," she sighed.

"The land agent said there's a creek on this new property, lots of tall grass for cattle, and a town just a few miles away. He said the crops would practically grow themselves!"

"Couldn't we settle in the town, at least until the baby is toddling? You could open a haberdashery shop."

"The town isn't big enough for that. Besides, you know how I feel about being a shopkeeper."

"But Robert, you would make a fine tailor." She took his hand and lifted it to her lips. Long slender fingers more suited to a needle and thread or a piano. His long, lean body echoed his hands, and his face had the aristocratic lines of his mother's people. "If the town has a church, perhaps you could play for services."

Robert pulled his hand away, "There's no church."

"Is there a town, Robert?"

"There's an assay office, and a railroad line goes through. The agent said new people are arriving daily. You'll soon have neighbors." No need to mention the saloon, which was also a house of ill repute.

He tucked a stray hair behind her ear, "This new homestead will pay off. I might even buy more land and run cattle. I can be as good as, I mean better than...." His voice trailed off, but the unspoken bitterness toward his father hung in the air.

Robert wished they still had the big Conestoga, but he had traded it last year for the buckboard and the horse he now rode. He hitched the oxen to the wagon. "There's a few hours of daylight left. Best we start."

"We're not ready."

"Ready enough."

Emma ran into the house and stripped the bed. She gathered the cast iron pot of stew and the bowls she had set out for dinner. Everything else had been packed earlier in the day. He motioned for her to get into the wagon while he finished loading it.

"I haven't said goodbye."

"Hurry up, then." He fiddled with the harnesses.

"Will you come?" She grabbed his arm.

"I have to cage the chickens and find that old rooster."

"I know the boys are in heaven, but I want to pick the buttercups growing on their graves. I'll press them in my Bible."

He thought about the other flower pressed in the sacred book, a delicate prairie rose. Their little girl, stillborn on the way to this homestead. They'd buried her deep in an unmarked grave to keep her safe from wild animals.

He watched Emma climb up the knoll—three boys in five years. A rattlesnake bite took the first boy before he was two. Samuel, born a year after that, had only lived a few hours. His third son died of a fever before he was six months old.

He watched Emma kiss each little wooden cross, and it pierced his heart. He wedged the caged chickens into the tightly packed wagon and whistled for her.

Each step she took toward the wagon was one step farther from their boys. Robert swallowed the lump in his throat and stared at the buttercups in her hands.

A few days later, they came to some low-lying hills. According to Robert's map, the assay office and railroad were just over the next ridge, still in Texas, with bluebonnets covering the meadows.

He unhitched the oxen and hobbled them near the creek. They placidly munched grass as Emma made a fire, then took a bucket to the stream.

A fish jumped out of the water. "Look, Robert, dinner!"

He untied his horse from the back of the wagon. "I'm going to the land office to see exactly where our claim is. I'll be back before dark."

She waved to Robert, then hollered to the fish, "Perhaps I'll see you at breakfast."

Emma set the full bucket near the wagon then stretched, making more room for the baby. She rubbed her chest. *I should be rubbing my backside after bouncing on the buckboard for days.*

She started a fire and set the kettle to boil. A cup of tea and a short nap would do her a world of good. Just a little rest, then she would tend to dinner.

She doubled over before the tea was ready. The oxen grazed as if her ear-piercing scream was nothing more than dinner music. She prayed Robert would come soon, and the baby would not. She watched the sun go down. Exhausted, she slept.

Sometime after midnight, Robert crawled under the blanket.

Fresh pain pierced her with the dawn. She shook him awake and asked for water.

"Is there coffee?" he mumbled. His sour breath told her he had visited a saloon.

She grimaced and crawled out from their makeshift bed under the wagon, put wood on the coals, and stirred up the fire. Soon the coffee pot on the grate boiled. Still in pain, she handed him a cup.

He leaned against the wagon wheel, not meeting her eyes. "Something's wrong. I lost the land."

"Something's wrong. I almost lost the baby."

"I spent hours at the assay office. The land's gone."

"I spent hours in pain. It's too soon."

"What?"

"What?"

Robert noticed her tear-stained, pain-ravaged face. He paced beside the wagon, sat down, and stood up. Emma pressed her arms against her stomach as if she could prevent the baby's arrival.

The day passed slowly as they tried and failed to reach out to each other. Eyes darted toward each other, then away, never making contact. Mouths opened, intending to speak, then clamped shut.

At last, his stomach let him know they needed food. "Emma, eat something. If not for yourself, then for the baby." Robert patted her shoulder and stirred a pot of beans. "I'll fix this, Emma. You'll see."

"Did you get a refund?"

He looked away.

"They must return our money if they gave our parcel to someone else."

Robert would not meet her eyes.

"They never heard of your land agent, did they?"

Robert jumped up and paced again. "He seemed honest. The paperwork looked real." He pulled his neckerchief off, wiped his face, and looked at his wife. If only she would get angry. "I did it for you." Even he didn't believe it. He kicked the dirt and swore.

"Robert! Such language."

Robert shoved his hands in his pockets and turned away, surprised he had said the words aloud.

"Surely, there is no need to curse." She grabbed her stomach and moaned.

"Is the baby coming? You said it was too soon! This can't happen again! I won't lose another one!"

She raised stricken eyes to him, "I don't know how to stop it."

The color drained from his face, and he broke out in a sweat. He bolted for his horse. "I'll get help."

He was gone before she could beg him to stay. Emma crawled under the wagon and drew the blankets up to her chin. What little strength she had, she used to beg God not to take her baby.

"You camped on the creek by that stand of birch trees?" The bartender spit toward the corner, missed the brass spittoon, and brown tobacco juice ran down the unpainted plank wall.

"My wife needs help. The baby's coming. It's too soon."

"Well," the bartender stuffed another wad of tobacco in his cheek, "a mile farther down the creek, there's a meadow with a lone pine tree in the center. An old medicine woman lives there."

"Isn't there anyone else?" Robert asked.

He wiped the counter with a dirty rag. "All we got here are Soiled Doves, and you don't want their kind around a good woman like your wife. Besides, they only know one thing, and it ain't doctoring." He laughed. "White Owl's tribe left when the fever took the chief's son. I guess they didn't think she was so good at doctoring. Ain't nobody else." Tobacco juice collected in the corners of his mouth.

Shoulders slumped, heart heavy, Robert stumbled to his horse. He galloped past their campsite without stopping. Best he fetch the medicine woman quickly.

"Bring water, bark, yarrow," White Owl pointed toward the edge of the creek and a tree near them. Robert obeyed her as he had the last two days, although he had little confidence in her Indian ways. Still, Emma seemed grateful for her presence. Between White Owl's medicinal efforts and Emma's prayers, the baby had not yet come.

However, seeing Emma in pain and hearing her moans unnerved him. He paced, he swore, he went for long rides and often stopped at the saloon.

The evening of the third day, White Owl pushed him down by the fire and thrust a cup of coffee into his hands. She shook her finger in his face. "Woman need strong man. Chief."

"I'm her husband."

"Weak." White Owl spat near his boots.

He clamped his teeth together and didn't answer.

"Baby, come."

"When?"

"Begin now."

"It's still too soon."

"Baby not care."

"I'll send for my father."

He saw the confusion on White Owl's face. "He's the chief." Robert threw the dregs of his coffee into the fire. He hated to admit it, but his father always knew what to do. It angered him, and he let the tin cup fall into the dirt and saddled his horse.

Emma moaned, and White Owl knelt before her, then turned to Robert, "Go."

The horse, lathered and spent, nearly collapsed before Robert reached that sorry excuse for a town. He pounded on the railroad shack door and did not let up until the telegraph operator opened it.

"Can't you see the closed sign? I'm on my way home."

"I need to send a telegraph now."

"Come back in the morning."

"Start tapping," Robert growled.

The telegraph operator looked at the desperate man and charged him double. As they left the office, Robert flung the reins toward him, "Take care of my horse. I'll be by in the morning."

"I ain't no livery stable."

Robert laid his hand on his holster. "When you're finished, hitch him outside the saloon."

He squinted against the sun and fumbled for the reins. It took several attempts to loosen them, even more, to hoist himself into the saddle. It must be midafternoon. Where had he spent the night? On the barroom floor, most likely.

Robert's drunken thoughts settled into the ruts he had developed over the years – like a well-worn wagon track that seemed to know what direction to take without any help from him.

He jerked the horse's reins when he saw a bramble of dewberries. Maybe they would take the sourness out of his intoxicated belly, although they wouldn't help the torment of his drunken mind. As the juice ran down his chin, he thought of Emma's pies. Whenever he was tired or angry, she baked, and words of encouragement and tenderness came with every slice.

He cursed as he wiped his berry-stained hands on his thighs. A man must make his way in the world. Become something. He'd show her.

Robert kicked his horse harder than necessary and vowed to give Emma a better life. He shook his fist at the sky. *I'll show You, too.*

Two days later, a weathered man on a black horse rode into the little campsite. White Owl looked at him with wary eyes. "You Robert chief?" she asked.

"I'm his father," The tall silver-haired man replied, "The telegraph operator gave me directions. Where is he? How is Emma?"

"Baby come. Man gone."

"What do you mean, gone?"

White Owl pulled a folded piece of paper out of her medicine bag. "Leave talking paper."

My dear Emma,

I have sent a telegram to my father. He will take you to the ranch.

I've heard rumors that there's silver in the Colorado mountains. I'll make my fortune and give you the life you deserve. Take care of yourself and the little one. I love you.

Robert

John crumpled the paper and tossed it into the fire. Emma held out her hand to her father-in-law.

"I took the train. Major rode in the freight car." The horse snorted, and Emma smiled.

"Can you be moved?" John knelt by her side.

"Bless you, John, no. I've been in labor for almost four days." She moaned and panted as another pain gripped her. When it passed, she whispered, "White Owl says one of the women at the saloon has a couple of nanny goats. The baby will need milk."

"You must live."

"White Owl says I've lost too much blood, and I believe her." Her words came almost one at a time as she tried to talk around the pain. "I'm praying God lets me live long enough to deliver this baby."

He paled. "You will, and then I'll take you home."

"Bury me next to my parents." Her eyes pleaded with him.

He nodded and squeezed her hand, "Your father was the best foreman I ever had, and oh, your mama could cook." John's voice broke.

"The foreman's daughter. I always wondered if you thought Robert had married beneath him, though you never made me feel that way."

"It was the other way around. When I find him..."

"Let him go, John. The shepherd went after the sheep, the woman after her coin, but the Father waited for his prodigal." She bit her lips until the pain passed and then continued, "He'll come home when he's ready. Forgive him and love him."

"He doesn't deserve you."

She sank back on the blankets, her strength spent, then screamed. The contractions were constant now, and she had no power to push.

John held her hand and prayed through the night. White Owl spooned an herbal mixture into Emma's mouth to help with the pain.

Near dawn, the baby arrived. White Owl wrapped the infant in the blanket Emma had crocheted months before. She handed the wee thing to John.

John held the baby close to Emma. "She's beautiful, and she has your eyes."

"I wish I could be there when you put her in your sister's arms. Elvira will care for her."

"We'll love her like our own, but she'll always know she's your daughter. I hope she inherits your sweet spirit."

White Owl lifted Emma and put a spoonful of broth to her lips which dribbled out.

"Not long now," the Indian woman said. She squatted by the fire, her back to them.

"I hope she'll inherit Robert's sense of adventure. He's always willing to go."

"Run away, you mean."

"Try again. Start over." She took a breath. Her shoulders shook as she let it out slowly and gazed at the baby, "She'll have Elvira's feistiness, and you, John, will give her the capacity to live in God's presence."

"You must name her," John said.

"Rachel, after your dear wife, and Ruth, after my mama." Emma's chest barely rose; her breath came shallow and faint.

"Did you know Rachel means lamb of God, and I think Ruth means companion or friend?"

"Rachel Ruth will be both." Her grip on John's hand slackened as her eyes looked beyond the morning sky.

PART
ONE

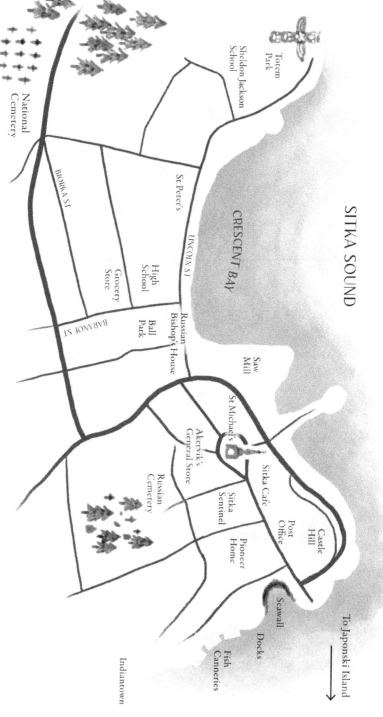

Map of Sitka, 1962

SITKA SOUND

CRESCENT BAY

To Japonski Island

Totem Park

Sheldon Jackson School

National Cemetery

BIORKA ST

St Peter's

LINCOLN ST

Grocery Store

High School

BARANOF ST

Ball Park

Russian Bishop's House

Saw Mill

St Michael's

Akervik's General Store

Russian Cemetery

Sitka Café

Sitka Sentinel

Pioneer Home

Post Office

Castle Hill

Seawall

Docks

Fish Canneries

Indiantown

ONE
Sitka, Alaska, 1962

Sam Mitchell Jr, the editor of the town's only newspaper, closed his eyes and leaned his head on the doorpost of the Sitka Café. In many ways, the Café had not changed since his childhood. Although Mick, the owner's son, had installed booths and table-top jukeboxes in the street-side dining area. His mother unplugged them several times a day and complained loudly whenever her customers played that horrible rock and roll. These few changes didn't register with Sam.

Same color paint on the walls, same oilcloth-covered tables. Same big round table in the backroom. The men who sat at that table had aged, some more than others, and a few had passed on.

The Café was what it always was, a mainstay in Sitka, a slice of his childhood. He saw it through the patina of the past.

Several days ago, Sam talked with Miss Ruth in Juneau and knew she planned to come back to Sitka soon; her mission in Nome was nearly complete. He blew out his breath and squared his shoulders.

Whatever had caused the accident, he did not believe Robert Nelson was at fault. Sam tapped his forehead on the doorpost several times, sniffed, and forced himself to open the door.

The warm smell of Agrefena's cooking, familiar and dear, welcomed him. He scanned the front dining area then gazed through the archway to the back room. The Café, always crowded and noisy, bustled.

Several years ago, Café owners Mike and Agrefena Evans sent their son, Mick, to college to study medicine. Unbeknownst to them, he took business and marketing courses instead. When his father died, Mick quit school and took over the financial side of the Café. Soon, he was behind the counter, coffee pot in hand.

The old-timers constantly razzed him, but Mick gave as good as he got, and soon folks had a hard time remembering he was not his father.

Today, vacationers spilled into town from a large ship anchored in Sitka Sound. The old men at the round table embellished their stories of the past—the Café's unofficial entertainment for the tourist trade.

Sam's heart pounded as he watched Mick deliver breakfasts to the overflow crowd in the front dining room. "What's wrong, Sam? You look like heck! Was the trial that grim?"

Sam shook his head, motioned Mick over, and explained. Mick took a step back and covered his mouth. His eyes darted to the kitchen door, "You sure?"

Sam nodded. Mick paled, then called his mother and whispered the news. She howled. All conversation stopped. Agrefena leaned on Mick as he led her to the center of the backroom. "I can make the announcement, Mom. You should go home."

The diminutive woman shoved him away and climbed on a chair. With tears streaming, she choked out the words, "Dear Miss Ruth and Robert Nelson fell out of the sky. He is alive. She is not." She fled to the kitchen.

Ivan leaned toward the others, "Miss Ruth, not fall."

"Feels like the sky itself is falling," Jake cradled his coffee mug and stared into the brown liquid.

"Rob's a great pilot. What happened?"

The diners slumped in their chairs. Food grew cold, and cigarettes burned themselves out. Heads bowed. Grief and silence settled on everyone except for a dozen tourists who wolfed their food, chatted about their vacations, and complained about Sitka's miserable weather.

"No respect," Ivan growled.

"Leave it alone, Ivan. They didn't know her," Ade said.

"Tourists, bah!"

"What are you talking about, old man?" A leather-jacketed teen, among the tourists, smoothed back hair that had flopped over his forehead.

"Respect," Ivan said.

"Be cool, man. It's not like a big jet plane crashed."

Ivan's chair fell to the floor as he bolted out of it. He shook his fist in the boy's face, "Evil boy." His speech descended into Russian curse words, which a few of the older Alaskans understood, and the tourists did not. All saw his rage.

Jake picked up the chair, and Ade guided a still cursing Ivan back to it.

Once again, the teen brushed his hand over the hair he had slathered with Brylcreem, "Ignorant old man."

"Paulie, be nice." His mother patted his arm.

Paul shrugged it off, straightened his leather jacket, and grabbed another piece of toast. "I'm cool."

Mick slid back the opening of the secret compartment and pulled out the ingredient. He held up the bottle. "Finish your coffee, folks. We'll drink a toast to Miss Ruth, straight up."

Paul laughed and said, "Don't you backwoods hicks know Prohibition was over a long time ago, before I was born, even."

The diners overlooked his rudeness and held their mugs high. "To Miss Ruth."

Ade put his mug to his mouth but couldn't swallow past the lump in his throat. Jake pretended his napkin fell to the floor then wiped his eyes with it as he bent to pick it up.

"To Miss Ruth," the teen stood and held up his mug in mock tribute. "That's all we've heard in this town. Miss Ruth this, and Miss Ruth that."

"Paulie, please." His mother, red-faced, looked at the local diners, who raised their eyebrows and stared back.

"Son," his father whispered.

"I'm only trying to figure out why everybody thinks that old lady was God's gift to Alaska."

"She was that," Ade said.

"I bet she was just a religious goody-goody." The boy tipped his chair back and glowered at the round table.

The men rose as one and stood in front of him. Across the table, Paul's father averted his eyes. His mother glanced at the men, picked up her coffee cup, set it down again, and chewed on the end of her thumb.

Paul scowled at his parents, then lifted his chin and tried to stare down the men surrounding him. Ivan, Jake, and Ade stared back. Stormy Durand and Mick joined them. Others at the Café moved in their direction, but Stormy, the retired Chief of Police, motioned them back to their seats.

He still commanded the people's respect. They obeyed but kept their eyes on the good-looking, arrogant, and disrespectful teen. The tourists' heads twisted back and forth from Paul to the locals as if they watched a tennis match.

"I'll take you on one at a time," Paul fisted his hands, and his veins bulged. "I'm not afraid," but his voice cracked, and his face reddened.

Agrefena raced out of the kitchen and pushed her way through the men. Eyes red and swollen, she stood in front of Paul and spoke over his head, "Thank you for visiting Alaska and my Café. Enjoy your breakfast. Young man, help me in the kitchen." She tugged on his arm.

Paul sneered and jerked away, "Look, lady, I didn't want to come on this trip, and I'm not your hired help."

Agrefena stood tall, all four feet, nine inches of her. "I said I need you."

It was only then that Paul and the others noticed the large butcher knife she wielded. Paul's father tried to stand, but a hand from Jake and Ade clamped on each of his shoulders restrained him.

Agrefena whispered in the father's ear, showed him the wooden spoon in her other hand, and winked. Understanding flickered in his eyes, and he nodded slightly.

"Go." Agrefena stabbed at the boy.

Paul's mother shrieked and kicked her husband under the table. She half rose, ready to protect her baby. Her husband grabbed her wrist and forced her to sit. She kicked him again.

Every few steps, Paul felt the prod of the weapon in his back and whimpered, "Mom, help me."

"Oh, Paulie."

Ade handed her his handkerchief.

Agrefena pushed the boy through the kitchen door, then

7

turned and raised the large wooden spoon above her head. Mick chuckled and held up the butcher knife.

Paul's mother continued to wipe her eyes, and his father blew out his breath and rubbed his chest. The tourists sat open-mouthed, and everyone listened to the sounds coming from the kitchen.

Crash!

"Pick it up!"

Pans smashed together.

"Mind me!"

Muffled cries came through the door. "Your mother must feel shame, despair; I don't know."

A yelp, then another.

"Do not disgrace your father."

A silence descended, so loud it hurt Paul's parents' ears. They sat stunned, frozen.

"Poor Paulie." His mother kicked her husband under the table again. "Go on!" she hissed and glanced toward the men at the round table. "Fix this."

"Excuse me, gentlemen, but I would like to apologize for my son."

"Psst. Don't apologize. Just make them rescue Paulie from that wild woman."

Ivan slammed his mug on the table. "No!"

"What?" Paul's mother and father cried in unison.

"What Ivan means to say is none of us will go against Agrefena," Stormy said.

"And your boy is old enough to apologize for himself," Jake added.

The man's shoulders slumped, "He never has."

A loud crash came from the kitchen. Agrefena yelled at the boy in several native languages.

8

"What? Speak English."

More yells and bangs.

"Please! Please!" the boy whimpered.

"My poor Paulie!"

Mick came around the counter and put his hand on the father's shoulder. "Your son has been alone in the kitchen with my mother for a while. I figure he's ready."

"Ready for what?" The father's eyes widened.

"Civilization," Ade said.

"She didn't hurt him, did she? He's such a sensitive boy," the mother wrung her hands.

Ade rolled his eyes, Jake choked on his coffee, and Ivan muttered his favorite curse.

Paul's mother scrunched the handkerchief, "Civilization, indeed. I knew we should've gone to Hawaii. I told you Alaska was too wild for my little boy."

This time the diners joined in the eye rolls. Most had finished their breakfast; none had left. All wanted to see the boy's condition once Agrefena had finished with him.

"They come," Ivan said.

Agrefena carried a large platter. The boy followed head down, shoulders slumped, and eyes red-rimmed. He brought small pots of butter and jam. She set the tray on the round table and said, "Paul has made this fry bread for you." She motioned to the teen.

"Excuse me, sirs." He swallowed, bit his lip, and swallowed again, "I, uh, sorry." His voice faded away. He set the jam and butter down, stepped back, and stared at his shoes.

"What are you apologizing for, son?" Ade asked.

The boy's head jerked up, and he wiped his greasy hair off his forehead. "Well, that is, I...."

"You want to say you're sorry for bad-mouthing Miss Ruth," Agrefena poked him with her wooden spoon.

"Insulting her," Jake added.

"And slandering someone who lived here for almost three-quarters of a century," Stormy shook his head.

"A friend to Natives and whites alike," someone yelled.

There were nods and affirmations about Miss Ruth throughout the Café. The boy's eyes darted about the room. "Yeah, that's it."

"You didn't know her," Mick said, "she wasn't a religious nut."

"But she knew Bozhe," Agrefena said.

"She shared Him with anyone interested," Jake added.

"And plenty of us who weren't," one of the diners at the back groused.

Sam caught his eye, and they shared a look.

"Shh," several others cautioned.

"She would have liked you, boy," Ade said.

Paul's head jerked up, and his eyes brightened but dimmed as his mother preened, "Everybody loves my Paulie."

"Miss Ruth would have found out everything about you," Jake said.

"Everything?" He glanced at his parents.

Jake slapped him on the back, "Miss Ruth knows everything, that is," he choked and wiped his eyes, "she knew everything about each of us."

"How'd she find out?" Paul asked.

"We told her," one of the Alaskans shouted.

"Despite ourselves, we always told her," Stormy Durand sighed and rubbed his red cheeks.

"Do you think she could have made me say stuff about myself," Paul whispered with another glance toward his parents.

"That's right, and she'd have helped you solve your problems."

"I don't have any . . ." Paul swallowed, scuffed his shoe on the worn wooden floor, and started again. "I mean, that would have been good."

"Shake, son." Jake held out his hand.

Paul rubbed his hand through his oily hair, then shook hands around the table but faltered when he came to Ivan, who sat with his arms folded across his chest.

"Sir?" Paul extended his hand.

Agrefena thumped Ivan with her wooden spoon. He peered at her, then stood. "I go to Olga, tell of Miss Ruth." He stood slowly, hanging onto the table for balance, then grabbed the cane he had hung on the back of his chair. He walked slowly and cautiously out of the Café.

Paul shoved his outstretched hand in his pocket, backed up, and slumped into his chair. He couldn't look at his parents. Agrefena brought them a small plate of fry bread. "Paul made this by himself." She patted the boy on his shoulder.

Paul's mother beamed. His father leaned back in his chair and closed his eyes, "I wonder if we could leave him here for a year or two."

He didn't realize he had spoken aloud until Agrefena leaned close and whispered, "Miss Ruth would say yes, so I say it also."

Now that the drama had subsided, the tour guide tried to hustle his little group out of the Café. They gathered themselves together and hoped for more drama as they slowly left. This would be a great story to tell when they got back home.

Mick poured another round, coffee this time, and the Alaskans quietly talked about Miss Ruth.

"What do you know for sure, Sam?" someone called.

"Alaska Air Rescue will do an investigation. There will be a death notice in this week's Sentinel. I'm working on the obituary. She'll be buried in Nome."

"Why Nome?"

"They don't have the facilities there to store the body. They've got to get it into the ground before the weather changes."

Agrefena, who had retired to her haven, burst through the kitchen door, her staccato voice issued orders. "She's been in Nome less than a year. This is her home. Sam, talk to the Fathers, the Episcopalian and the Russian, and that Lutheran Pastor as well. They will make an official request. Jake, call Alaska Air; we will take up a collection to pay for immediate transport," she choked on the words. "Ade, tell Ollyanna she and I will plan the funeral." She sank into the nearest chair.

The diners' sad applause covered her weeping. Paul's father reached for his wallet. After setting a generous donation in front of Jake, he told his wife and son they needed to catch up with their tour group.

"I want to stay here."

"Oh, Paulie." His mother grabbed her sweater and clutched her pocketbook as her husband pushed her toward the door.

Agrefena pulled the boy aside, "I talked with your father. You come back next summer and work for me. I will tell you stories of old Sitka."

Paul nodded, "Cool."

"I must get home before Ollyanna hears about Miss Ruth from

someone else," Ade nodded to the others as he reached for the money, "You know I'm always the treasurer."

Paul dropped a handful of change into Ade's hand, then ran out without a word.

Sam settled into an empty chair at the roundtable, "Well, guys?"

Stormy Durand shook his head and left, "Later."

Jake lifted red-rimmed eyes to Sam, "I need to get on the water."

"I thought you were retired. You said no more shore boats for you."

"I'll take my skiff to Silver Bay, where Miss Ruth and I fished," Jake stared through the Café's windows. Sitka Sound was calm today, peaceful.

Sam watched him shuffle out of the Café. *Why he's an old man.* In Sam's mind, the men at the round table were like Miss Ruth. Fixtures in this town, in his life. Their mortality shook Sam.

Sam sat mourning over his coffee, appetite gone. He listened to the other diners, set his mug down, none too gently, and rubbed his burning stomach. *Better slow down on the caffeine, Sammy Boy.* Like Jake, he needed to be alone. He spent the rest of the day hiking on Mt. Verstovia.

Sam had questions, and as always happened when he didn't find the answers quickly, it disturbed his sleep. He dreamt of his father, Miss Ruth, and Katharine Hepburn. Why her?

Sam woke early, skipped breakfast, and sauntered the sidewalks of Sitka. He stopped at the sea wall and gazed at the horizon.

"Get it together, Sammy Boy," he heard his father's voice, "there's a story out there. Go and get it."

"I wrote a great obituary, Dad. That's enough."

"It's not."

"I can't find the angle."

"It's right in front of you, son."

"The Department of Vital Statistics in Juneau has no record of her birth or a Social Security number, not even a driver's license. She's not listed in the census or on the payroll of the churches or missions she served."

Sam turned around, lit his cigar, and watched the people of Sitka go about their business. Most of them or their parents and even their grandparents had known Miss Ruth. He tossed his match into the gutter.

"That's the angle, Dad," he muttered to himself as he hurried to his office, "People gravitated toward Miss Ruth, and I want to know why? After all, she was just some kind of missionary lady, and nobody I know is particularly religious."

Nobody spoke to Sam as he made his way down Lincoln Street. Sitkans often saw Sam mutter to himself. They just assumed he was deep in a story, and usually, no one bothered him.

"What the heck does Katharine Hepburn have to do with it?" he asked himself. In Sam's world, religion and movie stars did not mix.

As he entered the office, Margaret Mary handed him several messages and story leads. Sam pushed Miss Ruth to the back of his mind and focused on his editorial duties. He was soon caught up in the town's current affairs, and Miss Ruth faded into the background.

TWO

Several of the town's churches held services. Each denomination tried to outdo the others in honoring the venerable old woman. Eulogies and speeches by dignitaries and notables. Flowers and banners everywhere. Songs sung by schoolchildren. The religious and not so religious came together to praise Miss Ruth and elevate themselves in the process.

The clergy argued over where she should be buried, finally settling on neutral territory, the City Cemetery. The Lutherans were angry; they had reserved a plot for Miss Ruth decades ago. The Orthodox were determined to place a Russian cross on her grave and a small fence around it. The Tlingits had carved a two-foot totem for her burial site. Other Natives brought a blanket to warm her soul and built a spirit house for the grave. The cemetery staff gave up. Rules were bent, if not completely broken. Miss Ruth's grave was covered with flowers and mementos of every kind. No one considered what the deceased would have wanted.

"Miss Ruth would hate all that nonsense," Agrefena grabbed the pot from Mick and sloshed boiling coffee into the men's mugs. "We planned a simple funeral."

"I don't know how it got away from you, Ma," he said.

"I blame all the preachers and church officials, even the governor's aides and legislators. She was our Miss Ruth, not those religious and political mucky-mucks." She handed Sam the cream, which he pushed away as usual. "What are you going to do about this, Sam?"

"Me?" Sam rubbed his burning stomach and wished he liked cream in his coffee.

"Yeah, Sam. What are you going to do?" Others in the Café added their outrage to Agrefena's.

Mick looked out the window and saw the crowd approaching the Café. "Ma, here come some of those mucky-mucks."

Agrefena stood in the doorway, knuckles white as she gripped the doorknob. "This reception is for locals only. Miss Ruth was ours."

"I'm from the governor's office. We've just come to pay our respects," the leader of the mucky-mucks stated and put his foot in the door.

The others nodded and said, "We heard the reception was being held here,"

"Sorry, gentleman, my dishwasher has the mumps. It's not good for men, real men, to be exposed." She gave them a long look.

They shuffled their feet, mumbled their condolences. Some still tried to enter, but Agrefena pushed the door closed an inch at a time. They were on the sidewalk before they knew it. The lock clicked.

"Ma, I'm your dishwasher. I don't have the mumps."

The old cook winked at her son. "I said my dishwater has lumps. Bad soap, I think."

There were grins around the room, and some lifted their mugs in a silent salute. Agrefena ignored them. "Now, Sam. What are you going to do about Miss Ruth?"

"What can I do? I wrote a long obituary, even added comments from some of you," Sam said.

"Don't print any of those mucky-muck speeches. They're only praising themselves," Jake said.

"I bet most of them didn't know the real her," Ade said.

"Do people expect me to devote a whole issue to her?" Sam muttered into his coffee.

"Yes. Good." Ivan said, "Is decided."

"Now, look, Ivan—"

"But not that drivel from the funeral," Jake said, "Let the other Alaska papers print that."

"Tell truth," Ivan said.

"When did she come to Alaska?" Mick wondered.

"I came in the 1920s to fish, and she was here," Ade said.

Despite his other pressing stories, Sam's curiosity was reignited, and his fingers tingled more than ever. "Was she born here?" he asked.

"I born here, see Miss Ruth all my days," Ivan said.

"Somebody in Alaska must know." Jake held up his mug, and Mick poured.

"You're a genius, my friend." Sam jammed his hat on his head, slapped Jake on the back, and hurried out of the Café.

"I the genius," Ivan muttered into his mustache.

Sam burst into the office. "Margaret Mary, get on the wire. Contact every newspaper and radio station in Alaska. I want everyone's story about Miss Ruth. I don't care if they heard someone who knew someone who thought Miss Ruth said something. They can write it down and send it to the Sentinel."

"You already printed a fine obituary. What more do you need to do?"

"The men at the Café want more, and I'm beginning to think they're right. Why does everyone hold her in such high esteem? It's not like many around here are religious, but they all seem to love Miss Ruth. It bothers me that I can't figure out why."

Margaret Mary shook her head. Once Sam fixated on an idea, there was no talking to him, "She was a nice old lady, a good Samaritan. Can't you leave it at that?"

"Most people might be a good Samaritan once in a while, but nobody makes it a way of life. It's not natural."

"You aren't going to let this go, are you."

"You know me too well, Margaret Mary. Now get on the wire."

"Yes, Boss."

Sam, balding but otherwise not bad looking for a man approaching his mid-forties, sat at the desk that once belonged to his father. He was getting a bit thick around the middle and knew he should be more active or deny himself Agrefena's fry bread. He blamed his limp for the inactivity and her for his expanding midsection. He sighed and reached for his ever-present coffee pot. *If I were taller, my weight wouldn't be a problem.*

He looked around the large room that housed the press, linotype machine, and a small smelter for melting the lead slugs. A tiny office in the back fleshed out the space. Sam used it to store rolls of newsprint.

His father, Sam Sr., the original owner of the paper, taught him that a real newsman remained in the middle of the chaos. Sam grew up amid that chaos and didn't know if he could think without it.

The linotype's clanking and clattering had ceased to penetrate his ears years ago. Without realizing it, Sam had learned to bellow over the machine.

"The 'sorry for your loss' and sympathy cards go right into the trash."

"That seems awfully harsh, I mean, she died and everything," Sarah said, one of the two teenagers he'd hired to deal with the responses about Miss Ruth.

He looked over at the skinny, dull-haired girl. She'd never get a story by trading on her looks. "Listen, kid. This is a newsroom, not a funeral home or a chapel. Toughen up."

Sarah ducked her head and let her hair fall across her face while her glasses slid down her nose. A tear escaped, but she ignored it. Sarah winced as she trashed the condolences. She separated the rest into categories: letters from businesses, churches, individuals, and her favorites, notes from school children.

"Mr. Mitchell?" She handed him a letter to the editor.

"I told you to call me Sam or Boss," Sam said, snatching the letter with the childish scrawl. "Mr. Mitchell makes me feel like my old man is leaning over my shoulder, correcting my grammar."

Sarah nodded. Sam waited. She gulped and whispered, "Okay, Boss."

"What?" he pointed to his ear and then the linotype.

"OKAY, BOSS"

Sam smiled, then laughed out loud as he read:

Dear Miss Ruth,

How are you? I am fine.
I am sorry you are dead.
If you get better, please write back.

Your friend,
Davey

"Why do you want me to print this one?"

"I thought about my mom. She'll shake her head and wonder out loud if it's in poor taste. Then she'll ask all her friends if they read it. They'll talk about it over their coffee."

Sam burst out laughing. "I like you, kid. Now find me something from somebody special. An old sourdough, Native elder, or lone trapper."

Sam poured himself another cup of coffee and looked out the window. The steeple of St. Michael the Archangel Church stood tall, and the church split Lincoln Street as it always had. *I wonder if the Russians planned it that way or if the streets changed when the Americans came.* He filed the question deep in his brain. He'd pull it out on a slow news week. Sitka history always made good filler.

He reread the letters he had chosen for the next issue of the Sentinel. They were heartfelt and honest, but he wanted more:

Office of The Governor:
Juneau, Alaska

I speak for all Alaskans when I say Alaska has had many pioneer women of valor, but none like Miss Ruth. She was indeed our Northern Light. We will miss her.

Governor Bill Egan.

Dear Sitka Sentinel,

My grandmother was a student at a government boarding school for Natives and was punished if she spoke Tlingit. She cried herself to sleep many a night, but quietly since crying was also forbidden. Miss Ruth often crept in and rocked her to sleep, singing, "Jesus, loves me." After many months, Miss Ruth asked her about Tlingit words. At first, my grandmother was afraid to respond. Eventually, she told her the Tlingit words to the song.

Soon Miss Ruth was fluent in Tlingit, which was no easy task. When discovered, Miss Ruth lost her job. To me, Miss Ruth is Tlingit. She is Raven.

Marie (Birdsong) Demidoff

Dear Editor:

Me and my old man was fisher folk. Came up from San Fran a couple of years after Alaska became an official territory, around ought fourteen, maybe fifteen. I know the Great War had begun over there. We had a contract to supply the cannery with as much salmon and herring as possible. We came for the season but stayed for the rest of our lives.

Once, my old man got ripped open by a gaff hook. I sewed him up, but it got infected. We put into Klawock on Prince of Wales Island and hoped we could get some help. Imagine my surprise to find a white woman there!

It were Miss Ruth. She opened his wound, drained it, packed it with some kind of moss, and put him in a tiny shack. The Natives kept a fire going. Miss Ruth wrapped hot rocks in seal skins and packed them around his body, and he sweats it out for the next three days. He had the prettiest scar and liked to show it off, too.

We asked about Miss Ruth in every village or port we stopped at for the next forty years. Everyone had a story about her, but we never saw her again.

My old man passed some years back, but he were convinced Miss Ruth was an angel sent to help us.

Mrs. Nels Bjorkson
English Bay

Dear Sitka Sentinel:

An upright white woman alone in Alaska was not a usual occurrence back in the day. Even though she wore long black dresses that covered her head to toe, Miss Ruth was a beauty, and occasionally some ne'er-do-wells were tempted and acted accordingly. If Miss Ruth could not stare you down and frost you with one of her icy looks, she had a sweet little derringer to help her.

In time, the men in the mining camps and fishing villages knew her by name and character and respected her. If the town had no doctor, she was the healer. If there was no dentist, she would pull your infected tooth. She would write a letter home for you, save your gold dust, help you recover from a hangover, always with a song, a smile, and a prayer.

When she first came to our mining camp, I thought she was just another cheechako out to make her fortune. That's the thing, Miss Ruth never charged for the help she gave. She said her Lord would take care of her, and I guess He did.

The rumor was her father left her a gold mine. I heard she was even kidnapped once by some crazy miner who had gone bust. He was going to make Miss Ruth marry him and get his hands on the gold.

If I remember correctly, that miner didn't live through the rescue attempt led by a young Irishman. I heard he followed her from village to village for years, protecting her.

To us sourdoughs, she was mother, sister, daughter, wife, and all the good women we left behind, rolled into one.

Sourdough Dan

To the Editor:

My husband followed his dream to homestead in Alaska. We started out in a little place north of Palmer in the Matanuska Valley.

I had four babies in five years. They all lived, thanks to Miss Ruth. I don't know how she knew when it was my time, but she was always there. She delivered them and stayed until I was back on my feet.

One winter, the darkness got to me, and I nearly went crazy. I was sick with cabin fever and so lonely with just my husband and babies. One day there was a noise outside, dogs barking, someone shouting.

Miss Ruth arrived by dogsled with books, a Bible, and newspapers. She stayed over four months, until spring breakup, in fact.

She taught me to look outside of myself to the God who created everything. She taught me about His Son, who would redeem me and save me from the blackness, who would love and care for me.

I genuinely believe I would not have survived that winter were it not for Miss Ruth.

Elaine Alexander

Matanuska Valley

Dear Sitka Sentinel:

I am a descendant of Changunak Antisarlook Andrewuk. You might have heard of her by the name Sinrock Mary. If not, surely you have heard of the woman they called Queen of the Reindeer. She became the owner of Alaska's largest reindeer herd. What many do not know is, this happened at a time when women were not allowed by law to own property.

Changunak was Inupiaq with some Russian ancestry, so navigating the white man's legal system was difficult. Miss Ruth helped her through the convoluted process of challenging the laws. It was quite a process and took a long time, but they won. Thank you, Miss Ruth.

Chris Andrews

Dear Editor:

I am an elder of the Yupik people. Long before laws and licenses and all that nonsense, Miss Ruth learned our traditional ways to treat sickness. She also taught us modern methods. She and I worked together and used the best of both worlds to bring health to many different Native peoples. We had a goal to make traditional medicine acceptable and legal. I am proud to say I was the first woman to be certified by the state of Alaska to practice traditional Indigenous medicine.

R P Blumefield

Dear Sam Mitchell, Jr:

My Grandmother was a great friend of Miss Ruth's. They had much in common. Oh, how I loved to sit around the dining table and listen to Gramma Cornelia Templeton Hatcher's stories.

Gramma Cornelia was an ardent Suffragette and temperance advocate with the Woman's Christian Temperance Union. She came to Alaska in 1909, where she met and married Grandpa Hatcher (Hatcher Pass was named for him).

Anyway, she and Miss Ruth lobbied the legislature for the women's right to vote. I am proud to say that was the first law passed by the new territorial government.

Our family is incredibly proud of that. We are not quite as proud of the work she and Miss Ruth did to get the Bone-Dry Law passed, although it did proceed and outlast the Eighteenth Amendment.

Alaska has many strong women. I am proud to have known both Gramma Hatcher and Miss Ruth.

Connie Herman

Dear Editor:

My Grandmother, Alberta Adams, is dictating this letter. She says she and Miss Ruth helped Elizabeth Peratrovich to integrate Sitka in the 1940s. They legally challenged the segregation policies of the territory and helped to pass the 1945 Anti-Discrimination Bill. My Grandmother is Inupiat and now lives at the Old Pioneers' Home. She loves having visitors and has many stories about Miss Ruth. Please visit her. I am sure it will be worth your while.

Tina Prescott

Dear Editor:

When Miss Ruth first came to our village, she was young. At the time, the Russian church did not allow other religions to preach or teach, especially our children. Miss Ruth was not Russian. She was not Native or Creole. She was the first white person most of us had ever seen.

As custom dictated, we gave her food and shelter, but we shunned her, as our priest ordered. We would not talk to her or look at her. She might be with us, but she was not of us.

She followed the women to the beach to dig clams and set fish traps. She was a good fish gutter, but we laughed as she tried to harvest herring eggs. She watched us and learned to do what we did.

She wanted to know our words and ways. Always, she wrote down what we said. I was a young child and had never seen a pencil or paper. The paper's marks fascinated me, and Miss Ruth began to teach me to read and write.

25

The priest did not mind having Miss Ruth in the village as long as she did not teach or preach about her God. I have to laugh. Miss Ruth sang and prayed. Out loud.

We children gathered around her. She hugged us and played with us while our mothers watched with pride.

Many years later, Miss Ruth returned to our village with Rev. Sheldon Jackson and his wife. He spoke of the Great Spirit and His beloved Son. Some were the same as our Native and Russian traditions, but the fact that this God wanted to know us and be with us and in us was a marvel. We were ready to accept this Jesus, not because of Rev. Jackson's words, but because of the prayers of Miss Ruth and the love she showed us.

Tikasuk Ivanoff
Chester Creek

"Here's a sympathy letter from a past president of the Sheldon Jackson school." Sarah waved the paper above her head.

"Keep digging. I need something unique."

She flinched at the editor's gruff voice. Chuck leaned across the table and spoke quietly. "Think of him like Perry White, the editor of the Daily Planet."

Sarah sniffed and straightened her shoulders.

"Do that, and you won't be afraid. Guaranteed." Chuck's lopsided grin turned Sarah's cheeks red. She grabbed a letter and held it in front of her face.

Chuck laughed and pulled another stack of letters from the box on the floor. His black hair and eyes hinted at his Native heritage, and his Slavic features showed Russian ancestry.

Chuck stared at the letter in his hand, focused, mute. Sam nudged the boy's chair with his foot. Nothing. The editor picked up his huge 1828 Webster's and let it drop. Chuck's head jerked up. "Huh?"

"What's so interesting, Chuck?"

"Boss, you ever heard of an old sourdough named Robert Merritt?"

"Nope."

"According to this letter, he was Miss Ruth's father."

"Sarah, have you come across the name Merritt?"

"No, Boss."

He motioned for Chuck to hand him the letter. After reading it, Sam folded it carefully and placed it under the scrimshaw paperweight on the corner of his desk. The ivory tusk came from a walrus his grandfather had killed decades ago. An old Native called Russian Joe taught him the art of scrimshaw. *File the thought, Sammy Boy, and concentrate on Miss Ruth.*

He shook himself, plopped down in his chair, and shuffled through the pile of papers. "What kind of newsman am I?" He grabbed the cigar from his mouth and threw it toward the wastebasket but missed. It lay behind the file cabinet, smoldering.

A minute later, he crawled behind the cabinet and reached for the cigar. *Can't think without the foul thing.* He chomped on it and glowered.

"Is something wrong, Boss? Can I get you a glass of water?"

Sam scowled; she better toughen up if she wants to be a real reporter, he thought for the second time.

"Boss?" Chuck raised his eyebrows toward the editor.

"There's no mention of a Robert Merritt in any of these letters," he waved the stack above his head. "How could she have lived here all these years, and no one knew her last name?"

"Did you check her birth certificate?" Chuck asked.

"She doesn't have one," Sam said.

"Not possible." The boy shook his head.

"It is," Sarah said.

"How?" Chuck asked.

"My grandmother was born at home and never got a birth certificate. Remember, Alaska didn't become an official territory until 1912, even though the Russians sold it nearly fifty years earlier. It's still difficult to get an accurate census in remote areas. Most old people don't care for a lot of paperwork."

Chuck stared across the table, "We have all the same classes at school, Sarah, and I've never heard you talk so much at one time."

Sarah blushed again and ducked her head. Sam looked at her with a hint of respect. "By golly, kid, you just might make a newspaperman after all. Follow up on that census thing. Give me a couple of story leads, a good angle, and we'll see. I might have to hire you as a stringer."

Sarah tucked her hair behind her ear and muttered to herself, "I'll be as brilliant as Lois Lane, and he won't call me kid anymore."

"What about me, Boss?" Chuck asked.

"I haven't heard any good ideas out of you," Sam turned back to the letter.

"But I just found Miss Ruth's last name."

"Maybe you did, and maybe you didn't." Sam, still irritated at himself for not realizing Miss Ruth had no last name, grabbed his hat, "Keep working, kids, and when you need a break, hustle over to the Café and ask Mick if you can approach the men at the round table. They all knew Miss Ruth."

Sam sat on the bench outside the Sentinel and waited. Sure enough, less than a minute later, he saw Chuck and Sarah rush out the door with their notebooks and pencils. Had he ever been that eager?

28

"In a hurry?" He grinned at the two teenage would-be reporters.

"Yes, Boss, but I still don't understand why you're interested in that old lady."

Sam pulled the cigar out of his mouth and threw it in the gutter. "Sometimes, Chuck, you just sense there's a story and follow it without knowing why."

"That doesn't seem very practical. Doesn't it lead you on a lot of wild goose chases?"

"It does, but every once in a while, you hit the jackpot."

"Okay, Boss. You're the boss." Chuck shook his head. He and Sarah had orders to scour the letters to the editor, which they had done all week. At least now they got to interview the old men at the Café.

"I'll be a better reporter than Lois Lane," Sarah said.

Sam laughed, and Sarah blushed when Chuck said, "Does that make me Clark Kent?" Chuck's eyes twinkled.

She ducked her head and mumbled, "Maybe."

Chuck had jogged ahead and didn't hear. Sarah clutched her notebook and hurried after him.

"Just remember, everything is on the record!" Sam yelled.

THREE

Sam crossed the road and, despite his limp, practically ran to the Pioneers' Home.

His nose twitched, and his fingers tingled the closer he came to the large cement building, home to many of Alaska's aged and infirm. His nose and especially his fingers always informed him when he had a good lead. He patted his vest pocket to ensure he had a fresh supply of his beloved cigars.

"I'm here to see..." Sam dug into his pocket and pulled out the letter. "Sean Connor."

The receptionist pointed to the large glass doors at the end of the room. "Outside, wheelchair, white beard." She didn't even look up from her reports. Sam shrugged and crossed the room.

He looked at each wrinkled face and wondered what their stories were. *Sammy Boy, imagine if you could crawl deep into their hearts and mine their stories.* He made a note to send Sarah and Chuck to do some preliminary interviewing.

He stepped outside and called, "Sean Connor."

The old man in the wheelchair turned, squinted, and growled. "I don't know you."

Sam grinned. *Nothing wrong with his hearing, and he says what he thinks. We're going to get along just fine.* "I'm from the Sitka Sentinel. You can call me Sam."

"Got my letter, did ya?"

"Yes, Mr. Connor and..."

"Just Connor."

"Connor, then, I'd like to ask you some questions about Robert Merritt."

"Who?"

"The Rev, I think you called him." Sam waved the letter.

Connor's old eyes twinkled. "Da called him the Rev. Everybody else called him Denver Dan, almost didn't remember his real name. He came to Alaska with me Da, don't remember when exactly."

Sam lowered himself into an uncomfortable wooden chair and prepared to spend the next couple of hours pulling whatever facts he could out of the old man.

"You still have a touch of the Irish in your voice, Connor, but mostly you sound like the old sourdough you are."

"Let's be straight, boy-o." Connor replied, "Me Da was the sourdough, came as an ignorant immigrant from Ireland, worked his way across America, and ended up in the silver mines of —" Connor scratched his head. His eyes clouded for a moment— "Colorado. When Da got too friendly with some dynamite, Robert Merritt sewed him back together. Preached the whole time, so Da called him the Rev. I have his account somewhere in my papers."

"I'd like to read those papers."

"Make no mistake, sonny. Denver Dan may have spent a lot of time preaching, but he was more about the gold than God. Least-ways that's what me Da said."

"And you know for a fact this Robert Merritt was Miss Ruth's father?"

"I could tell you the whole story, boyo, but I got me a power-ful itch." He pulled up his trouser leg to reveal a highly polished wooden leg.

Sam looked at the homemade leg and then at Connor. "Make that yourself? Good workmanship. Now about Robert Merritt."

"Got trapped in a mine on Chichagof during the war."

"I thought the government closed them."

The older man's eyes twinkled. "They did. But I wasn't looking for gold."

Sam threw him a questioning look.

"I found a skeleton and a pocket watch. Yessiree, I did."

"Robert Merritt? Miss Ruth's father?"

Conner ignored Sam's question. "This here is leg number three. I even got me a knee hinge. Want to hear the story?"

"I do, but not today."

"Then scratch right here." Connor sighed and pointed to a spot just below the hinge.

Sam grinned, reached over, and scratched. "About Merritt and those papers?"

Connor leaned back in his wheelchair and closed his eyes. After a minute or two, Sam began to gather his things. Connor opened one eye and said, "I ain't sleeping, getting it straight in my head."

The Irish pioneer, son of one of Alaska's early sourdoughs, reached into his vest pocket and pulled out an aged leather pouch with a patina soft and pliable as butter. Connor's fingers had that same buttery look. He proceeded to roll a cigarette.

Sam listened and tried to think of a way to gain access to Connor's papers.

FOUR

Johnny, the Bear Boy, paced outside the Sitka Sentinel and hoped the man would come out. Newspapermen knew if things were true, and Johnny needed to know. Others came and went, the canneries' afternoon whistles blew, and Johnny's stomach rumbled. He took a swig from the flask he carried in his back pocket.

He cleared his throat and spat on the sidewalk. The Tlingit women sitting there squealed and shook their fists. Johnny glared. His saliva was a good hand's breadth away from their beaded pouches and woven cedar hats. He ignored the curses that followed him into the office.

A Native boy and a white girl sat at a table in the middle of the room. They took papers from boxes on the floor and arranged them in piles on the table. Johnny's eyebrows merged when they took writing sticks and made scratchy noises on the papers.

In the back, an older woman faced a big black machine. She put little pieces of metal in a tray and then slid them into the machine. It clicked and clacked. Johnny put his fingers in his ears and looked for the man.

He saw the editor bent over his desk, writing furiously. Johnny cleared his throat, then coughed. A polite way to get someone's attention. No response.

He coughed louder. When the man at the desk did not move, Johnny pounded his fist on the counter. The man continued his work. Johnny, the Bear Boy, swept his arm across the counter, and the stacks of papers sitting there filled the air like gulls in flight.

"What are you doing?" Sam yelled.

Chuck, alerted by Sam's yell, crossed to the old Tlingit, who roared at Sam and waved his hands above his head.

Sam bellowed back, "Don't come in here and destroy every..." Sam took a breath and nodded at Chuck to pick up the scattered papers. "Crazy old coot, nothing but trouble," the editor muttered.

Chuck replaced everything on the counter and leaned over it as Johnny whimpered. Chuck held his breath. It was apparent Johnny had not yet had his spring bath.

"Johnny wants to know if Miss Ruth walked into the forest."

Sam stopped himself from yelling, 'dumb Siwash.' "Tell him there was an airplane accident. She died."

"When someone dies, we say they walked into the forest. Johnny wants to know if it's true. His speech is a mixture of Russian and Tlingit, hard to understand."

"Tell him what happened, then back to work. There are a lot of letters left in that box."

"Yes, Boss," Chuck spoke haltingly to the aging Native. Johnny slid to the floor, tears waterfalled down his cheeks. He pulled his knees up, wrapped his arms around them, and began a low keening.

Chuck turned to the editor. "Boss, I think you might want to head over to the Café. Johnny's going to be here for a while."

"See if you can get him to the bench outside."

"He won't budge."

"I can't see him, and the linotype covers his moaning." Sam focused on his typing and hoped the old man would just go away.

A shriek erupted from deep within Johnny the Bear Boy. Torrents of his anguish filled the room. The clacking stopped as Margaret Mary jerked around and glared, then lifted her eyes to the sign above the linotype, FIRST THE NEWS. Shutting out everything, she turned back to her beloved machine.

Sam grabbed his hat and raced out the door.

Sarah took her hands off her ears, "Is he okay? Should I get him a glass of water?"

"He's not really here. All the conversations he's ever had with Miss Ruth are marching through his mind. As he relives each one, he sees her turn and walk into the forest." Chuck pulled another letter from the box at his feet.

Sarah's glasses fogged, and she took them off. As she wiped them on the edge of her shirt, she peeked over the counter. "How sad."

Chuck shrugged his shoulders. "He'll remember all they shared, and that's not sad."

"But seeing her walk into the forest over and over must break his heart."

"It makes it real, and for someone like Johnny the Bear Boy, it needs to be real."

Sarah sniffed and sat on the floor next to Johnny. The shrieking gave her a vile headache, and the odors wafting from his unwashed body and clothes made her nauseous, but she stayed.

"Crazy white girl." Chuck tuned out the noise and went back to work.

Sam, irritated with himself as he left his office, didn't know the entire reason for it. *Come on, Sammy Boy, you're a reporter. Figure this out.* Several blocks later, he turned toward Crescent Bay. Despite his limp, a souvenir from boot camp twenty years before, he almost sprinted, trying to outpace his agitation.

Sam took off his shoes and socks and rolled up his trousers. The cold, damp sand between his toes eased the tension in his mind. How many big-city editors could do that?

A recent snowfall had dusted Mt. Verstovia, and a thick fog formed a belt of clouds around the mountain's mid-section. He pictured Mt. Edgecombe, its classic volcanic shape rising out of the sea on the southern end of Kruzof Island to the west of Sitka. Seagulls would soon head toward the docks on that side of town. The birds thought the seiners and trawlers went out solely to collect their dinner.

Sam scratched his jaw. Fact one: the Sitka he grew up in was segregated, but no longer. Sam ran his hand over his eyes. Fact two: Johnny the Bear Boy made him uncomfortable. Johnny couldn't speak English or think clearly. He was often unkempt and drunk, roaming the sidewalks of Sitka. Sam always crossed the street when he saw the old man coming. Most people did.

Sam walked the beach as far as St Peter's by the Sea, crossed the street, and entered the tiny stone church. He sat on one of its hard-wooden pews. The rich oiled wood reflected the light shining through stained-glass windows. Sand from his bare feet sprinkled the floor.

Sam didn't think the Carpenter from Nazareth would mind. After all, He was an outdoor kind of guy. That's what Sam remembered from those long-ago Sunday School stories. He looked up and saw a painting of one man caring for another: a Jew and a Samaritan, bitter enemies.

Was he like those who had passed by the wounded man? The thought stung, and Sam winced. Whites took care of whites, and Natives took care of their own. That's just the way it was.

As a boy, Sam attended the white school while the Native kids attended their own; separate churches, too. Even the theater had an invisible line down the middle. Each group barely acknowledged the existence of the other.

In the late forties and early fifties, signs in store windows saying NO INDIANS ALLOWED were removed. Alaska passed integration legislation while still a territory, decades before the United States. A memory tugged at Sam, but he couldn't catch it. Summer, ice cream, Miss Ruth, all the kids in town. He rubbed the back of his neck and filed the thought.

Was he prejudiced? He didn't think so. Perhaps indifferent. He'd never done anything to help the Natives retain or recover their rights. He hadn't done any investigative reporting about their issues. They lived their lives in Sitka, and he lived his.

Sam dusted his cold feet with his socks and put them on. As he tied his shoes, he thought: *You've taken your eyes off the person in your quest for the story. It's time to get back to basics and find the humanity in human interest stories, Sammy Boy. The Natives are just as human as you.*

His thoughts and feelings percolated. He felt himself change course. Perhaps he should come back to this little church on a Sunday to see if it would speak to him when it was full of people. *Okay, Sammy Boy, let's get moving. Time to interview the men at the Café.*

Years of habit influenced Sam, and he ducked behind a telephone pole when he saw Johnny the Bear Boy outside the eatery. Chuck emerged with a brown paper bag. Johnny reached in and soon had a hamburger in each hand. Chuck patted the old Tlingit on the shoulder and slipped him a few bills, then headed back to the Sentinel.

Sam jammed his hands in his pockets and hung his head. Chuck could teach him a thing or two about humanity. Sam was uncomfortable and didn't like it. He vowed to do better. His thoughts were heavy as he entered the Café.

"Hey, Sam, the usual?" Mick called.

"Just coffee, and ask the round table if I can have a bit of their time."

Mick slid the coffee mug down the counter like a beer down the bar. It landed in front of Sam without a drop being spilled. He grabbed it and gulped.

Mick returned to the counter, "They want to know the reason...."

"Just tried to give them time to grieve," Sam interrupted.

Mick smiled. "They told me to tell you you're about a week late. I left out the words that are not fit to print."

"So, they're ready to talk?"

"I think they need you to open the floodgates." Mick wiped the already clean counter.

Sam motioned for a refill, took it, and made his way through the crowded room. Mock indignation that he had not interviewed them earlier gave way to recommendations for running the paper and his life.

Sam listened in silence and nodded. A little trick he'd learned from his father. Soon their complaints dwindled. "About Miss Ruth," Sam said.

Ivan tapped his spoon on his mug. Sam wondered if the old man knew he tapped SOS in Morse code. "We say how make news better."

Sam signaled Mick for more coffee. The men talked, and Sam nodded.

"Now, about Miss Ruth."

"You send children. Insult us," Ivan said.

"Just a minute," Jake objected, "Sarah's my niece and top of her class."

Ivan ignored Jake, leaned across the table, and asked, "What you want of Miss Ruth?"

"What kind of woman was she? Why was she so important?" he pulled out his notebook and a stubby pencil.

"Don't play dumb, Sam. She was here your whole life," Jake said

"I was just a kid and concentrated on sports and girls. She was just an old lady in black wandering the streets."

"She was Miss Ruth, our Miss Ruth," Ade said.

"Come on, fellas, was she genuine, or a do-gooder and busybody like that tourist kid thought?"

Ivan slapped his fist on the table, "Do not disrespect. I think Miss Ruth Russian. "

Sam patted the old man on the arm, "Calm down, Ivan. I didn't mean anything by it. Tell me about Miss Ruth."

"She talk to number one daughter. Stop sneak with evil Sven Anderson. Keep girl on straight narrow."

Ade slapped Ivan on the back. "Don't forget, Sven Anderson is now your son-in-law and father to your three grandsons."

The men around the table laughed.

"Boys big trouble. Girls better."

The men groaned. Ivan had spent decades complaining about his daughters. Around this very table, in fact.

"Before Rob took over the business, Bob Nelson used to pilot Miss Ruth all over the Alexander Archipelago. Such a shame," Jake tapped his forehead, "he's not with it anymore."

"The nurses at the Pioneers' Home called me a couple of times when he was lucid, but by the time I got there," Sam shrugged.

"When Bill Wall's wife died, Miss Ruth organized everything, held them together for years. Have you talked to Our Firy?" Ade said.

"Got a letter from her. It told me nothing." So far, this was not going the way Sam planned. "Come on, fellows, give me something. Didn't any of you have a real encounter with Miss Ruth?"

Ade leaned forward, winked at the men, and asked, "Is there a statute of limitations on rum-running?"

"What?" Sam's fingers tingled, and he dropped his pencil, "You mean like, during Prohibition?"

FIVE

Sam licked the tip of his pencil. "Ade, the law can't go after you for what you did back then." Sam hoped it was true. He'd find out before he printed the story, of course.

"I heard it happened like this," Ade said.

Jake punched him on the shoulder, "It happened to you."

"Maybe it did, but I'm not admitting anything. Mike was short of the ingredient, and we were sick to death of running to the bathroom every time we had a bottle of bitters."

"Bitters?" Sam looked up with a question in his eyes.

"At Wellerton's drugstore, you could buy a quart of bitters; port wine with enough laxative added so Wellerton could sell it legally as medicine," Jake said.

"With toilet all night," Ivan shuddered at the memory.

"The fish weren't running, and we had too much time on our hands," Ade said, "and not enough money."

"Who's we?" said Sam.

"Don't ask."

Sam nodded.

"Where was I?" asked Ade.

"Thirsty," Ivan answered.

"Right. I knew a guy who ran cheap Canadian whiskey from Prince Rupert into Ketchikan and from there up to the mines on Chichagof. He said I'd make more money if I bypassed the guys in

Ketchikan and brought it all the way from Canada. He set me up to make a run.

"As I readied the boat, here comes Ollyanna, who thought I was going to Rupert for a boat part. She had brought Miss Ruth, who had a bad tooth. I offered to drop her in St. Petersburg or Wrangell, but the wife says Prince Rupert is the closest port for the kind of dental work she needs. Miss Ruth didn't look too good and spent the entire trip below deck.

"When we docked in Prince Rupert, I escorted her to the dentist's office, and we agreed to meet at the boat that evening. I bought the booze and cached it on board." Ade shivered and clamped his lips together until Jake nudged him under the table.

"Miss Ruth looked terrible and seemed worse. I figured her wooziness could work in my favor. I gave her two aspirin, and she lay down, not knowing the booze was under the bunk's false bottom. She dozed through the night and into the early morning hours when we left Prince Rupert.

"Late that evening, we came through the Biorka Channel at fifteen knots, but there was a revenue cutter in the lee of Little Biorka. I knew it spotted us and I swore. Miss Ruth stumbled topside. I told her I was nervous about running the boat after dark."

"Did she believe you?" Jake asked.

"She gave me the look."

"What look?" Sam asked.

"I tell," Ivan said.

"Not now, Ivan," Jake said.

"I hid among the rocks near Redoubt Bay." Ade drained his coffee and held the mug out for Mick to refill.

"What happened? Did the revenuers catch you?" Sam asked.

Ade shook his head. "Miss Ruth fetched a kerosene lantern. She said the Lord had given her a word."

"A word?"

Jake slapped Ade on the back. "Seems like the Lord gives Ollyanna a word whenever you argue with her."

"Then we do it the Lord's way, which is the same as Ollyanna's." Ade sighed.

"Get back to the story." Sam scribbled as fast as he could.

"We doused every light on board, then Miss Ruth climbed into the skiff and wedged the lighted lantern tight in the rocks."

"You should have done it," Mick said.

Ade threw the young man a dirty look, "Persuading Miss Ruth is like arguing with your mother."

Mick shivered and shut up.

"So, the cutter's captain thought the lantern was a light from your boat." Sam looked up from his notes.

"Yeah, we drifted away in the darkness. Her ruse was a success."

Sam's grin split his face, and his cigar fell into his coffee cup. He paid for everyone's breakfast and left in a hurry as usual. "Great job, Ade. This is good stuff."

"But, Sam, there's more to the story," Ade called after him.

On Saturdays, the mail plane usually arrived around six in the morning. Sam looked at his watch, just past eight. A little too early for the post to be fully sorted. Still, he grabbed his hat, gulped the rest of his coffee, and left the Sentinel. He yelled to Margaret Mary that he would have breakfast at the Café. She waved but didn't turn from the clacking of her beloved linotype.

Sam whistled as he walked, happy about Ade's boozy adventure. He had deciphered his notes and written the story. It was ready for the next issue.

"Sam! Sam!" Ivan ran down the sidewalk as fast as his short, arthritic legs could carry him. Red-faced. Cheeks puffed.

"Calm yourself, old man. You don't want to have a heart attack."

Ivan grabbed Sam by the arm. "Ade talk to children. Is too much."

"What?"

"Ade tell of revenuers."

"Chuck and Sarah are at the Café again?" Sam shook his head then laughed. He remembered his enthusiasm at their age, "It's okay. I've got the story."

"Ade say revenuer board boat."

"What? Why didn't he tell me?" Sam yelled.

Ivan patted the editor's arm, "You young. Always hurry. Leave too soon. Your Papa, he get story from rock or walrus. Is okay. One day you learn." Ivan continued to pull Sam toward the Café.

Sam stood mute in the middle of the sidewalk. Had he been insulted or encouraged?

"Why stop? Come."

"Tell you what," Sam said, "let's give the kids a chance. When we get to the Café, you sit at the round table and get Ade to repeat the story."

"What you say?"

"Have him start where he left off the other day. I'll sit in the front dining room where the kids can't see me. You know how everybody listens when you old sourdoughs tell your stories."

Ivan nodded. "That is sure. One time..."

"Not now, Ivan. We need to get to the Café pronto."

The short, stocky Russian ran, albeit slowly. His cane dangled uselessly from his wrist. The editor loped along, ignoring his limp.

Ivan slipped into his place. "What I miss?"

Chuck kept writing and did not look up.

"It's the most exciting story," Sarah said in a rush.

"Start from light in rock."

Ade sighed and reached for his coffee. "Ivan, I've already told the story more than I care to."

"Oh, please, Mr. Bunderson, I want to make sure everything I've written is accurate," Sarah said.

"You kids sure you're still on assignment from Sam?"

Chuck nodded, but Sarah hung her head, face flushed. Sam had not authorized this additional interview.

Ade finished his coffee and said, "Miss Ruth had wedged the lantern tight in the cleft of the rock. Even to me, it looked like the light from a boat. I raised the anchor, and we drifted away. The cutter's lights remained still. I knew every current and shoal, every outcropping of rocks and narrow channels, every shallow strait between Redoubt Bay and Sitka. The revenuers weren't going to get me."

"I'm so glad," Sarah whispered.

Chuck glared. "Shh."

"It was almost dawn when we approached Japonski. That's where the cutter caught us. The captain stomped aboard and demanded my papers; boat registration, license, fishing permit, port of call transcripts, everything." Ade grabbed his empty mug and held it high. Mick filled it.

"The captain opened his coat and showed a revolver tucked into his belt. 'I ought to blow you out of the water,'" he growled.

"His three deputies, armed with clubs and gaff hooks, looked more like wharf rats than lawmen."

"What did you do?" Sarah squealed.

"I kept my mouth shut and handed over my papers. Those goons searched topside but didn't find anything. I followed the captain below deck. I wanted to see his face when he saw Miss Ruth. Even in her early fifties, she was a beauty."

"Ma always said she looked twenty years younger than she was," Mick added.

"Olga say movie star," Ivan said.

"She could have been Katharine Hepburn's sister," Jake said.

Sam, hiding behind the half curtain that separated the two dining areas, drew in his breath. Katharine Hepburn!

Ade leaned back in his chair, "Miss Ruth rose from her bunk, hair all tousled. I knew what the captain thought as his head swiveled from her to me and back again."

"What?" Sarah asked.

Chuck rolled his eyes and looked at Sarah's Uncle Jake, who growled, "Never mind."

"Miss Ruth stood tall, but I knew she still didn't feel good, 'Who is this man, Ade? Why has he boarded your boat?' she said.

'Now look here, lady,' he waved his revolver at her.

'Careful there,' I said. 'Don't you know who this is?'

'For all I know, she could be the brains behind the whole operation.'

Miss Ruth stood and reached into her pocketbook.

'Watch it!' the captain yelled.

'I am only getting my papers, as you seem to have some sort of authority over us.'

'I am an agent for the United States Revenue Cutter Service.' He sucked in his gut and puffed out his chest.

"Miss Ruth held out her hand, 'I assume you have papers documenting such a claim. Your paperwork, sir.'

"The captain blustered and threatened, but Miss Ruth remained adamant. 'Captain, I will not show you my papers until you show me yours.'

"He took out his wallet and produced a card for her inspection."

Ade took out his handkerchief and wiped his eyes. His shoulders shook, "She dumped her pocketbook on the galley table, found a piece of paper, handed it to the captain, and said, 'Here is my dentist bill from Prince Rupert. Notice the date, and here is a receipt showing I paid this gentleman twenty dollars, round trip'.

Ade slapped his knee and laughed until his face flamed. "That was such a lie, and I knew I would burst out laughing if I caught her eye. She must have known it, too, because she kept her gaze firmly on the captain who brushed her paper aside and growled, 'Don't you know this boat is full of booze?'

"Miss Ruth adjusted her spectacles. 'Are you insinuating I am complicit in the importation of the demon rum? I assure you, I am the most temperate, law-abiding person in the territory. In fact, I worked with the legislature to pass our dry laws.'

'Look, lady, all I know is there's booze on this boat, and I aim to find it.'

"Miss Ruth's spine stiffened. She stood in front of the captain and gave him the look."

Sam stood in the doorway between the two dining areas, then eased himself into an empty chair at the round table, "Tell me about the look." Those around the table acknowledged him with a nod.

Ivan shuddered, "Eye on fire."

"Glacier ice," Jake corrected.

"It's like the wind from the Arctic blowing over you. One wrong move, and you shatter." Mick said.

"How would you know?" Agrefena said, coming out of the kitchen, "When did Miss Ruth give you such a look?" She grabbed her son by the ear and pulled him toward the kitchen.

"Ma, I'm a grown man. It was years ago."

He howled as she yanked on his ear. The diners stopped chewing and stared. Agrefena raised her eyes heavenward and murmured, "Thank you, Bozhe; Miss Ruth was there."

Mick escaped from his mother and poured Sam a cup of coffee.

"Anyway," Ade continued, "The captain sputtered and spewed as Miss Ruth raised her hands over her head. 'Perhaps you would like to search me, as well as the boat. After all, perhaps I am hiding bottles of the vile stuff under my skirts.'

'No, ma'am, that won't be necessary.'

"Then Miss Ruth ordered him to tear the boat apart but warned him she'd be watching, and as agents of the United States government, they needed to treat my property with respect. She told the captain to be sure his deputies replaced every can and jar in the galley."

Ade was beside himself again. "Here's the kicker, kids; Miss Ruth folded her hands in her lap and said, 'I alphabetized them.'"

"What?" Sam said.

"Huh?" Ivan hiccupped into his coffee.

"Miss Ruth had alphabetized all the food stores. Every last can, jar, and every single packet of spices. Then she told him she categorized all my fish hooks by size and bait, by species. The captain tried to stare her down but failed. He wrote all my information: license, registration numbers, custom's permit, in his little notebook, then said, 'I think we're done here.'

"When they left, Miss Ruth made soup for herself and sandwiches for me. She handed me one and said, 'I wonder why he thought you would engage in such a vile, illegal activity.'

"I shoved the sandwich in my mouth. I tell you, kids, I had that booze offloaded, and the money spent twenty times over by the time Miss Ruth stuffed everything back into her pocketbook.

"We pulled into Conway's dock, and I helped her up the galley stairs. She pulled a pair of gloves out of her coat pocket, turned to me, and said, 'Your wife Ollyanna is such a lovely woman, and your young son is getting to be more like you every day.' Miss Ruth shook her head, then raised it heavenward, 'Dreadful.'

"She looked at me for so long I had to ask, 'What, Miss Ruth?' She gave me a tiny smile and said, 'Not to worry, Bozhe knows.'"

Ade scratched his chin and shook his head.

"Then what, Mr. Bunderson?" Sarah asked.

"Miss Ruth left, and I ripped the mattress off the bunk and removed the false bottoms. I don't know if I cried because she saved me from the revenuers or because my booze was gone."

"What happened to the booze?" Sam asked.

"I never asked."

"What did your partner in crime do to you," Jake asked.

"Nothing," Ade muttered, hiding behind his coffee mug.

"No possible!" Ivan hollered.

Stormy Durand sat at the counter, his back to the men. He finished his coffee, turned on the stool, leaned his elbows on the bar, and drawled, "Relax, Ade, your miserable attempt to break the law was a failure. No booze, no crime. You can thank Miss Ruth."

Ade's head jerked up. He wondered what Stormy knew and when he knew it. Before he could figure out a subtle way to ask, he heard Jake say, "What happened to his partner? Why didn't he beat him up, smash his boat, something?"

"Where booze?" Ivan asked.

Stormy walked to the table, coffee mug in hand. "You want to know the rest of the story?"

Sam wrote furiously. "Never mind him. I want to know."

Stormy laughed, snatched the last of Ade's toast, and said, "Again, Miss Ruth."

Ade looked up, and the color drained from his face. "What did she do?"

Stormy leaned back in the chair and hooked his fingers in his belt. "Even though the pain medication made her thinking a little muddled, she saw you load the booze onto your boat. She stayed in the shadows until you were done."

"She never said a word," Ade moaned.

"After she wedged the lantern in the rock, she went below." Stormy finished his coffee and set the mug on the table.

Ade nodded, "I remember she wanted to sleep off the pain."

Stormy grinned, "Instead, she found the booze bottles and dropped them out of the porthole."

The men laughed, and Ade dropped his head in his hands. "The revenuers must have found them, but why didn't they arrest me?"

Stormy's eyes twinkled, "She pulled the corks out so the bottles would sink."

Ivan's shoulders shook, his belly bounced, and tears ran down his face. He laughed so hard he lost his breath.

"What's so funny?" Ade growled.

"Miss Ruth. Get fish drunk."

The others joined him and gave Ade a hard time, then Jake asked, "But what about Ade's partner in crime?"

Ade's head jerked up, "Stormy said no booze, no crime."

Stormy nodded and turned to Sam. "Miss Ruth gave me a name."

"How did she know?" Ade asked

Stormy shrugged, "Some things Miss Ruth didn't share."

"Come on, Stormy, what did you do then?" Sam rattled his papers.

Stormy enjoyed Ade's discomfort and Sam's eagerness. "The lout had only been in Sitka a few weeks. The law had chased him out of St. Petersburg and Wrangell."

"Could you talk a bit slower, please, Mr. Durrand. I mean, Chief." Sarah said.

Stormy, who had finished Ade's toast, snagged a piece of his bacon. Ade slid his plate toward the hungry chief. "Miss Ruth gave me a one-way steamship ticket to Seattle, and I encouraged this fellow to use it and never come back."

"How encourage?" Ivan asked.

"Never mind, Ivan. You don't want to know." Stormy laughed.

"For months, every shadow made me jump." Ade shook his fist at Stormy, "even now, I get nervous in dark alleys."

"Miss Ruth said it would do you good to be a bit fearful for a while."

Ade dropped his face into his hands. "A while?"

"It's been decades since Prohibition," Sam laughed.

"You say nothing?" Ivan stared at the lawman.

"Slipped my mind." Stormy grinned, and Mick refilled his coffee. "I retired this week, been thinking a lot about the old days."

"Old days good, even when bad," Ivan said.

Jake looked at his Café cronies, then at Bill Wall's unoccupied chair. They nodded. "Chief, on behalf of the roundtable, I'd like to offer you Bill's chair."

"It's been empty too long," Ade said, "it would be good to have someone that remembers the old days."

"He was a good man. I'm honored."

"That's a great story," Chuck looked at the editor. "I bet you'll want to print it."

"I do," Sam said, "You and Sarah each write an article, and we'll see what happens. And Ade, next time you tell me a story, tell the whole thing."

Chuck and Sarah eagerly gathered their things to head back to the Sentinel.

Ade cried, "Wait. You haven't heard the end of the story."

Sam's head jerked up, "You've got to be kidding me!"

"What's that?" Chuck said.

"There's more?" Sarah sat down.

With a grin that almost split his face, Ade slapped a twenty-dollar gold piece on the table. "After Miss Ruth left, I found this in the galley. I've been carrying it in my pocket ever since."

SIX

Sam started a fire to warm the cold house. His mother's ancient calico, Sadsack, sat on the back of the couch in front of the window. The last rays of the evening sun warmed the feline. He opened one eye, his look said, what took you so long?

Sam sighed, "I swear, Sad, you're worse than a nagging wife. Come, let's see what kind of supper Agrefena's made."

The cat didn't move except for two twitches of his tail, which told Sam dinner was acceptable, and Sad would like it delivered. Sam opened the cartons he had picked up at the Café. He spooned a generous amount into the cat's dish and set it on the windowsill.

Sam put his portion of stew and buttermilk biscuit on the side table. The aroma from the venison and root vegetables made his stomach growl. After the first spoonful, Sam sighed and patted his stomach. *Sammy Boy, if Agrefena weren't such a good cook, you'd probably be married by now.*

After eating, Sam lit a cigar and picked up the first of several papers he'd read tonight. Seattle Times, Anchorage Daily News, and the Vancouver Sun. They came by mail a few days late, so Sam forced himself to watch broadcast news. Television had come to Sitka several years ago. One station, broadcasting five hours a day. Other than the news, he didn't bother with it.

As he finished each newspaper, he let it fall to the floor. Sadsack shook his head, then turned and gazed out the window.

"I am not a slob," Sam said. The cat didn't respond.

He pulled his briefcase out from under the Times' sports section, anxious to see what Chuck and Sarah had done with the story about the revenuers. *Not bad for a couple of high-schoolers*, he thought as he scanned them.

It was the sheet of paper behind Chuck's article that stunned him. Sam chewed on his cigar, sat up straight, angled the page toward the light from the fireplace, and read:

ALASKA'S PREMIER PIONEER WOMAN SETS EXAMPLE FOR THE SOUTH

With racial tensions high in the Southern United States, it would behoove leaders from both sides of the issue to take a lesson from the peaceful and passive integration of Sitka, Alaska, in the late forties and early fifties.

In the 1920s, 30s, and even before, tensions rose as more people from the lower forty-eight settled in Southeastern Alaska. Many businesses posted signs saying, "No Indians or Dogs Allowed."

Decades ago, the federal government passed a law that Natives could become United States citizens if they rejected their culture and became civilized.

The Alaska Native Brotherhood agreed and pushed for total assimilation. Many elders preferred their traditional hunter/gatherer ways and rejected the government's offer and the ANB's pressure.

After Japan attacked Pearl Harbor and the Aleutians, many Natives, including our own Tlingits, enlisted in the various armed services. They were not separated or segregated like black Americans. They did their duty with diligence, honor, and respect. Some were even trained as Code Talkers, much like the Navajo.

Those Code Talkers and other Native military returned home after the war and were unwilling to accept separate places of education, worship, or entertainment. No longer content to live on the edges, these returning veterans refused their elders' advice to proceed cautiously.

The Alaska Native Brotherhood had changed its perspective. They no longer agreed with the United States government that Alaska's Natives needed to be— highly civilized and fully assimilated—to be good citizens.

Sam reread those pages. *Pretty impressive for a high school kid.* He continued with the article.

Raven elder Petrov Bravebird did not know the number of years he held in his aching bones. Although his wisdom was valued, he could not find the bridge over which the young veterans and the elders could travel together.

He walked the beaches of Crescent Harbor, Jamestown Bay, Silver Bay, Sandy Beach, and Halibut Point. He took his small cedar canoe and paddled the placid waters around Sitka for a week.

Petrov Bravebird knew something must be done, or cultures might clash in violence. Bravebird wanted his children to pledge their allegiance and loyalty to the United States of America. However, he wanted them and their children to know their clans' history, respect their art, and retain their language. He wanted them to participate in potlatch celebrations, listen to their ancient stories, eat some of their traditional food, and sing their songs. He wanted them to be Tlingit as well as American.

Raven is cunning. Raven is wise, even sly. Raven elder Petrov Bravebird knew Miss Ruth's powerful God could do this thing without violence. But Miss Ruth was at English Bay on the Kenai. The ANB must think it their idea to send for her.

Raven accomplished this.

Miss Ruth traveled to Juneau and met with Elizabeth Peratrovich of the Alaska Native Sisterhood. They visited Native mothers and discussed their children's futures.

Then Miss Ruth returned to Sitka with a plan. She borrowed Petrov's cedar canoe and paddled to Japonski Island and back. The Natives marveled as this older white woman expertly handled the craft. She was accompanied by a half dozen canoes on her second trip.

That evening at the meeting house in Indiantown, the clans gathered. Miss Ruth said. "Give me your children for the next ninety days."

Petrov Bravebird rose and spoke for a time in Tlingit and Haida. Miss Ruth understood most of the speech and was relieved when she saw heads began to nod. Somber. Stoic. Little hope in their eyes. The Natives shuffled out without speaking.

Miss Ruth took their children to Wellerton's Drugstore and Soda Fountain every day. She ordered ice cream cones and handed them out individually. If there were any white children in the store, she randomly called them over and gave them ice cream.

Soon lots of white kids showed up for their free treats. A mixed group of children crowded around Miss Ruth, shouting out their favorite flavors.

True, some old-timers made rude and crude comments. Miss Ruth handed an ice cream cone to each negative person and said, "People come in different flavors, just like ice cream. We are all delicious."

Mr. Wellerton was irritated but unwilling to confront her. Miss Ruth bought a lot of ice cream, and he soon changed his mind and quietly removed the NO INDIANS ALLOWED sign from his store window.

After several weeks swarming the drugstore, playing at the ball field, or on the beach, her little group had grown to include most of the white kids in town in addition to the Tlingit, Haida, and Tsimshian children.

Many mothers opened their doors in the morning and said, "Go, find Miss Ruth." Children whooped and hollered and ran to the beach or the ballpark. Both white and Native mothers closed their doors with a sigh and began their housework and laundry or, more often, put on the coffee and called the neighbors for a chat.

Miss Ruth umpired ballgames. She refereed Simon Says, Red Rover, and Mother May I. Petrov Bravebird supervised traditional Native games.

My older brothers were some of those children. Of course, they were just kids. All they knew was they were having fun with Miss Ruth.

They told me about a Flash Gordon movie Miss Ruth took them to. As the kids rushed through the theater doors, they dutifully arranged themselves into two groups: one white and one Native.

Miss Ruth sat on the invisible dividing line of the theater. She handed out bags of popcorn by calling their names in such a way that the kids crawled all over each other to get to her outstretched arm. She would not allow them to pass the bags. By the time she was done, whites, Natives, and Creoles sat together and watched the movie, imagining themselves in outer space.

Miss Ruth held a Sunday School class on the front lawn of the Pioneers' Home. Old Sunday School songs were sung in Tlingit and English. Soon, some of the old sourdoughs attended, then whole families.

Picnic baskets appeared as if they were loaves and fishes provided by the Lord himself, and afterward, strawberries and ice cream. No one knew for sure where Miss Ruth got all her foodstuffs that summer, although pots and pans banged at the Sitka Café and Agrefena's muttered complaints that Sitka had better integrate soon, or she'd go broke, led some to speculate.

Miss Ruth took her little group to every church's Daily Vacation Bible School. As they approached, they sang: "Jesus loves the little children, all the children of the world, red and yellow, black and white, all are precious in His sight."

If any minister, priest, or teacher objected, Miss Ruth raised her hands, and the children sang all the louder.

If there was a picnic or fishing derby, they were there. When the VFW and the American Legion played baseball, they were there. If there was a potlatch or salmon barbecue in Indiantown, they were there. The townspeople got used to seeing Miss Ruth and her flock of brown and white children.

With their parent's permission, Miss Ruth took eight Native children to the public school in September. The principal and the head of the school board met her on the sidewalk. When the white students saw their Native friends, they escorted them into the school as the adults watched.

Once the Native children were inside, Miss Ruth stretched out her hand. The president of the school board shook it and walked away, not quite sure what had happened.

Imagine how different things would look in the South if only there had been a Miss Ruth in Louisiana, Georgia, Alabama, or even Mississippi.

Alaska has lost a great woman. Our Northern Light.

Sam leaned back, cigar smoldering in the ashtray. He remembered that summer; one of the few times he had been aware of the old spinster missionary. He had asked his father if there was a story there and if he should check it out.

His dad had put his feet on his desk, clasped his hands behind his head, and said, "Miss Ruth's a wily old bird. I see what she's doing, and I'm glad. But Sammy Boy, if we report too much, too soon, we could change the outcome. We're going to leave it alone."

Sam shook his head and reread Chuck's article. Of course, there were some grammar issues, and technically Chuck hadn't used the sacrosanct journalistic pyramid, but Sam didn't care. He'd print the article as is and give Chuck a by-line.

"What do you think, Sadsack? Chuck's on his way to being a darn good reporter, and I don't mean, for a Native. Yep. A darn good reporter."

"Let me ask you something, Chuck."

"Yes, Boss?"

"What do you think of white people?"

Chuck set his pen down. "I don't understand the question."

Sam crossed his arms and sucked on his cigar in frustration.

"Sure, you do. White people, non-natives, how do you feel about them, about us?"

"Boss, I could tell you how I feel about you or what I think of Margaret Mary." He gestured to the older woman clacking away on the linotype. "If you pressed me, I could even tell you how I feel about Sarah."

Sam glanced at Sarah, who picked up a tattered copy of Strunk and White and stuck her nose in it. He wondered if Chuck knew Sarah thought of them as Lois Lane and Clark Kent.

Chuck continued. "You're all different. I don't think of you as a group."

"Chucky boy, you're very wise," Sam said around his cigar.

"For a Native?"

"For a wet behind the ears, 17-year-old kid who thinks he's going to set the journalistic world on fire."

"I'll take it."

SEVEN

For the past two weeks, Sam had taken Sean Connor a coffee and Agrefena's Indian fry bread before making his way to the Sentinel's office. Some days he didn't get to his typewriter until noon, but it was worth it. The old man seemed to know everything about Sitka's history. He was evasive about Miss Ruth.

The cagey older man gave sparse answers and hinted he knew more. Sam suspected Connor did it deliberately to ensure more visits. No matter, Sam was happy to spend his mornings with the old sourdough.

Sam gathered enough stories about Alaska's early days to fill a dozen books. More often than not, some of the other pioneers joined them, and the storytelling expanded, but they knew nothing of Miss Ruth's life before she came to Alaska. Connor hinted that he did, but he was stingy with the details.

Still, these sourdoughs were living history, and their stories would disappear with their deaths. Sam sent Chuck and Sarah to the Pioneers' Home a couple of afternoons a week. They filled notebook after notebook. Then Sam took samples of their work to their English and history teachers, who designed a project to capture and save these stories. Sam felt he had done his good deed of the decade.

This morning, Sam added a jar of wild blueberry jelly to the coffee and fry bread. He'd ask Connor about those papers again.

The receptionist was not at her desk, and Sam didn't wait to check in. He made his way to Connors's room. Empty. The old man wasn't in the dining room or on the terrace.

Sam gulped down Connor's now lukewarm coffee and threw the fry bread into the trash. He put the jar of jelly into his jacket pocket. Sam didn't like his thoughts and looked for a staff member to tell him where Connor was. The infirmary, maybe. Sam headed in that direction.

"Mr. Mitchell. Mr. Mitchell."

He turned and saw a nurse at the end of the hall. He hurried toward her and saw tears in her eyes.

"Connor?"

"He passed away sometime in the night. Just worn out, I think."

"He didn't have a family?"

"There's no mention of any in his records. You were his only visitor. You brought him joy."

"Thank you," Sam looked at the nurse's name tag, "Miss Blakely. What will they do with him?"

"He was a veteran, WWI. They'll bury him at the National Cemetery at the edge of town."

"When?"

"This afternoon. No need to wait." Her voice caught, and her eyes filled again, "No one will be there."

"I'll be there."

"Would you mind very much if I went with you? Connor was one of my favorites," Alice Blakely's lips formed a sad smile.

"Not at all," Sam looked at her for the first time. Short, dark-haired, a little plump, mid-thirties. Connor had mentioned the new nurse was feisty and true, even though a cheechako.

She put her hand on his arm to get his attention. "Mr. Mitchell, I don't quite know how to say this. It sounds so odd."

"Call me Sam, and say it like it is."

"All right, I will. Connor left you something."

The papers. Connor had come through.

"He wants you to have his wooden leg," Alice almost smiled. "He wants you to keep it in your office where you can see it every day and scratch it when he gets an itch."

Sam gulped, "Don't you think they should bury it with him?"

As they headed toward Connor's room, Alice stopped and pulled a piece of paper out of her pocket. "No, I don't. Connor dictated this a couple of weeks ago. He must have had a premonition," she scanned the letter, mumbling aloud.

"See," She pointed to the second paragraph—*I insist Sam keep my leg. Don't let him talk you out of it.* Alice looked at Sam and said in an official voice, "Mr. Sam Mitchell of the Sitka Sentinel, will you take Connor's leg?"

He nodded.

"And will you keep it in your office?"

Sam gulped and nodded again, "It will be a conversation piece, at least."

"Oh, I'm glad. I think Connor wanted you to remember him." Alice took the wooden leg out of the closet and handed it to Sam.

He wiped his eyes and cradled Connor's limb in his arms. "He was an interesting, cantankerous old guy. I am going to miss him, and I will remember him."

Alice handed him the rest of the letter and pointed, "Read this," she said.

'...and Alice, my dear, if you think Sam is a good man (as I do) and if he honors my request (which I think he will), then give him my box of papers. As for you, my dear, please visit my leg every week. But don't let Sam give you any of that awful frybread. Tell him you want Agrefena's French crullers instead.'

"I thought he loved that bread."

"Perhaps he didn't want to hurt your feelings."

"I expect you to honor his final wishes. You must visit his leg every week."

"I will." Alice reached over and patted Connor's leg.

"I'll have the coffee and crullers waiting."

Connor's leg leaned against the metal filing cabinet, where all could see it. Sarah wouldn't look at it. Chuck tended to scoot his chair close and read his stories aloud while scratching Connor's shin as if asking its opinion. On her way to the linotype every morning, Margret-Mary just waved and said, "How's the leg, Con?"

After a week or so, it seemed as if it had always been there.

The carved wooden box nestled among the papers on Sam's desk. It had been a week since Connor's funeral, and Sam couldn't bring himself to see what was inside. If the box didn't give him the answers he sought, he would be bitterly disappointed. Perhaps, that made him reticent.

He had watched Connor hold this same box many times, but the old man had never opened it. Now Sam turned it over and over. He looked toward Connor's leg. *You old coot. Why do I feel like you're still here giving me a hard time?*

The sun twinkled off the hinges; he opened the box. Sam sorted and separated the jumble of papers. He piled them into several groups—personal and business documents. There was a letter from J. Merritt to Robert Merritt in care of Jack Connor, saying he was bringing Rachel to Alaska, nothing personal about Miss Ruth.

Sam swiveled his chair toward the window where his percolator rested on the sill. More caffeine might help him think. The box, which had been sitting on the edge of his desk, crashed to the floor. It broke, and a false bottom jarred loose. Sam found a small journal written by John Merritt and two gold nuggets.

Sam thumbed through the journal. Who was John Merritt, and how was he related to Robert Merritt and Miss Ruth? Sam's stomach growled. He ignored it.

He wanted to explore the journal. His stomach growled again, and he imagined Sadsack's doing the same; he had promised his mother he'd be kind to her cat. He stubbed out his cigar, muttered curses about that wretched feline, stuffed the papers into his coat pocket, and left the broken box on his desk.

"Little late tonight, aren't you, Sam?" Agrefena said as she handed him his thermos and dinner. "Fried halibut cheeks. Sadsack will be pleased."

"That's all that matters." Sarcasm made his tongue thick.

"True." Agrefena looked at her lazy tabby sitting on the Café's window sill, watching the sun reflect on the waters of Sitka Sound. "At least, that's what they want us to think."

Sam read well into the night. He found several entries that mentioned Sean Connor as a teenager. The journal's pages were onion paper-thin, the writing faded and spidery. The diary ended with this John Merritt near death in the Hawaiian Islands, cared for by his granddaughter, Rachel Ruth. Was this girl Alaska's Miss Ruth?

Near midnight Sam yawned and rubbed the sandpaper out of his eyes. He couldn't fill in the blanks. *Go to sleep, Sammy Boy. It will be apparent in the morning.*

Sadsack endured Sam's snoring as long as he could, then rose, stretched, and headed to the living room, where he curled up on the braided rug in front of the fireplace. He stared into the dying embers until he too began to snore.

Sam tossed and turned as the journal's pages flipped through his mind. He rolled over. Moonlight struck the clock—two in the morning. Sam groaned, grabbed his extra pillow, cradled it, and fell back to sleep.

In his dreams, he saw a young woman in a faded calico dress climb into a hayloft.

PART
TWO

EIGHT
Bar M Ranch, Texas, 1888

Rachel Ruth Merritt took her Bible, journal, and fountain pen to the hayloft. Setting her thoughts on paper always revealed what was in her heart.

She stood in the opening where the hay was lifted into the loft. The ranch was situated in that undefined topography between two areas of Texas. Hilly and green to the east, semi-arid and dry to the west. The Bar M was the biggest ranch in the state. You couldn't ride across it in three days, although Rachel Ruth had tried. She much preferred the east when the bluebonnets covered the hills.

The sweet hay prickled through the saddle blanket as she plopped down on it. She lay back and laced her fingers behind her head. Surprised, she woke an hour later.

Swallows in the rafters twittered, and Rachel Ruth saw a mama bird bringing breakfast to her hungry babies. Their tiny peeps spoke of their eagerness.

"Your children don't know how blessed they are to have you to guide them through life." She tapped her fountain pen against her cheek and read what she had just written in her journal:

I have decided I am an odd duck with no duck pond in sight. Growing up on an isolated ranch in Texas with Aunt Elvira as a teacher and Grandpa John as a parent has not prepared me for life.

We didn't even have a town until the railroad came. I was so glad when we finally built a church and called a minister. The church became the center of our ranching community, religious and social.

Two years ago, the Millers arrived, and Mr. Miller opened a bank. I remember the first time they attended the church. The eight or ten unattached females took one look at the Miller's son, Thomas, and practically swooned. He was a slim, elegant gentleman from the East, impeccably dressed with gold cuff links and not a speck of dust on him. Feminine eyelashes batted, and handheld fans fluttered.

He seemed amused and flirted with each girl for a month or two, and then last year settled on me. Those girls don't speak to me anymore, although they had always been friendly.

I did nothing to attract Thomas. At least, I don't think I did. He seemed polite, charming, cordial. He said all the right things, but his tone was off.

Sometimes when he looked at me, I shivered, and it wasn't with excitement or anticipation, not totally. The glint in his eye was—calculating, as if he expected a particular response. I felt like he sized me up as if I were a prize heifer at the Texas State Fair.

He makes the long ride out to the ranch a couple of times a week even though I've told him repeatedly I have chores and work to do. He follows me and points out all the improvements and ideas he has for the ranch. I grit my teeth and don't answer. I've learned it's best not to argue with him.

Of course, Aunt Elvira is over the moon. Thomas gushes over her and constantly compliments her cooking and how she has done an excellent job raising me. She overrides any doubts I have about him until I begin to doubt myself. I cannot talk to her.

Rachel Ruth breathed in the warm summer day and prayed. *Lord, If I'm not careful, Aunt Elvira will have me married to Thomas before my eighteenth birthday, and that's only a few months away.*

Soft peeps came from the rafters. Rachel Ruth watched the baby birds as she tried to separate the confusing sensations running through her body and the musings of her heart. The thought of asking Grandpa John about any of these feminine notions made her blush, "Oh little birds, I wish I had a mama like you."

Rachel Ruth thought about how every Sunday, Aunt Elvira maneuvered her and Grandpa John into the same pew as the Millers.

Thomas, slender and several inches shorter than Rachel Ruth, scooted close. She glared. They shared a hymnal, and he touched her hand. When she snatched it away, he laughed. She couldn't concentrate on the sermon.

All the unmarried young women of the church and even those who didn't attend were jealous of Rachel Ruth. They considered Thomas her beau, as good as engaged. Rachel Ruth's protests fell on deaf ears.

Whenever Aunt Elvira invited the Millers to Sunday dinner, which was almost every week, Mrs. Miller twittered, "We couldn't possibly impose."

"Of course, we can, my dear," Mr. Miller always said, "That hired girl of yours can't cook a lick."

"It's no imposition. Send your hired girl out. I'll teach her to cook," Aunt Elvira replied.

Mrs. Miller sniffed and put her nose in the air. "I can teach my own hired girl to cook if need be."

"Really, dear?" her husband raised his eyebrows.

Thomas laughed, rubbed his pencil-thin excuse for a mustache, and complimented Aunt Elvira on her cooking while kissing his mother's cheek and whispering in her ear that he didn't mean it.

Rachel Ruth pushed her honey-streaked, coffee-colored hair out of her face, chewed on the end of her pen, and watched the barn swallows cuddle in the rafters. How uncomplicated their lives, if only she were like those little brown birds.

Confusing thoughts and feelings swirled through her in a maze of emotions. Her journal was full, and she needed more paper. She sighed and scrambled down the ladder. Aunt Elvira, so efficient, always had paper for ordering supplies and pretty stationery for writing her old school friend in Wyoming.

"Aunt Elvira? Auntie?" The empty kitchen said her aunt was probably gathering eggs or working in the garden.

There was no paper on the sideboard or in the Hoosier cabinet, so she looked in the parlor where her aunt's huge rolltop desk sat opposite the fireplace. Aunt Elvira did all the paperwork for the ranch. Surely there would be paper there—nothing in the first two drawers.

The bottom drawer wouldn't open. Rachel Ruth knelt and used two hands to pull. The drawer flew open, and papers scattered everywhere. Most seemed to be receipts and other documents, but she saw the stationary and a tablet of blank paper. She tore several pages from the tablet and stuffed the rest back in the drawer.

Aunt Elvira, her cheeks mottled, chins quivering, shrieked from the doorway, "What are you doing?"

"Looking for paper."

"Get away from my desk," the older woman strode across the room, arm outstretched. "Give me that!"

Rachel Ruth picked up the document lying face down at her feet. *Why was Aunt Elvira so agitated and angry? Her blue eyes darkened, and she practically shrieked at me. I've never seen her like that.*

Rachel Ruth quickly turned the document over. She gasped and raised wide eyes to her aunt. "This is about my father."

Elvira stopped mid-stride. "It's nothing."

"What do you mean nothing? This has my father's name on it." She scanned the document. "It was dated just a few years ago. Was he here? Did you see him?"

Elvira, a tall and sturdy woman, almost stout, nearly lost her balance. She grabbed the edge of the rolltop desk. "I said it's nothing!" She held out her hand, "Give it to me."

"No," Rachel Ruth slowly folded the paper and put it into her apron pocket while she stared into her Aunt's fearful eyes.

"Please, dear, nothing good will come of this. Can't you trust me?"

Rachel Ruth chewed on her bottom lip, backed up against the wall, reached into her pocket, and slowly pulled out the paper.

"I knew you'd do the sensible thing." Elvira extended her hand.

"How could you keep this from Grandpa and me?" Rachel Ruth clutched the paper and pushed past the grey-haired woman.

She found her grandfather at Jed's place. Any other time, Rachel Ruth would have played with the foreman's two young children. Not today.

She handed Grandpa John the document. He sucked in his breath, finished giving Jed his orders for the day, and led an angry Rachel Ruth back to the house.

"Let's not go in yet, dear. I want to understand this document before we talk to Elvira," he said.

They sat on the swing on the side porch while Grandpa John studied the paper. It was a bill of sale for a quarter share of the Erin-Go-Braugh, a silver mine in Colorado. The seller, Robert Merritt. The buyer, Elvira Merritt.

"What does it mean, Grandpa?"

"He's alive." Tears formed in John's eyes. He leaned back and stared at the clouds. His face, weathered by sun and wind, had a dark honey hue. His laugh lines today were merely crow's feet. He sucked in his breath and rubbed his chest.

"Can we go? Will you take me?"

John put his arms around his precious granddaughter and rested his chin on her head. "I must talk to Elvira, and then I must pray."

She nodded and said, "The date was three years ago, so we know he was alive then." The girl's face shined with a sad innocence, then confused anger as she asked, "Why didn't he stay? When I was born, I mean?"

John's eyes echoed her feelings, but he did not speak.

He took her into his arms when she sobbed, "Why didn't he want me?"

Rachel Ruth and her grandfather made do with bunkhouse victuals and waited for Elvira to come out of her self-imposed exile. On the third day, she was in the kitchen, as usual, making breakfast.

Rachel Ruth slid into her place, silent and avoiding her aunt's eyes. Her own were red and swollen. She folded her hands in her lap and sniffed.

John came in, poured himself a cup of coffee, and glanced at his sister. He laid the bill of sale on the table, never taking his eyes off of her.

"I can explain."

"Please do," John said.

Elvira placed a large bowl of oatmeal in the center of the table and sat down. "Several years ago, I got a letter from an old school friend in Cheyenne. Robert had written to her and asked her to contact me, find out how we felt about him."

"And?" John said.

"I didn't answer."

"Her second letter said Robert was on his way to collect his wife and child."

"Where was I?" John asked.

"Cattle drive." Elvira turned toward her niece and answered the unasked question. "You were staying with the minister and his wife, helping with their new baby."

Rachel Ruth gazed out the window. "What did he look like?"

"Like the photograph in the hallway only older." Elvira brushed their other questions aside.

"What did he say?" John insisted on knowing every detail of Elvira's conversation with Robert.

"The mine was a success, and he had enough to give Emma and the child the life they deserved, but they needed equipment to extract the deeper silver. I offered him the money if he would go away. He wanted to wait for you, John." Elvira buried her face in her apron. "I didn't want him to take Rachel Ruth away. I said his wife and baby died all those years ago."

Rachel Ruth continued to stare out the window while the tears fell down her face. Her father was alive. Joy. He left her when she was born. Rejection. He came back for her and her mother. Elation. He didn't know mama was dead. Sorrow. He didn't know he had a daughter. Misery. She faced her aunt and screamed, "You're a nasty, wicked woman!"

Elvira held her arms out, "Please."

Rachel Ruth turned back to the window, shoulders hunched; she leaned her head on the glass.

Elvira, pale and shaking addressed John, "Robert said there was no reason to stay unless you had forgiven him. I told him you blamed him for Emma's death."

John ran his hand through his thick, still dark hair. Looking older than his sixty-some years, he slumped in his chair, silent. They all looked at the document on the table.

"He wouldn't take my money unless I took a share of the mine. Hence, the bill of sale." Elvira whispered.

"He must have felt awful about my mama." Rachel Ruth wiped her eyes.

"I'm sorry." Elvira sighed.

"Are you?" John asked.

Elvira burst into tears and pushed her face in her apron again.

"You did a terrible thing," Rachel Ruth scrubbed at her own tears.

Elvira twisted the corner of her apron around her fingers, then wiped the tears on her face. "I did it for you. I did it for the family."

He's Grandpa's son!" Rachel Ruth howled, tears accumulated and spilled over again. "My father!" All the anger Rachel Ruth felt about her father's abandonment rose up and spilled out onto Elvira.

"Your very own nephew, Elvira," John said with a deep sadness.

Rachel Ruth turned away from her aunt, "Grandpa! He thinks

you hate him. We must go to him right away." Her thin voice rose an octave.

John took her hand; it was as cold as his own. "I'll go into town tomorrow and telegraph the...." He picked up the bill of sale, "the Erin-Go-Braugh mine."

"I'm so sorry," Elvira repeated.

"Don't talk to me." Rachel Ruth shot a look of venom at her Aunt.

NINE

The first telegraph went unanswered, so did the second.

Several days later, John led a brace of mules out of the barn and hitched them to the wagon. "Come on, Agnes," John struggled to get the bit into her mouth, "Cooperate. We need to get going before Elvira sees us. I don't need to explain myself to her."

Agnes clamped her teeth together and snorted. She raised her head and waited as Elvira ran out of the house. Elvira pulled an apple from her apron pocket, gave it to Agnes, then patted her on the nose.

"Where are you going, John?" She whispered, seeing the valise in the back of the wagon.

"I left a note on the sideboard."

She didn't hear over Elsie's bray, "Hush, Elsie. I didn't forget you." She pulled a carrot out of her other pocket and gave it to the impatient mule.

"I'm going to Colorado to find my son," John said.

"He didn't respond to either of your telegrams."

"All I said in the telegram was to come home," he explained. "I didn't tell him he had a daughter."

"He's made his life elsewhere."

"I must see him and tell him he's forgiven."

"Don't go, John. I'm sure Thomas is going to propose soon. I have Rachel Ruth's wedding all planned."

John leaned against Agnes's neck, sighed, and finished harnessing the mules. He turned and faced his sister. "Ellie. I have forgiven you, but I'm still angry. My son doesn't know he's a father."

She blushed and looked at her shoes, "I'm truly sorry, but what about the wedding?" She pulled at his arm. "Is it worth disrupting your granddaughter's life?"

"You've already done that. Besides, the girl does not plan to marry. She wants to serve the Lord."

"That's no life for her. She has too much love to give."

John pulled himself into the wagon and picked up the reins. "I'll not give my blessing to a marriage between Thomas and Rachel Ruth." He slapped the reins harder than he had intended. "I'll leave the wagon at the livery for Jed to pick up. Don't know when I'll be back."

The mules hee-hawed as they lunged and trotted out of the corral, "Don't complain to me. I wanted to get away without Elvira's knowing," John said to the mules. "This is your fault, Agnes."

The jenny turned and gave him a reproachful look.

"Don't give me that look, you no good...." He stopped himself. It wasn't the mule's fault he hadn't left before Elvira noticed.

"You see, Agnes, and you too, Elsie, I need to find my son, tell him about Rachel Ruth," John pulled his neckerchief free and wiped his eyes, "I don't like Thomas. Soft hands, weak chin. He sits in his father's bank and takes people's hard-earned money. I'm sure Rachel Ruth sees through him. She just doesn't have the experience to handle him."

The mules nodded and hee-hawed to the tune of the hymns John sang as they traveled the dusty road.

He ordered a load from the feed store and picked up several things at the mercantile for Mary, his foreman's wife. The storekeeper threw in some penny candy for Mary's children. After accomplishing everything on his list, John drove to the livery stable and gave Agnes and Elsie a sugar lump, cautioning them to mind their business until Jed came for them. Agnes snorted and stomped her feet as if to say, when do I not?

The whistle blew, and he boarded the evening train. John hoped for his granddaughter's sake that Robert would return with him. It was in the Lord's hands, and he trusted those hands. He sighed and reached into his vest for the small pocket Testament he always carried.

John Merritt looked at the three-story structure with multiple porches and the ornate trim and wished he had packed his suit. He swiped his dusty ranch pants with his hat and sighed.

He had left the mine early this morning. It was a dusty ride back into the city. He should have bathed and climbed into some clean clothes after registering at the hotel. Too late now.

The door opened slowly, and a tall skinny manservant sniffed and said, "Yes?" He looked John up and down and sniffed again. "Tradespeople use the back door."

John handed him the card he had received from the manager at the Erin-Go- Braugh mine. "I'm here to see Mrs. Jack Connor."

The servant took the card with the tips of his gloved fingers. He glanced at it and then at John, "Humph." he snorted.

There was a bustle behind him. "Who is it, Braxton?" asked a fine-looking woman in a fashionable dress.

"Nobody, I'm sure, Madam," he said under his breath. He started to close the door.

"John Merritt, ma'am," John said, holding the door open with his foot.

"Merritt," she exclaimed, "that's a name I've not heard in a long while."

John's heart sank, and he wondered if this was the end of his journey.

"Don't be rude, Braxton," she continued, "Let the gentleman in."

"Madam?"

She pushed past the butler, flung the door open wide, and said, "Welcome, Mr. Merritt. It's a pleasure to meet you, I think." She appraised him with frank eyes, but John couldn't tell what she thought.

She led him through to the parlor and threw staccato orders to the aggrieved butler. "Shoo, Braxton, make yourself useful. We will have tea in the parlor." She looked at John. "Better yet, coffee, make it strong and bring some of that butter cake I know you've been hoarding."

Braxton's face reddened, and he opened his mouth. Maureen Connor waved him away. "Go. Go. Go."

He shot John a look that would've put a lesser man on the floor. John looked at the retreating servant, then at Mrs. Connor, as she led them to the frilly, over-furnished parlor.

"He came with the house, poor man. He tries to civilize me every time I come outside."

"Come outside?"

"Sit," she commanded, indicating the dark leather chair next to the delicate brocade settee.

"That's Jack's chair," she added, "Braxton hates it. To tell you the truth, it's the only comfortable chair in the house."

John, who had settled into the soft leather, started to rise.

"No, no. You sit there. A man needs a real chair, and something tells me, Mr. Merritt, that you are a manly man."

John blushed, but Maureen Connor ignored it. "Now, where was I?"

"Outside?"

"Outside is what we call any place that's not Alaska." She laughed.

There was an Irish lilt and a Celtic cadence to her voice that John found delightful. This Mrs. Connor appeared to be about his daughter-in-law's age, that is, if Emma had lived. John pushed the thought away as the word Alaska resonated within him.

"Alaska? **Alaska?**"

She jumped up and ran to the hallway. "Braxton, hurry up with that coffee, and don't you be eating any of that cake behind my back."

"He wouldn't dare, ma'am, and if he did, I would have a word with him." Despite his anxiety about Robert and his confusion about Alaska, John chuckled.

She tossed her red curls, and her green eyes sparkled as she returned to the settee. "I think I'm going to like you, John Merritt, and I know my husband, Jack would." She gave him a long look and said in a quiet voice, "Robert has the look of you, around the eyes, especially."

John's face revealed his pain.

"Ah, it's like that, is it? I was thinking so," Maureen reached over and squeezed his hand. "Sit back and get comfortable, John Merritt. We have a lot to talk about."

"Just tell me he's alive!" John blurted.

"Oh, Mary and Joseph, did you think he was dead then? No, he and Jack are mining partners...."

"The manager at the Erin-Go-Braugh said he had never heard of Robert Merritt." John sighed and brushed his hand across his eyes. "I guess he saw a father's desperation, and that's why he gave me your card. Otherwise, I would have gone straight back to the ranch."

"He's a new man and wouldn't have known your son. Robert was always the quiet, almost silent partner. Jack has the personality and the public face of the company. We thought the Erin-Go-Braugh had played out. But there was silver down deep. Since Robert wanted to go north, we installed a manager at the Erin. We have several placer mines in the mountains above Juneau."

"I don't know where that is," John said.

"Juneau's in the southern part of Alaska. It backs up against British Columbia on the edge of the Alexander Archipelago," she laughed, "No polar bears or Eskimos, although we do have our very own glacier."

John nodded. He would stop at Denver's library, if they had one, and find a map. "So, you live in Colorado, and my son and your husband live in Alaska?"

"Heavens, no," she squealed, "Alaska's my home. I'm only outside a month or two every year. I check on the Erin-Go-Braugh and expand my son's horizons. He thinks Alaska is the world. To prove it's not, I'm taking him to Ireland."

"Ireland?" John scratched his head.

"I want him to know my people and what's left of Jack's family. I'll bring as many of them to Alaska as will come, now that the gold is flowing."

John shook his head. This woman talked of Alaska and Ireland as if they were as close as neighboring villages instead of half a world apart.

Maureen Connor caught herself. "Forgive me, Mr. Merritt. You've come to learn about your son, not my travel plans."

"I find your many topics of conversation entirely fascinating, ma'am," he said politely.

She threw back her head and laughed, most unladylike. There was some blarney behind the sound. It delighted him.

Braxton set the tray on the side table and picked up the silver coffee pot and a delicate china cup. "It's okay, Braxton, I'll pour," she said.

He retreated but hovered in the hallway.

As she handed John a bone china cup that held a thimbleful of coffee, she whispered, "One day I'm going to drink out of a tin mug and dress as I do in Alaska, and Braxton is going to have a heart attack."

"Ma'am?" John said as he swallowed the meager portion and held out his cup for more.

"Do you think I wear fancy dresses in the wilds of Alaska? I wear clothes similar to yours."

"Levi's?"

"My favorite," she tugged at the starchy collar of her high-necked velvet dress. "Levi's sound really good about now. I'm ready to rebel."

"Rebel against what," a freckled young man with the same fiery red hair and lilt to his voice entered from the hallway.

She patted the cushion next to her. "Come and meet Mr. Merritt, Sean."

The boy shook the rancher's callused hand, then turned his attention back to his mother. "Rebel against what, Ma?"

"Those highfalutin' Denver society dictators; *Sacred Thirty-Six* indeed."

"I'll join you, Ma," he pulled at his wool suit.

"No," his mother said, "When in Rome...."

"But Ma, you and Molly Brown talk all the time about staging an Irish uprising."

"Shush, Sean, Mr. Merritt doesn't want to hear our silly talk."

"On the contrary, ma'am," John said despite his impatience to know about his son, "I'd love to know what you're planning. Even I've heard of the matrons that rule Denver."

"I'll wear their frivolous styles and go to their endless bridge parties, which I loathe, but only because they do a lot of charity work, and I want to be involved in that while we're here. But I will say what needs to be said."

Sean reached for more cake, then turned his attention to John, "Excuse me, Mr. Merritt, are you a cowboy?"

"I have a ranch."

The boy peppered John with questions. How big was it? How many cows did he have? How did it feel to look from east to west and know all that you saw was yours?

John shook his head. "It belongs to the Good Lord who made it. I'm just his manager."

"I want to see Texas. Of course, Alaska is bigger, but we have mountains at our back and the sea before us. Sometimes I feel I could stretch out my arms and touch both at the same time. I've heard, in Texas, you can look east to west and see forever because no mountains get in the way."

"Sean, me boy-o, you're here to keep me on track. I must say you're doing a poor job," Maureen said.

Sean smiled at the old cowboy. "She's right, Mr. Merritt. She'll talk your ear off and never get to the point."

Maureen swatted her teenage son with her napkin. "Is that any way to talk to your dear, sainted mother?" She placed her hand dramatically over her heart and then winked at John.

"Ma, I'm almost a man. You can't treat me like a little boy."

"You will always be my little boy, even when you're an old man." She turned and winked at John, "Isn't that right, Mr. Merritt?"

Sean sighed and asked for the rest of the butter cake. At his mother's nod, he scooped it up and said, "Ma, it's time to tell the man what he wants to know."

"It might go a little faster, Mr. Merritt, if you asked me questions."

John leaned forward. Hands clasped, knuckles, white, "How did my son and your husband meet, and how did they end up in Alaska?"

He wanted to ask how Robert seemed emotionally and spiritually, but he couldn't find the words. The Irish mother turned to her son and said, "You know Robert Merritt, but not by that name."

The boy opened his mouth, still full of butter cake. His mother closed it with her fingertips. John's eyebrows nearly disappeared under his hairline, but he said nothing.

"I'll be trusting you not to ask any questions until Mr. Merritt has finished asking his," Maureen said.

The boy frowned but nodded.

TEN

"My Jack worked on the railroad many miles from here. There were rumors of silver in the Colorado mountains, and many a man ran off in the night. Jack dreamed of striking the mother lode as much as the next man, but he wasn't willing to leave his hard-earned wages behind. The railroad didn't pay until the job was complete, and Jack had been working for them for nearly a year."

John sat back and hoped Maureen would soon get to the point. She was a good storyteller, and from the look of rapt attention on her son's face, he had not heard this before.

"As you can imagine, the railroad became extremely short-handed. The foreman took over demolition when the dynamite-man left. Is that what they call the man that blows things up?"

John didn't think so but nodded anyway. He didn't want her distracted.

"Jack didn't think the foreman knew one end of a stick of dynamite from the other. More coffee?" She asked, holding up the pot.

"Ma!" Sean yelled, "What happened next?"

"I don't like the next part of the story." She set the coffee pot on its silver tray and pulled a handkerchief from her pocket. "There was an explosion, and everyone except your father died; even so, he was seriously injured. Robert Merritt rode into camp that evening, looking to earn a stake. He found your father almost gone. My, but that man had some serious sewing skills. Jack's scars are practically invisible."

"His mother insisted he learn even though Robert considered it girly," John said. "I must say it came in handy when the stock or even the wranglers were injured."

"I'm grateful to her; it saved Jack's life. He could have been a surgeon." Maureen continued her story, "They lived on the food-stuffs from the cookhouse, and when Jack was able to travel, they found a wee bit of dynamite and blew open the office's safe. Jack was determined to leave with his wages, but they decided to take all the money, along with shovels, picks, whatever they thought would be useful for prospecting."

She saw the look on her son's face. "Don't worry, me boy-o, once the mine began to show silver, they paid back all the money, plus the cost of the tools and the food."

"But still," said Sean, "didn't they get in trouble or arrested or something?"

"It was done anonymously through a lawyer, and you don't need to be speaking of it. Although it is a good story," she grinned, "and the rest, as they say, is history."

"What about Alaska?" John asked.

"After several years, Robert wanted to pull up stakes and move on, but Jack was convinced there was more silver, deeper in the Erin. They just needed extra capital for some costly extraction equipment, and Robert said he knew someone."

John gave a slight nod, his lips tight. Maureen reached over and laid her hand on his arm. "He returned a broken man."

"Did Robert get the money, Ma?"

"From his aunt. Robert gave it to your father then went on a drinking spree worthy of an Irishman. We couldn't stop him from going into the mine in that condition. It seemed he had nothing to live for."

"He thought his wife and child were alive at the ranch," John said.

"I didn't know he was married, much less a father."

John wiped his hand across his eyes. "His wife died in child-birth, but his daughter lived."

"Then why..."

"He was told they were both dead and that I never wanted to see him again." John's eyes glistened with tears.

Maureen let hers fall freely and pulled her son close. He squirmed.

"There were reasons Robert felt the way he did," John said, looking down at his hands. They trembled. He met Maureen's eyes, green as lush prairie grass. "And ma'am, my son has a right to know he has a daughter. She would go to the ends of the earth to meet him, even Alaska."

Maureen nodded. "When Robert heard rumors of gold in Alaska, he convinced us to go with him. We tried to keep the drink away. But it was Sean here who changed him."

"How's that?" John asked.

Sean sat open-mouthed.

"Before our cabin was built, we lived in a tent, and I cooked over an open fire. Sean was playing with a small wooden horse and bumped Robert, who held the coffee pot. It went flying, and when the hot coffee scalded Robert, he threw the toy into the campfire. Sean lunged after it and fell into the flames. Robert pulled him out. The poor man sobbed through the night and never touched a drop of drink again."

"I don't remember," Sean said.

"That's how you got the scars on the back of your legs."

"I knew I'd had an accident when I was little, but I never heard the whole story."

John told them about Robert's marriage to the foreman's daughter and their attempts at homesteading. How John had offered to stake them, give them a start, but Robert refused. Robert said he was going to be a vast land-holder. Important. Successful. Instead, his efforts failed, and their first-born daughter and three sons had all died. John fell silent, lost in the past and what might have been.

"Sean, go bother Braxton for a while," Maureen said.

"I want to know what Mr. Merritt's going to do."

"It's not your business. Go." She gave him that look that mothers do. Sean stood and shook hands with John, "Goodbye, Mr. Merritt."

At the doorway, he turned and said, "You will love Alaska, sir, and so will your granddaughter."

"Sean!"

"I'm going. I'm going."

Maureen leaned forward and spoke quietly to John, then yelled, "So help me, Sean, if you're in the hallway, I'll make you do all of Braxton's chores."

"I'm gone!" came the laughing reply.

Maureen picked at the stiff pleats of her full-skirted dress then said, "I'm a plain-spoken woman, John, but I'll not share my thoughts without your permission."

"You have it, of course."

She tilted her head, and her red curls caught the light from the sun streaming through the open window. "You might not want to hear what I have to say."

"I'll listen." The grim-faced cowboy settled himself in the soft leather and prepared himself to hear the worst.

Maureen leaned forward. She clasped and unclasped her hands. John put his own large hand over hers. "Just talk, Maureen. Tell me about my son."

"He seemed to be a lost soul. Now I think he was looking for something to replace his dead family."

John shuddered and squeezed his eyes, feeling his son's pain.

"Your son was always ready to move on to the next big scheme or enterprise, the next big deal. He was a seeker but didn't know what he was looking for. He had an instinct for finding the silver and gold but had no interest in the day-to-day operations of running the company. Jack did all of that."

"I see," John said.

"Jack and I became involved with the Rev. Sheldon Jackson, a minister and government agent who traveled throughout the southeast islands, establishing schools, some funded by the government, some by churches. Whenever he was in Juneau, he told the most interesting stories of his travels."

"I suppose Robert wanted to travel with him."

Maureen nodded and picked up the coffee pot once more. It was empty, so she set it down and continued her story. "When Robert heard the Rev. Jackson was compiling a dictionary of Tlingit, Haida, and other Native words, he was excited. It seems your son has an ear for languages. He picked up Russian words almost instantly. Most of the Natives speak it."

"He learned French and Italian from his mother and Cherokee from old Tobacco Joe. He always had an affinity for languages, but I can't imagine...."

"I suspect it was more the idea of being on the move. I suppose seeing our family, especially young Sean, reminded him of all he had lost."

John rubbed his hand over his chest. His heart ached. "I confess we never understood each other. The ranch was enough for me. I think Robert felt like he needed to compete, be more important. Sometimes I think he believed he needed to earn my love."

"Perhaps." Maureen used the the handkercheif again and dabbed her eyes.

"So, he's traveling with this preacher?"

"He did one excursion throughout the southeast with the Jackson party, but Robert wanted to concentrate on the languages, not the schools, so went off on his own. We haven't seen or heard from him in nearly a year."

"What?"

John closed his eyes and breathed a prayer for his only son. Maureen rested her hand on his shoulder.

"I pray he is alright. Mr. Merritt, Alaska is not as civilized as it will be one day. As I said before, your son goes by a different name."

"But why?"

She patted his knee. "Many Alaskans do. Some want to leave behind a painful past. Others are running from the law, most from themselves." She smoothed the folds of her dress. "I hope you'll take my advice."

"Yes, ma'am."

"Maureen."

"Maureen, ma'am."

Maureen picked up the china cup. "Jack and Robert are wealthy men."

"I have no interest in my son's gold, I can assure you."

"I didn't think you did, but others will. And they might use your granddaughter. After all, she will be his heir."

John thought of Thomas and his schemes, although this sounded worse. "How does Jack protect his son?"

She reached into the pocket of her fancy Denver dress and pulled out a small derringer.

John's eyebrows rose. "How's your marksmanship?"

"Good. Better with a rifle. I've killed deer, and once I shot a bear. Jack had to finish him off. In Alaska, I strap on a revolver whenever I go out. Sean is almost as good with guns as I am. And Jack surrounds us with bodyguards."

John smiled, "I assume Braxton isn't one of them."

Maureen inclined her head and looked at him through her lashes.

"You're kidding." John almost snorted his coffee through his nose.

"Shhhh." she grinned, "he's a Pinkerton man. He has great fun playing the snooty butler, but I trust him with my life and, more importantly, with my son's."

"I'm glad you're protected, but I'm sad that Robert changed his name. What does he go by?"

"Denver Dan."

"I knew it!" A shriek from the hallway startled them.

"Sean, get in here!" His mother yelled. Her eyes apologized to John.

"Sorry, Ma."

"You need to apologize to Mr. Merritt."

John gave the boy a long look. "Can you keep this information private, especially if my granddaughter and I come to Alaska?"

"Yes, sir." The boy extended his hand.

"When a man in the West gives his word and his hand, it's a serious thing. Sacred."

Sean stood tall. "On my honor, of all that's good in Alaska, sir."

"He can't make a vow any stronger than that, John. Alaska holds his heart."

John nodded and shook the boy's hand.

Sean turned to his mother. "Ma, I'm a much better shot than you."

As Maureen was about to respond, John hurriedly said, "Ma'am... Maureen, thank you for taking the time to see me." He reached for his hat.

"Oh, you will not be leaving yet, John. I've more to tell you. I'll be talking until dinnertime for sure. You'll stay."

It was a command, not a question, and John rightly assumed the Irishwoman wouldn't take no for an answer. He settled in the comfortable chair and listened in amazement as Maureen told him about Denver Dan and life in Alaska.

Dinner was served in a stuffy dining room by an equally stuffy Braxton. The food, excellent and the company, better. John did his best to keep his spirits up, but all the time, he wondered about Robert's whereabouts and if his son was still alive.

After dinner, Braxton handed John his hat and held the door open.

"Thanks, Mr., er, Braxton."

The butler looked down his nose at the old rancher, and John wanted to comment. Instead, he turned Maureen. "I'd like to invite you to stop at the ranch on your way to Ireland. You can tell me more about my son," he looked at Sean, "and you can tell me more about Alaska."

"I'd like to go, Ma."

John smiled at the boy. "I'm sure Rachel Ruth would pit her shooting skills against yours any day. She's pretty good."

"We'll see about that."

Maureen looked at the horrified butler, winked at her son, and told John they would be delighted.

ELEVEN

John had left for Denver several days ago, and since he wasn't there to root her emotions, they blew along like tumbleweeds. Rachel Ruth couldn't plant them and didn't know when they would sprout and grow, twisting and turning, dragging her places she didn't want to go.

This morning she could neither choke down the breakfast Aunt Elvira prepared nor could she bear the woman's over-solicitous comments. Rachel Ruth pushed her bowl away and stomped from the ranch house. Chickens scattered, and the dog slunk behind the woodpile. Jed's children ran from her scowling face, and the wranglers looked at her with concern as she passed the bunkhouse. Even the horse barn provided no solace.

She heard Jed yell, "Stay on him, Orly. Don't let him toss you."

She turned in time to see the wiry cowboy fly through the air. He scrambled to his feet and pivoted, intending to escape, but the bronco's hind foot caught him in the stomach. Orly bent over; the wind knocked out of him. Two wranglers grabbed him and pulled him to the corral's fence out of the bronc's dangerous path.

Rachel Ruth grabbed her own stomach. The truth had bucked out of the past and kicked her in the gut. She couldn't breathe.

"Miss. Miss." Ling Si's cabin was adjacent to the corral. He ignored the cowboys' everyday chaos and brewed his tinctures and cure-alls over an open fire outside his door. He ran to Rachel Ruth, a bottle held high.

"You drink. Good for heart. Drain anger. Put feet in creek. Feel better."

Rachel Ruth nodded but did not answer. The old man's foul-tasting tea could not cure what ailed her.

She sat at the creek's edge near an old cottonwood and took off her cowboy boots. The frigid water tingled then burned, and she focused on its icy sting. Perhaps the cold would put some distance between her and the hot anger within.

After a time, she pulled her feet out, dried them with her skirt, and let the sun warm them. She leaned against the cottonwood's trunk and watched ivory clouds move across an indigo sky.

What she saw were images of her and Grandpa John. He had perched her in front of him on the saddle before she could even walk. He'd taught her to read weather signs in the sky, identify plants on the prairie, and everything there was to know about ranching.

She pictured the times he had assigned her to care for newborn calves who had lost their mothers. She bottle-fed them, petted them, loved them. She became their surrogate parent, poor things. She supposed that's what Grandpa John and Aunt Ellie had become, and she was the poor thing.

The day she found the bill of sale, she was thrilled to know her father was alive and horribly angry that Aunt Ellie had sent him away.

Her face contorted, and she spat out the last of Ling Si's tea. It was as foul as the truth. She wanted no more of it.

She threw the bottle across the creek. It smashed on the rocky bank, and she felt a twinge of guilt. The old Chinaman treasured those hard to come by bottles. She felt even more guilty that she couldn't pardon Aunt Ellie. Her aunt loved her, but Rachel Ruth was too angry to forgive. She couldn't forgive her father either, although she longed to love him.

She clenched and unclenched her fists as the rage within rose like wildflowers on the prairie after a good rain. She picked those loathsome blossoms until she had a whole bouquet. There was no need to pluck the petals; he loves me, he loves me not. The man who fathered her could not possibly love her.

She climbed the cottonwood and searched the horizon. There were no answers. The sky, a vast blanket of blue, separated her from the God she knew she should talk to.

A tiny brown blur fell in front of her. Rachel Ruth looked down then raised her eyes to the branches above. The nest, empty now, once cocooned that little life. A peep and a soft blur of feathers hobbled a few steps, then fluttered its wings and lay still—no need to try to rescue it. No mama bird in sight, no papa came.

Rachel Ruth clung to the cottonwood's trunk and let her tears flow until her eyes were as empty as her heart. Drained, she wiped her face, blew her nose, and stuffed the handkerchief into her pocket.

She wanted to let go of her anger. She wanted a reason to love her father. She wanted to know that in some small corner of his heart, he carried her. She wanted to pound on his chest and demand answers. Maybe then she would understand. Perhaps then she could release the hurt.

Jonas McGregor, telegraph operator and railway ticket master, was privy to the small town's current and unusual events. His wife expected a full report each evening.

Last week, she was displeased when he told her John Merritt, silent, serious, and grim-faced, bought a ticket to Denver. She wanted to know why and withheld dessert when Jonas couldn't tell her.

This morning he received a telegraph from John requesting a buckboard and a saddle horse be ready at the depot this evening. Jonas ran to the livery stable while eating his lunchtime bread and butter. Why hire a team and wagon? What was John bringing back from Denver that wouldn't fit in his saddlebags? Something was up, and he, Jonas McGregor, had better pay attention.

Jonas kept an eye on the track all day and finally heard a long whistle. He checked his pocket watch; only six minutes late, not bad.

He directed the freight as it was offloaded and saw three passengers disembark with John. The first, a wiry man in new duds, strolled through the station, eyes darting in every direction. He surveyed the street outside and gave a slight nod to John.

"Evening, Merritt," Jonas called as John led a fine-looking woman and young man across the lobby.

"This is sure different from Alaska," the young man said with a slight accent.

"Don't gawk, son. Remember your manners. Your father..."

Jonas missed the last part of the conversation. Alaska? Father? What? Could John have gone to fetch a wife? Not likely. Elvira wouldn't stand for that. Were they already married? And what did she say about Alaska?

He watched John help the redheaded woman into the wagon. Although taller than his mother, who looked of average height, the carrot-top boy seemed relatively young. Jonas wasn't sure of the boy's age. It was hard to tell these days.

"Not to worry. Rachel Ruth will love you." John slapped the young man on the back.

That's it. The wedding bells were for Rachel Ruth. No wonder the young man turned as red as his hair at every mention of her name. What about Thomas? Everyone in town knew he had his cap set for Rachel Ruth or rather the Bar M.

Jonas smiled until his teeth hurt; he would earn all the extra pies and cakes he could. He took a notepad from his pocket and listed everything he could about the strangers.

Of particular interest was the slim man who followed them on the horse while John drove the buckboard. Those new duds proved him a tenderfoot even if he looked more like a gunslinger as his eyes darted everywhere, hand on his holster, snarl on his face.

Rumors spread through small towns like tumbleweeds. No roots, nothing to attach them to reality. They blew about like the wind, catching leaves and debris as they somersaulted down the main streets. By the time this particular rumor reached Thomas, it burned like a prairie fire.

Rachel Ruth and Elvira greeted their guests with enthusiasm, but their eyes told John they required an explanation. The sooner, the better.

He nodded and brought the luggage in with Sean's help. Cows were much easier to deal with than people. John imagined he heard a chuckle from heaven.

Maureen and Sean refused offers to rest and freshen up. Elvira took Maureen to the kitchen, where she plied her with tea, buttermilk pie, and questions.

Sean wanted to see some actual cowhands. John gave him directions to the corral and told him to ask for Jed. Sean hooped and hollered. "Come on, Braxton, we're going to see some real cowboys."

Braxton sniffed and followed him out the door.

"Grandpa, who are these people?" Rachel Ruth demanded, hands on her hips, foot tapping on the polished wooden floor.

"Rudeness from my granddaughter?" His eyebrows lifted as he settled in his chair.

She answered in a softer tone. "Sorry. I'm sure they're nice, but what about my father?"

Rachel Ruth's disappointment tore at John's heart. He told her what he had learned. As he finished, he saw a faraway look in her eyes.

"Slow down, girl. I haven't received any direction from the Lord. I don't know how He wants us to proceed."

"He wants us to do whatever it takes to find him! He has to, Grandpa. He just has to."

"Come here."

Rachel Ruth crossed the room and stood before the old man. She felt like a 12-year-old girl instead of a nearly grown woman.

"Sit," he said gently.

She sat on the large footstool that matched his worn leather chair.

"Look at me."

She met his gaze.

"Have you prayed about this?"

"Of course, Grandpa. I've done nothing but pray since I found that bill of sale."

"Did you tell God what you wanted, or did you ask Him what He wanted for you?"

Rachel Ruth searched her pockets and nearly dragged her sleeve across her nose. John handed her his handkerchief.

"Oh, Grandpa, don't you want to see your son?"

"About as much as you want to see your father. But let me ask you this, my dear—."

"Yes, Grandpa?"

"Is God sovereign even over this?"

"Yes."

"And is His heart kind?"

She nodded, and the tears slipped down her cheeks.

"Do you delight in Him?"

"Yes, Grandpa."

He lifted his eyebrows.

"I try to, anyway."

"And when you delight in Him, what happens?" The old man, whose years of living had given him much wisdom, asked.

"The Bible says He will give me the desire of my heart."

He cupped her cheek with his hand and smiled at her. "What is the best that your heart could ever desire?"

With closed eyes, Rachel Ruth felt her intense longings. Desires so deep she couldn't describe the feelings they produced: finding her father, serving God, and being a force for good in the world; She opened her eyes and looked straight into her grandfather's, "I know it's God, Himself, but sometimes, most of the time, I want what I want."

"That's the struggle of every believer's life, best you learn good battle tactics now when you are young. We will pray for the next two weeks and then...."

"Two weeks!" She shrieked. She recovered almost immediately. "I'm sorry, Grandpa, but two weeks is a long time."

"Mrs. Connor and Sean will be here for two weeks. If we're going to journey to Alaska, and it's still a big if, she'll be able to advise us, and she knows your father quite well."

Rachel Ruth almost smiled, "Okay, Grandpa, she can tell me all about him."

Thomas fumed and whipped his horse repeatedly, although the poor animal galloped at full speed. No one was going to take the ranch away from him, which meant Rachel Ruth could have no suitors but him.

Thomas kicked the horse again, and it thundered into the corral. Everyone except John had gathered behind the barn. Thomas jumped off his horse and threw the reins in Jed's direction.

Jed's shoulders stiffened, but he bit his tongue and led the poor animal to the barn.

Rachel Ruth's smile faded as she saw Thomas striding toward her. "What are you doing here, Thomas?"

"Is that any way to greet your fiancé?" He grabbed her and kissed her. Rachel Ruth struggled, and her face became hot and red.

Thomas saw a redheaded woman frown then lay her hand on the slim man next to her. "No, Braxton, we're not sure what's going on here."

The man stepped back but made a great show of pulling his revolver from the holster and spinning the barrel as he stared at Thomas. Thomas licked his lips and tried to smile.

Sean, sensing the tension, stepped over to his mother. "What's going on, Ma?"

"I don't know, but I will find out."

Aunt Elvira scooped up Rachel Ruth and spun her around. "Finally! Thank you, Lord. I'm so happy."

"But I'm not, we're not," Rachel Ruth sputtered.

Thomas stared at Sean, much too young to be a potential suitor, but he'd have a word with the boy anyway. And the slim man with the gun? Thomas turned away and frowned.

Elvira invited Thomas to dinner. He winked. "Thanks, **Aunt** Elvira."

She giggled, then asked the Irish woman to help her in the kitchen. She didn't notice Maureen's silence and chattered about wedding dresses and veils.

Thomas could tell Rachel Ruth was livid. He didn't like her whispering to that Braxton. Perhaps he was the potential suitor. With his obviously new western clothes, the man looked like a tenderfoot, albeit menacing. Thomas took a step forward, and Braxton stepped in front of the girl.

"It's okay, Braxton. You go help Jed in the barn."

"You sure, ma'am?"

"Yes."

He tipped his hat to her, glared at Thomas, and drifted slowly toward the barn. Rachel Ruth watched him go, then spun around, "Thomas, you made me so mad I could...I could..." She stomped off.

Sean started to follow, but Thomas threw his arm around the boy's shoulder, "That's how to keep your woman in line. Keep them speechless."

Sean clamped his lips tight as Thomas squeezed his shoulder hard.

"Let me show you around the ranch," Thomas said.

"I've seen it." Sean shrugged off Thomas's overtures.

"Oh, but let me describe the plans I have for it."

Thomas knew the boy felt trapped as he led him around the stables, bunkhouse, and various outbuildings. As Thomas questioned the boy about his life and his reason for visiting the ranch, Sean squirmed and answered evasively and reluctantly, but Thomas praised him and complimented his answers. Soon Sean responded honestly to everything he was asked. As Sean relaxed, the wily banker's son slipped in seemingly innocent questions.

Thomas, satisfied that he had pulled everything of interest out of Sean's brain, told the boy to tell Elvira he suddenly remembered he had urgent business at the bank.

Thomas's mind raced as he forced his tired horse to gallop back to town. As the poor beast lunged forward, so did the thoughts and schemes in the rider's mind. He must force Rachel Ruth's hand. Public pressure would help; everyone already assumed they were engaged. He relaxed as a strategy formed in his mind, and his grateful horse slowed to an easy canter.

Robert Merritt, alive and in Alaska of all places? Gold and silver mines? *I'll have the ranch and the mines as well. If the price I have to pay is marrying goody two shoes, Rachel Ruth Merritt, so be it.*

Thomas stopped by the church and had a word with the preacher, emphasizing Rachel Ruth's shyness and reluctance for a long engagement. Next stop, the newspaper's office.

With those tenets of his plan put into action, he confided in his mother. Although she didn't think anyone was good enough for him, he had always bent her to his will. She agreed to do his bidding.

With his mother and Elvira planning the event, the wedding would occur soon. He would be heir to the ranch and the mines.

A few days later, John yelled as he entered the ranch house. "Rachel Ruth! Elvira! Come into the kitchen!" They came, and so did Maureen. "Jed brought the Chronicle back from town."

John spread the weekly newspaper on the table. The three women bent over it and read:

Mr. and Mrs. Owen Miller
Announce the engagement
Of their son
Thomas Andrew Miller
To
Miss Rachel Ruth Merritt
Granddaughter of Mr. John Merritt
Wedding imminent!

Elvira clapped her hands and hugged her great-niece.

Maureen snorted and said, "What does he mean wedding imminent?"

Rachel Ruth blanched, and the blood drained from her face. She fell into the chair and lay her head on the table.

"That's not the worst of it." John flipped the paper over to the front page where the headline read:

BANKER'S SON AND RANCHER'S DAUGHTER HEAD TO ALTAR.

The article interviewed Thomas, who described how friendship had developed into a passionate flame. "After all," the paper quoted Thomas, "We must obey the Holy Scriptures: it is better to marry than to burn, although we are all sinners."

Rachel Ruth wailed, "That makes it sound like we...that I...I've told him no over and over. He didn't listen."

"It's because he knew you didn't mean it." Aunt Elvira patted her shoulder.

Rachel Ruth glared at her, "I'm so mad I could spit nails."

"Nonsense," Elvira said. "You're just nervous. All brides are."

TWELVE

Evenings were usually spent around the piano in the parlor. Once again, Elvira excused herself; she had so many patterns to choose from and must begin sewing the wedding dress immediately. There was no point in asking Rachel Ruth's opinion. The girl had no idea what she wanted. No matter, Elvira would have her looking like a queen.

Elvira's enthusiasm and excitement blocked everyone's objections, and they gave up trying to convince her the wedding was not happening.

"Everyone in town feels the same way," Rachel Ruth wailed, "no one believes me."

John paced, slapped his thigh, and growled, "I ought to take a horsewhip to him. He can't do this to my granddaughter."

"Anger won't solve anything, John."

"I confess, I'm too angry to pray."

"Go for a long ride. Let the Lord settle you."

Maureen watched Elvira spread patterns for a lavish wedding gown across the kitchen table. "I must decide on a pattern today and begin sewing." She said

"Mind if I put the kettle on?" Maureen asked.

"I know Thomas was a bit forward placing the announcement in the newspaper. John should have done it. Thomas just got impatient, perfectly understandable. Everyone knows they're getting married."

"Are they? What's the rush?" Maureen asked.

"You know how young men are, but I don't understand Rachel Ruth or the rest of you. Why is everyone so touchy?"

"Perhaps you should do your sewing in your room for now."

Elvira, cheeks puffed, muttered about pushy houseguests, gathered the patterns and yards of lace and satin, and slammed the door of her bedroom.

Maureen poured her tea and thought long and hard.

Two days passed, and everyone's touchiness increased.

"What's wrong with everybody," Sean shoved one of Elvira's cinnamon rolls into his mouth.

"Just a lot of grown-up drama that your dear, sainted mother is going to interfere with," Maureen said with an exaggerated Irish brogue and a flash of Celtic feyness in her eyes.

Sean laughed and hugged her with sticky fingers. "They won't know what hit them, will they, Ma? I'll make myself scarce."

"I'm sure Jed could find something for you to do."

"He said I could help brand calves today."

Maureen looked at her son. His fiery red hair had turned strawberry blonde, and his freckles had multiplied into the millions.

"Wear that Stetson Grandpa John gave you, so you don't burn. And don't come back until supper time."

Sean swiped another roll from the sideboard. "How about I eat at the bunkhouse with the wranglers, ma'am?"

"Ma," she laughed.

"Yes, Ma. Ma'am."

Maureen shook her finger at the boy, "Mind you, don't pick up any bad language."

Maureen cringed when she passed Elvira's door and heard the old woman hum Mendelssohn's Wedding March. She continued to the parlor where Rachel Ruth sat at the piano and sang about love lifting her when nothing else could help. The girl sounded melancholy and weary. Maureen settled on the piano bench next to her.

"He won't take no for an answer."

"What do you think you should do?"

"I don't want to be cruel, Maureen. He's so stubborn and thinks he's always right."

"You have a deep kindness in you and also the Spirit."

"Do you think so? I'm glad it shows."

"Do not let your fear of hurting someone's feelings override the Spirit. Speak the truth. Gently when you can, boldly when you must."

Tears came from deep within Rachel Ruth's soul. "I often feel God is moving me to speak, but I hold back."

Maureen's heart ached for her new young friend, "Have you wondered about the Almighty's feelings when you refuse to do as He asks?"

Rachel Ruth's eyes widened, "You mean it's possible to hurt God's feelings?"

The Irishwoman nodded with sad eyes. "It happens all the time, and yet He continues to care for us."

Rachel Ruth's tears soaked the front of Maureen's dress.

The Irishwoman reached into her pocket. "Lemon drops, prayer, and a good cry can make almost any situation better."

Rachel Ruth rested her hands on the piano keys, shoulders sagging, "I don't think a piece of candy can help."

Maureen took the girl's chin in her hand and looked into her eyes, "So, you're thinkin' this wee yellow drop is merely a confection?" Her Irish eyes sparkled.

"What else could it be?"

"A good question, lass," She held it high between her thumb and forefinger. "'Tis round and yellow like the sun, is it not? And the Good Lord promised the sun would rise and set until the end of time, did He not?"

Rachel Ruth nodded.

"Sweetness on the outside and tartness within, enough to make you pucker. When you let it melt in your mouth, you taste both."

"Sweet and sour together."

"Never bite down on the lemon drops. They will fill your mouth with grit."

Maureen popped a lemon drop into the girl's mouth, "In life, when you gnash or grind your teeth, you're not allowing the Good Lord to unfold things smoothly."

"You mean, do nothing?"

Maureen laughed, her red curls shaking, "Oh my no. Many a plan has come to me while savoring these wee drops."

Rachel Ruth reached for another, "We don't let our lives melt away, then?"

Maureen laughed again, "It's not a perfect metaphor, but it has helped me." She played a Celtic hymn, the lemon drops melted, and the Good Lord dropped a plan into Maureen's heart.

Rachel Ruth placed her hands over Maureen's and stopped the music, "I've hurt the Lord's feelings, Maureen, and now my heart hurts."

"There now, that's proof of your repentance, and with repentance comes forgiveness. He will give you the courage to do what must be done."

Rachel Ruth gave the smallest of nods and then stammered, "How will I know what that is, exactly?"

"Live your life to please Him. When you do that, others will either respond well or turn against you. Both responses are under His sovereignty."

Rachel Ruth straightened her shoulders and declared, "I pledge to please Him."

"As you learn to live this way, you'll enjoy His freedom, but I warn you; some will be angry that you are not pleasing them." She paused and then added firmly, "Do not let anyone manipulate you."

Rachel Ruth bit her lip, thought for a long minute, and then faced Maureen and said, "I'm determined and a little afraid."

They prayed, played the piano, and sang hymns while the lemon drops melted. The music drew Grandpa John, sweaty and tired from his ride. He sat in his favorite chair, laid his head back, closed his eyes, and let the music wash over him.

After a time, he called to his sister, "Come join us, Elvira."

"Can't," she responded. "Too much to do... What kind of lace should I sew on the veil? Flowers? I haven't even thought about the flowers." Her footsteps slapped across the kitchen floor, and the screen door slammed behind her as Elvira went to see what was in bud and bloom.

John clenched his hands and clamped his mouth shut. Maureen came and knelt beside him. "Come now, John, you believe the Lord is in control, do you not?"

"I always believe it, but right now, I don't feel it."

"I didn't think you'd let your emotions get the best of you."

"Not usually, but Rachel Ruth is my heart."

The Irishwoman thought of her son, "Picture God's heart. Rachel Ruth is there."

"Still..."

"Take heart, Mr. Merritt. We are about to fight fire with fire."

"Do I sense you have a plan, ma'am?"

"Maureen."

"Maureen, ma'am. What's the plan?"

"First, tell me, are you two going to Alaska?"

The piano bench flipped over as Rachel Ruth raced across the room and threw herself into his arms when he said, "We are."

"Soon, I hope," Maureen said.

"That depends on what you have in mind."

"Timing is everything, and we're going to have to work out the details, but this is what I'm thinking."

Maureen explained, then leaned against the couch cushions. She saw a movement in the corner of the room. Braxton. No matter, they needed him as well.

"Are you sure I couldn't just take Thomas out behind the barn and horsewhip him?" John asked.

"If I thought it would do any good, I would join you," Braxton, his chair obscured by the large potted plant, stood and faced the others.

"It would be an honor," John laughed.

"Do we dare do this? Imagine what people would think." Rachel Ruth put her hands up to her hot cheeks.

Maureen looked intently at Rachel Ruth.

The girl blushed, "I will learn not to care about people's opinions. Really, I will."

They bowed their heads.

Braxton shifted uncomfortably. Maureen often stopped and raised her voice to heaven at the oddest moments. He had assumed she was an odd duck. Now the old man and the girl were doing the same thing. He squirmed again. He felt left out and didn't like it. When they finished, he surprised himself by whispering amen.

Then the Pinkerton man addressed the group. "It is a good plan, and I think it will work. Those that know you best will understand. Those that know Thomas will hoot and howl, but I worry about Elvira."

"She's stronger than you think," Maureen said.

"I know my sister. She's stubborn, once she's made her mind up—"

Maureen interrupted. "I will ask you to trust me on this, John. It takes a woman to look deep into the heart of another. I have a plan for Elvira, but I'm going to need a few days alone with her."

"Tell us," Rachel Ruth demanded.

Maureen turned to John, "Why don't you organize a campout for everyone?"

"Me too?" Braxton asked through gritted teeth.

"We'll make a cowpoke out of you yet," John laughed.

THIRTEEN

The late afternoon sun continued to warm her skin as Maureen sat on the west-facing side porch. She rocked on the porch swing and almost fell asleep. She yawned, opened her sleepy eyes, and decided the plan was good. She picked a huge bouquet of lilacs, also known as Mexican lavender. They were Elvira's favorite flower, and the smell would invade the house.

Elvira had spent the last day and a half banging pots and pans in the kitchen, yanking weeds, beating rugs thrown over the clothesline. She ranted and raged at the chickens and ripped up the pattern for the wedding dress. She did her chores with a tight jaw and pinched lips. Maureen had left her alone.

John had taken the others on a campout, but they were due back tomorrow. Maureen stood outside the kitchen door with her arms full of the flowers and sent a quiet request heavenward. The time had come to see if the upset ranch woman would cooperate.

Maureen breathed deeply, squared her shoulders, and entered the kitchen. Elvira sat with a big bowl of green beans in her lap.

"Elvira, can we talk?"

"Haven't you said enough?" Snap.

"About the plan, yes, but there are other things."

"That plan will rob Rachel Ruth of her future." Snap. Snap.

"Can you not stop for a cup of tea?" Maureen put the flowers in the sink and looked for a vase.

"These beans won't snap themselves!"

"Please, Elvira. Sean and I will be leaving soon."

The older woman, still angry, rose and put the kettle on. "It would've been better if you'd never come."

"Pardon me. I didn't hear you," Maureen moved the bowl of beans to her own lap.

Elvira frowned and reached for it, but Maureen moved it farther away. "I'll help you snap them later. I've come to talk, and I will have my say." She knelt before Elvira and took her hands, "You carry a lot of guilt."

"They hate me."

"They don't hate you, but sending Robert away was wrong."

Elvira's head shot up, and she met the Irishwoman's eyes, ready to defend herself.

Maureen continued, "I'm not saying I wouldn't have done the same to protect my child."

"Then, you understand?" Elvira's voice cracked.

Maureen rubbed her thumb across the old woman's knuckles. "Aye, I do, but still."

"They hate me, and now I'll be left alone!" Elvira pulled her hands away and reached into her apron pocket for a handkerchief.

Maureen cradled the crying woman in her arms. Elvira stiffened and did not respond.

"I do believe John and Rachel Ruth will go to Alaska, and I do not think they will return," Maureen whispered into Elvira's ear.

"What about me? Oh, I wish you had never come here." The tears started again.

Maureen swallowed and forced a cheerfulness into her voice, "I have a gift for you, dear one. I'll be right back."

When Maureen returned to the kitchen, she saw the lilacs in a white pitcher on the sideboard. That was a good sign. Elvira, up to her elbows in dishwater, was not.

"No time for gifts. I've work to do."

"I'll just fetch a stool and sit near you because there's always time for gifts."

Elvira rubbed her dishrag across the plate harder than necessary. She glanced at the many envelopes and folded pieces of paper in Maureen's lap. Maureen held up a half sheet of paper, smudged, creased, and scribbled on. "This one is my favorite:

Dear Miss,

I can hear the rooster crow in the morning and see my baby sister in the afternoon. Thank you for not making me go into the mine. I love you. Ian

"I have no idea what that's about."

"Elvira, I know about your school and the home for aged and injured miners."

"What school and home?

"At the Erin-Go-Braugh."

"I just told the lawyer to put my share of profits from the mine back into the community. Anonymously. I'll fire that darn man," she thrust her hands deeper into the soapy water.

"Your lawyer didn't tell me. I figured it out."

"You seem to figure out a lot of things," Elvira hissed through tight lips.

"Did you know most boys follow their fathers into the mine, some as young as eight?"

Elvira's hand stilled in the dishwater. "Poor little things."

Maureen rose and gave the older woman a soft kiss on the cheek. "All the sons of the Erin-Go-Braugh's miners are in school."

"But how?"

Maureen laughed. "It's simple. You pay them."

"What?"

"As long as they stay in school and earn passing grades, your lawyer pays them the same wage they would earn in the mines. Straight A's earn a bonus."

"I knew that man was a genius." Ellie grabbed the pump handle and added more water to the dishpan.

"Old and injured miners would be in want if it weren't for you. Ellie's House is open to everyone, not just those that worked at the Erin-Go-Braugh."

"Ellie's House?"

Maureen nodded. "Rumors are, Ellie is a crazy, rich woman in the East who doesn't know what to do with her money."

"Let's keep it that way."

"Jack and Robert have followed your example and diverted a large portion of their profits to Ellie's House and the school."

"Read me another." Elvira wiped her hands on her apron.

The two sat at the table and took turns reading the letters out loud. The unsnapped beans and unwashed dishes were forgotten, but the kettle frequently whistled, and the china teapot was often filled.

With tears in her eyes and warmth in her heart, Elvira gathered the letters, pulled the pale blue ribbon from her braided bun, and tied the precious messages together. "I especially like the ones from the children."

"You've given mothers hope for their children's futures."

"I wanted a future, a wedding for Rachel Ruth. Children."

"I know, but I want to talk about the things you can still do for others." Maureen patted the older woman's arm.

"Give more money?"

"May I call you Ellie?" Maureen patted her hand. "Giving the money was a lovely thing."

The older woman smiled, but it faded as Maureen continued. "It was loving, but from a distance."

"I don't understand."

"Look around, Ellie. There's more love for you to give right here."

"What can I do with John and Rachel Ruth leaving?"

"There are all those empty bedrooms," Maureen raised her eyebrows.

Elvira thought of the six bedrooms upstairs plus hers on the main floor. She couldn't even imagine climbing the stairs once her brother and great-niece were gone. "You don't think I should invite the wranglers to live here, do you?"

Maureen pointed out the window where Jed's two little ones pulled a string. They had tied several sticks to it, the ducks waddled after it, chickens followed, and the cat attempted to pounce on it.

"I have the children in for milk and cookies as often as Mary allows. But she says they mustn't get above themselves, being the hired help and all."

"What do you think, Ellie?" Maureen asked, then held her breath.

"It makes me downright mad. My granny was a poor washerwoman straight off the boat, and my mama worked in a mill before she married and came west. Above their station, indeed."

Maureen smiled and released the air trapped in her lungs. "Ellie, you know I'm Irish, don't you?"

"Yes?"

"My grandmother's grandmother was a fey gal, out of the ordinary. She had second sight. Some say I've got it, too.

"What?"

Maureen leaned closer and took one of Ellie's hands. "It means I see things."

"We all see things, although I admit I need spectacles when I read." Elvira rubbed her hand across her eyes and sighed.

"I sometimes see things before they come to be."

Ellie got up and refilled the china teapot. She poured herself a cup and drank the scalding liquid. "You are an exhausting woman, Maureen Conner."

Maureen laughed and continued as if Elvira had not spoken, "I visited Jed's wife yesterday. Her pregnancy is taking all her strength."

"I know, but she won't let me help."

"She's barely four months along and as big as a barn. She needs you."

Elvira pulled the bowl of beans into her lap, "I've tried, and don't think I don't know what you are getting at. Do you think you can manipulate me?"

"Would you let me manipulate you for the sake of three bairns?"

"Three barns? What?"

"Bairns! Babies. Mary will deliver three wee ones."

"Three?" Elvira's eyes widened, and she swallowed.

Maureen saw the confusion on Elvira's face. She reached over and grabbed a handful of green beans. "I know you don't understand but thank you for believing me."

Elvira took a deep breath, "What can I do?"

"Mary needs to stay in bed until the wee ones are born and after. I doubt she will ever fully recover her strength. The babes will come early. One of them will be so small that you must wrap him in lamb's wool and lay him on the oven door of the wood cookstove. It's the only way to keep him warm.

"I've heard of that. What else?"

"Mary's proud. You will have to make it seem like she's doing you a favor."

Elvira's brow furrowed, and her lips puckered.

"Empty bedrooms," Maureen prompted.

"How can I convince her to move into them?"

Maureen leaned forward and looked deep into Elvira's eyes. "When John and Rachel Ruth leave, shuffle over to the foreman's house and tell Mary you need Jed close, tell her how lonely you'll be for a woman to talk to."

"Once I get her here, I'll keep her in bed even if I have to sit on her. I'll ask her to help with the ranch accounts. That will make her feel needed, and I dislike the paperwork even though I'm good at it."

Maureen drank her tea and listened to Elvira's plans about who would get which bedroom and how she'd turn the library into a schoolroom. Ellie and John had taught Rachel Ruth her letters and could do the same for Jed's oldest.

Maureen's hand trembled, and the hot tea sloshed out of her cup. She saw darkness and despair amid high waves. John. Rachel Ruth. She hated the second sight when it brought confusion instead of clarity. The Irishwoman silently prayed for the Merritt family.

Maureen finished her tea, "Ellie, we need to review the plan."

Ellie laid her lists aside. "I don't agree with any of it, but I will do my part."

"I'm afraid you are going to bear the brunt of Thomas's anger. He's so mean-spirited."

Elvira shook her head and snapped, "I've never seen him angry, and I daresay you haven't either. I know what to do, and you have my word, but I don't like it."

Maureen sighed, then pulled three pairs of tiny blue booties out of the knitting bag hanging from the back of her chair. "Look, Ellie."

"Oh, my goodness!" Elvira cradled them in her hands. "I bet Mary has been too tired to knit three of everything."

"I haven't told her she's having three."

Ellie's head jerked up, "She doesn't know?"

"No."

"Did you tell Jed?"

"No."

Elvira set the booties aside and picked up her lists. "That's probably wise. I'll have everything ready in triplicate."

The two women grinned at each other, toasted the three bairns, and drained their cups.

FOURTEEN

John planned a huge sendoff for the morning's departure. Friends and as many ranch hands as possible would gather at the railway station to say goodbye to mother and son. Sean, excited to see Ireland was, nevertheless, loathe to leave the ranch. As the Connors boarded the train going east, John and Rachel Ruth would slip away on the stage going west.

Jed moved his family into the ranch house right away. It kept Elvira busy and distracted. By Maureen's calculations, those in the ranch house would have three days of peace before Thomas arrived.

Sure enough, several days later, Thomas stomped into the ranch house kitchen and yelled for Rachel Ruth. Elvira spun around. The dirty dishwater sloshed onto her clean floor. "Thomas. Shush. You'll wake the children."

"Children? You don't have any children!"

"Actually, I do, and I just settled them down for a nap. Poor things are tuckered out."

He shook his head. It was apparent old age had addled Elvira's mind. "Do you know what they've done? Have you seen this?" He slammed the week's issue of the Chronicle on the table without waiting for an answer. He stabbed his finger at the announcement:

Mr. John Merritt
Is pleased to announce
His granddaughter, Rachel Ruth,

Is not and has never been
Engaged to
Mr. Thomas Miller,
Son of Mr. and Mrs. Owen Miller
Wedding nonexistent

Elvira put her hand over her heart. "Oh, Thomas, I am sorry."

"Just look at that headline."

RANCHER'S HEIR RENOUNCES INHERITANCE, PLANS LIFE OF SERVICE

"When I get my hands on her," He left the threat unsaid.

"Let me see the article, Thomas." Elvira pretended she didn't know anything about it.

He crumpled the paper and screamed, "That girl wouldn't know a good thing if it was standing right in front of her – and I was."

"Thomas, calm down."

"I'll not calm down." Thomas looked at her with wild eyes. "Nobody makes me look the fool. She'll pay for this." He slammed his fist on the table.

"What's going on?" A thin voice called from the downstairs bedroom.

"Nothing, Mary, just a rather loud deliveryman from town."

She turned to the furious banker, "Thomas, please, settle yourself." She pulled on his arm. He jerked it away and knocked the lilacs off the sideboard and onto the floor. The vase shattered, water puddled, lilacs scattered across the floor.

Elvira's heart thumped; this is what the others had seen in him. "She's gone, Thomas. It's over."

"It's not over! This ranch is mine!"

"But Thomas..."

"The ranch is mine, I tell you!"

"Actually, it's mine," a soft voice behind him said.

Thomas spun around and saw Jed standing in the doorway. "You're nothing but a cowhand."

"Maybe so," Jed drawled, "but before he left, John signed over the ranch to me. He will receive a portion of the profits, of course, but I hold the title."

Thomas, his face mottled, turned toward Elvira.

"I will live out my natural life in this house," she smiled and hoped she would have many years watching Jed and Mary's children grow.

Thomas sank into a kitchen chair, put his face in his hands, and then lifted his head with a sly smile. "It doesn't matter. My father has an outstanding lawyer. I'm sure John's mind had gone soft, or perhaps Jed, here, blackmailed him. I will have the ranch and the mines in Colorado and Alaska."

"Nobody was supposed to know about them," she whispered.

"You can thank that Irish whelp. It was easy to get him talking."

"Thomas, that was unkind. Poor Sean."

He ignored her and continued thinking out loud, "I think they've gone north to find her father. Nobody's stupid enough to give up a goldmine, not even a holier-than-thou gal like her."

"Thomas, no."

"Robert Merritt will be happy his darling daughter has a wonderful fiancé. We'll marry, even if I have to drag her to the altar in the middle of the night."

Elvira wracked her brain as she picked up the pieces of broken glass. She set the shards on the edge of the sideboard. "Did you know there is an English Duke in Wyoming territory buying up all the small ranches?" Elvira kept her voice low, calm.

"What's that to me?"

She ignored his ugly tone and forced herself to remain cheerful. She pulled a letter from the sideboard, scanned the first few paragraphs as Thomas paced the kitchen. Elvira tugged on his sleeve, "Look." She pointed:

> *... And Elvira, you wouldn't believe what a beauty his daughter is, an authentic English rose! She's barely 17, and all the young bucks in the area are after her. She turns up her nose and says she doesn't want anyone dusty and smelling of cow dung. She's waiting for someone who knows how to dress and which fork to use. Don't that beat all?*
>
> *The Duke, a widower, invites us to their place often and—*

Thomas crumpled the letter in his fist.

Elvira swallowed. "You have such lovely manners and a sophisticated way about you. Maybe an English Duchess is more suitable to you than a silly girl that's overly religious. Henrietta says the Duke plans to become a citizen and run for governor when Wyoming becomes a state later this year."

"Power, prestige, politics. Lots of opportunities in a new state." Jed drawled.

Thomas ignored him, but his eyes glistened as the words penetrated, "My dear Elvira, you are going to write me a letter of introduction to...." he unrumpled the letter, "to this Henrietta Myers, and she can present me to the Duke."

Elvira reached around Jed as she fetched her writing materials. Thomas dictated a lengthy and glowing message. Elvira's hand shook, and she bit the inside of her cheek. As she stuck the letter into the envelope, she smiled at Thomas, "That should do it."

He snatched the letter, stuffed it in his vest pocket, and turned to go.

Elvira tugged on his sleeve, "I heard there is a tailor in the town, fresh from New York. Imagine how impressive you would look with a new wardrobe."

Thomas brushed his dusty suit, pushed past Jed, then turned and said, "If the Duchess doesn't work out, I can always go north, **Aunt** Elvira." He slammed the door behind him.

Jed turned to Elvira, who was at the table writing furiously. She held up her hand as he began to speak, "I know it was wrong to put Thomas on the trail of that young Duchess, but I had to direct his attention away from Rachel Ruth."

Jed shrugged. "It's not my place to comment. But I'm sure I'd do the same to protect my children."

"From what Henrietta has written, Thomas will be no match for the Duke. Give this note to Orly. He used to ride for the pony express, didn't he?"

"Yes, but he's older now, and the railroad's faster."

"He can take the railroad to Cheyenne and hire a horse for the last 150 miles to Henrietta's place."

"Yes, ma'am."

"I think it will take Thomas a week or so to get a new wardrobe. My note warns Henrietta about him. She'll delay his meeting the Duchess, even refuse if she can think of a reason."

"But Ma'am, Thomas said if he can't get the Duchess, he'll go after Rachel Ruth."

"Pursuit of the Duchess will buy them time, perhaps permanently. I just didn't see him for what he was."

Jed nodded and reached for the letter.

Elvira handed the taciturn foreman some cash. "Give this to Orly for expenses."

Jed left to do her bidding, and Elvira mopped up the water, disposed of the lilacs, and put the kettle on. She was glad Jed's children had slept through the whole episode. As the water heated, she brought in some new lilacs. She buried her nose in them and breathed deeply, covering the ugly scent Thomas left behind. She took her tea and settled into the old oak rocker on the porch.

Thomas, enraged, left the ranch house. *Make a fool of me, will she? Take the ranch away from me? Humiliate me before the whole county? I'll have her, the Bar-M, and the mines, too, before I'm through.*

His mottled face showed his anger, and the spurs sank into the horse's flesh. Thomas pictured the English beauty on his arm and Rachel Ruth safety locked away on the ranch.

His eyes squinted as he passed grazing cattle on a nearby hillside. Everyone knew how much Rachel Ruth loved cattle drives. Accidents happened, didn't they? He laughed aloud and kicked his horse again. All it would take was a stampede, a fall from her horse, a shot from a rustler. So many things happened on the trail.

And the old man? It would be a good thing if he just got sick and died. *I could probably arrange that too.*

The horse stumbled, and Thomas spurred it viciously. The dust flew up from the poor animal's hoofs. Thomas coughed and looked at his dusty attire.

He'd order the new wardrobe Elvira suggested; that way, she'd think he was on his way to Wyoming and never know he was going to San Francisco. He was sure John and Rachel Ruth were heading to Alaska and would take a ship from that port city.

"Thomas, I can never show my face in this town again! "His mother waved her handkerchief in front of her face, a sure sign of agitation. "How could the Merritts have humiliated us like that. You were much too good for that holier-than-thou snippet. But what are we to do?"

"Sit, Mother, let me fix you a pot of tea." Thomas knew he could turn his mother's embarrassment and agitation to his advantage. The words galled him, but he smiled and said, "You warned me, Mother. I should have paid more attention to you."

His mother preened as she accepted the delicate china cup. She began to speak, but he hurriedly told her about the English Duchess in Wyoming. He assured her he would return with the young beauty on his arm. All he needed was money for a new wardrobe and to set himself up in style in Cheyenne.

"But, dear, what will I do? I can't face anyone. We'll go together."

Thomas had no intention of going after the English beauty until he had dealt with Rachel Ruth Merritt. He patted his mustache with the napkin and poured his mother a third cup of tea. It gave him time to think.

"How would it look if I set out to court this noblewoman and my mother tagged along? It wouldn't work Mother, she has to see me as a man's man. You do agree, don't you." He kissed her heavily rouged cheek.

"Don't leave me in this god-forsaken hick town."

His eyes hardened, and his fists tightened. He clenched his teeth and paced the room. Twice around the purple velvet settee.

"Please, Mother, you know this is the best thing for us."

"It's a lot of money, dear. More than you've ever asked for before."

He sat with a sly grin and said, "Ask Father, no, tell him in that special way you have, that you need a new wardrobe and new furnishings; everything here is so shabby. I'll take you to your cousins in Denver, and you can have a spending spree while I go on to Cheyenne."

His mother bit her lip and fingered her necklace, "That would cost a fortune."

"You are worth it, Mother. Besides, what's the use of being a banker's wife if you don't have access to the money?"

"Are you sure, Thomas?" She looked at him over the rim of her teacup.

"Imagine how you will feel if we hold the wedding reception here. You in your new clothes, a houseful of new furnishings, and a real Duchess as your daughter-in-law."

"But, Thomas—"

"Everyone will be so envious of you. I already have a glowing letter of introduction, and I've been assured the British beauty wants a gentleman in elegant dress, not a dusty, smelly cowboy. You will feel like a queen, Mother."

Mrs. Miller looked at the son she adored. "I'll begin working on your father tonight."

"Don't take too long. I need the money now."

FIFTEEN

"Grandpa, do you think the driver will let me ride up top?" Rachel Ruth asked after several hours of jostling on the hard leather bench of the stagecoach.

John grimaced as the front wheel dipped into a rut. The coach lurched awkwardly then stalled. At the slap of the reins and a roar from the driver, the powerful horses surged forward. John tried in vain to find a position that would ease the pain in his back.

"Grandpa?"

"I'm sure the stage line has rules about that, my dear."

"But you wouldn't mind if I asked? The worst they could do is say no."

John nodded. If anyone could talk them into it, it would be his granddaughter. Two hours later, when they changed horses, the ex-Confederate guard sat across from John, giving him a lecture about how the South still suffered under Yankee rule. The war had been over for years, but the memories were ever-present and bitter.

John closed his eyes and tried to nap while the old soldier continued his litany of complaints. He hoped his granddaughter was having a better time topside.

It took over a week for the arid sandy browns of West Texas to meet the Colorado foothills' verdant greens. When the soft blue-grays of the Rockies appeared, Rachel Ruth was amazed at the immensity and stability of mountains she had never seen and couldn't imagine.

Dinner at each of the changing stations along their route was similar, usually ham and beans, light on the ham. The tenderness and flakiness of the biscuits depended on the deftness of the cook. None matched Elvira's.

After supper, the two travelers always walked around the station. The sky was close, the stars bright, the air fragrant with pine and sage. John stretched his arms over his head and leaned against the corral's rails. He was glad he only had one more day in the coach. One more day of listening to the old soldier. One more day of being jostled. "I can sit in the saddle all day with no ill effects, but being bounced around in that coach has rattled my old bones."

"You should ride up top, Grandpa. It's not as bouncy."

"I don't think it will make a difference, and I don't want you to miss any of the driver's stories."

She hugged him tightly, "Thank you for coming with me. I know modern young ladies travel alone, but I'm glad you're here."

"Don't forget, I'm as anxious to see my son as you are to see your father."

She hugged him again. "Soon."

By mid-afternoon, the next day, the horses, as ready to reach their destination as the weary travelers, sensed their journey's end. They strained against the reins, nearly pulling the driver's arms out of place. To avoid injury to his anatomy, he let the reins slacken.

After bouncing in the stage for endless hours, they elected to walk to Maureen's house from the station and have their luggage delivered. Maureen's description did not prepare Rachel Ruth for the gaudily trimmed homes and even gaudier-dressed ladies. Those ladies looked at her dusty calico dress and even dustier face and put their noses in the air.

Maureen had given John a key. He pulled it from his vest pocket, clicked it into the lock, and called out a greeting to Barnabas, the caretaker. The old man shuffled into the foyer and told them a pot of stew simmered, biscuits were ready to pop into the oven, and he would serve them in ten minutes. His eyes were rheumy with some kind of palsy, and his hands shook, but his tone was cheerful, and he welcomed them with Maureen's strong Irish brogue.

They ate in the kitchen with him, and he entertained them with stories of Miss Maureen. Tales of when she lived in Denver full-time. Her battles with the *Famous Thirty-Six* rivaled Molly Brown's.

"Are you sure you don't want to rest a day or two before you visit the mine?" Barnabas asked.

"We'll go in the morning," John said.

"I've hired a buggy for your trip to the mine," Barnabas said.

John groaned and said, "I'd rather have two horses, western saddles on both."

"Yes, sir. Would you like me to provide a packed lunch?"

"Thanks. We'll leave early, so don't get up for us."

"You'll have a good Irish breakfast before you go, or Miss Maureen would have my hide."

John retired early. Barnabas told him all the bedrooms were made up, and he could have his pick. The smallest, in blues and browns, appeared to be Sean's. John found the bed soft and comfortable.

Rachel Ruth had a long soak in Maureen's copper tub. The steam rose from the hot water and eased her aching muscles. She could have planted an acre of potatoes in all the dirt she washed off.

Instead of going to bed, she explored the house, admiring Maureen's sense of understated elegance. The front parlor, filled with lace and gaudy fancies, seemed out of place. Grandpa had told her it was a sop to the *Famous Thirty-Six*. Rachel Ruth spent the evening in the library and fell asleep over a stack of books.

Dawn came all too soon. Irish oatmeal and stewed apples filled and warmed them. Rachel Ruth shivered as she climbed into the saddle. She could hardly wait for the sun to come over the mountains. The air was thin and crisp, and she wished she had bundled up a bit more. Barnabas saw her shiver and brought her one of Maureen's jackets.

As he stepped into the stirrup and threw his other leg over the gelding, John regretted not taking a turn in the copper tub last night. He felt old and creaky.

"How long until we get to the Erin-Go-Braugh, Grandpa?"

"It's about a half a day's ride," he said.

"And how long will we stay?" she asked.

"As long as we like. Ellie's lawyer has arranged a tour of the school and the mine if we want. We'll lodge at Ellie's House."

"I'm excited to meet the children and the old miners," she said, "but every day we spend there is a day later finding father. I'm so anxious to get to Alaska."

"The timing is all in God's hands, my dear."

"I know, Grandpa. I guess I just haven't learned patience yet."

John smiled to himself and remembered his own youth. Many things came more naturally with age. Living one day at a time was a hard lesson to learn, "Perhaps patience is one of the things our Lord will teach you on our journey."

She gave her grandfather a big smile, but inside she told herself the last thing she wanted was an opportunity to practice patience.

"My goal is to get on the ship and sail north as quickly as possible."

Grandpa John just smiled.

Rachel Ruth blew out her breath and prayed a prayer she didn't feel. *Lord, don't let the goal of finding my father rob me of the things happening now. Help me enjoy tomorrow when I meet the children.*

As they neared the Erin-Go-Braugh, they saw gaping holes left in the hillsides where no ore had been found. The nearby town of the same name had survived the boom or bust era, and most tents had disappeared. Many of the saloons and ladies of the evening that had occupied them were gone as well.

Hastily thrown up log cabins and crude two-room houses lined the rutted main street. Dusty in summer. Muddy in winter. There was a church, a post office, a mercantile, Ellie's House, and the school.

Rachel Ruth stood in the stirrups, "It's a hard life, isn't it, Grandpa?"

He nodded, then pointed to a larger building at the edge of town, "I think that's the school."

The school was everything Maureen had said and more. Mr. Blackmore, stern yet cheerful, presented his students one by one, youngest to oldest.

"Please," five-year-old Miranda said, "Are you, Miss Ellie?"

Rachel Ruth bent down to take the wilted flowers from the little girl's hand. "No, sweetie, but she asked me to come and see you. Is there anything you would like me to tell her?"

Little Miranda nodded, then hung her head.

"Come, Miranda," Mr. Blackmore urged. "These are important visitors. They haven't got all day."

Rachel Ruth, on her knees, gathered the little girl in her arms. "Actually, Mr. Blackmore," she said, looking at him over Miranda's head, "We do." She turned and whispered in the little girl's ear, "You're important to God, you're important to me, and you're important to Miss Ellie."

Miranda took her thumb out of her mouth and said, "Blue."

Rachel Ruth smiled and said, "Blue is Miss Ellie's favorite color, too. Is there anything else you want me to tell her?"

Miranda shook her head as Rachel Ruth started to rise. Then the little girl grabbed her in a fierce hug and whispered in her ear, "Tell Miss Ellie I don't pee my pants no more."

Rachel Ruth smiled, "Miss Ellie will be so proud of you."

Miranda hurried back to her desk and put her thumb back in her mouth. She saw Mr. Blackmore frown in her direction, pulled it out, and sat on it.

One at a time, the children came with a picture, an agate, a note, a bird's feather. All had messages for Miss Ellie, whispered in Rachel Ruth's ear.

John stood near Mr. Blackmore's desk. He watched his granddaughter's affinity with the children and marveled. She seemed to enter into their world with empathy and clarity.

"Your granddaughter is a natural-born teacher. I do believe she could secure a position here on her merits." Mr. Blackmore said.

"If we didn't have pressing business elsewhere, I'm sure you could tempt her."

Mr. Blackmore handed John a packet. "Here is the report on all the children and my recommendations for those I think would benefit from higher learning."

"Miss Ellie will enjoy seeing these."

"Normally, I would have given it to her lawyer, but since he said you're her brother, please tell her I would be happy to correspond with her directly if she's willing. Each life is a story, and she is changing the rather bleak endings these children would have had," Mr. Blackmore smiled.

John scribbled the ranch's address on the envelope, gave it back to Mr. Blackmore, and said he was sure Ellie would be delighted to hear everything from him directly.

The children sang several songs and recited Psalm 23. Then they encircled Rachel Ruth with hugs and tugs.

She had difficulty untangling herself from them until she pulled a small box of lemon drops from her bag and tossed it to Mr. Blackmore. "Here's a little treat for the children when they're seated and quiet."

He caught it and waved it above his head—the children hurried to their seats.

"Grandpa," Rachel Ruth said as they walked down the only street of the small mining town, "Do you think Aunt Ellie would be interested in providing sidewalks for this town?" She peered at her muddy boots and held her skirt above her ankles.

"I think if Ellie paid for the lumber, the men of the town should build the sidewalks themselves. When you help people, my dear, always try to give them some responsibility. It preserves their dignity."

"I'll remember. Even the children have to garner good grades to earn their wages. How proud they must be. But let's hurry," she said, taking his arm, "that dark cloud looks like it's ready to let loose."

The welcome at Ellie's House rivaled the one at the school. John and Rachel Ruth spent the afternoon with the men playing checkers, chess, and poker. Some sat on the porch and watched the rain as they whittled small toy animals or whistles.

After dinner, the housekeeper showed them a massive garden in the back. Several of the men tended it daily. Others took care of the chickens and goats. There was even a sow with twelve little shoats.

The housekeeper shooed John and Rachel Ruth into the parlor. They joined the men in a sing-along. Fiddle, guitar, and harmonica blended perfectly with the old miners' voices.

John marveled at these men who had spent most of their lives deep underground with pick and shovel. A rare individual might strike it rich, but most work for wages and poor ones at that. He was grateful he had lived his life in the saddle. He might swelter in the summer and freeze in the winter, but at least he wasn't in the dark belly of the earth, filling his lungs with its foul dust.

A miner in a wheelchair took Rachel Ruth's hands and said, "My son is a miner like me. He and his wife have eight children. The youngest, little Mandy, just started school."

"Miranda?"

"Yes, Miss, named after my wife, may she rest in peace. Anyway, they all live in a tiny two-room house. There was no room for me. I would not have gone there anyway." He rubbed his hand across his eyes, "Ain't about to be a burden. Here at Ellie's house, I organize the weekly schedule of who does what. Always wanted to be a boss man." He chuckled. "My grandchildren come to see me every day after school. And my son takes me to their place for Sunday dinner. You tell Miss Ellie, you tell her she saved my life." His eyes, full of grateful tears, spilled over.

The next day John toured the Erin-Go-Braugh while Rachel Ruth went to a quilting bee. A dozen women crowded around a quilt frame that filled the tiny living room. Each woman's stitches were as small and precise as the next.

Questions about Miss Ellie and herself came fast and furious. Rachel Ruth laughed and said for every question she answered, she got to ask one. In this way, she found out about the hopes and dreams these mothers had for their children.

"You tell Miss Ellie when my Mandy comes home; she tells me everything she learned in school," Miranda's mother said.

Several women in the group nodded, and a mousy woman in the corner spoke, "I know my letters now, Miss, every single one."

Another said, "I can write my name, and by this time next year, I bets I can read. You tell Miss Ellie it ain't only the children what's getting educated."

"Yes, tell her that," others chimed in.

Rachel Ruth nodded, unable to speak around the large lump in her throat.

John and his granddaughter stayed longer than they intended. Everyone wanted an opportunity to talk to them. Rachel Ruth enjoyed every moment, but the north still tugged at her heart.

"We love Miss Ellie. Tell her to come to visit."

"Please give Miss Ellie this apron. I made it out of my best flour sack."

"Tell Miss Ellie we got us a Bible, and my boy reads to us every night."

"Tell Miss Ellie..." Rachel Ruth's ears were full as she jotted down every message. She smiled, nodded, and hoped she wouldn't run out of paper and stamps before boarding the train.

How her heart could hold the desperate longing to find her father and grasp these beautiful people as well, she didn't know. Often these conflicting emotions confused her, and she longed to feel one thing at a time.

The train from Denver chugged along, clinging to the side of a cliff with a steep incline, bare-faced with few trees, awe-inspiring but terrifying. "I'll be glad when we're out of these mountains," Grandpa John said.

The next leg of the journey was hot and dry, the landscape arid. They peered through the train windows and saw evidence the pioneers had passed this way. Sun-bleached and wind-weathered pianos, sideboards, brass beds, even a cradle were scattered across the plains. They gave mute testimony to the harsh realities of those who had gone before.

Rachel Ruth saw the fatigue on her grandfather's face. The big strong cowboy that raised her looked like an old man. She hadn't realized the toll the journey would take, even though they had the luxury of stage and train travel, unlike the pioneers who spent months on the trail.

Late tomorrow evening, they would arrive in San Francisco. Rachel Ruth knew grandfather needed a rest. She tried to convince herself a few days in San Francisco wouldn't matter.

"Miss, excuse me, Miss," a little boy across the aisle said, "Are you a cowboy?"

"Why do you think I'm a cowboy?"

He pointed to her boots.

"I'm a cowgirl. I live on a ranch."

"My name is Anthony. When I grow up, I'm going to be a cowboy."

"You'll be a wonderful cowboy Anthony. Where are you going?"

"My papa went across the ocean, and then he went to look for the gold and pirate treasure and mama didn't know I would be born, and Papa didn't either, or he wouldn't have gone away, and he didn't find any treasure, so now he works like a steve, like a steve a more."

The shy woman looked up from her knitting.

Anthony said, "Mama does not speak the English. Our priest taught me so I would make good in America."

The boy's mother bent and whispered in his ear. Her voice melodious, her language musical.

"Mama tells you my papa works on the dock of San Francisco." Anthony continued to chatter, "He had to work a long and then another long time more because he didn't have any treasure and it cost a lot of money to send for Mama and me, and now I wished he was a cowboy." Anthony eyed her boots.

"Anthony," Rachel Ruth said in a solemn tone, "A stevedore is a significant person. He loads cargo on all the big ships. He puts on the trunks and suitcases for all the people that are going to faraway places."

"Are you going far away, lady?"

She leaned over and looked into Anthony's dark brown eyes. "Just like you, my father went away before I was born. I'm on my way to see him."

"Is he in San Francisco, too? Maybe my papa is a friend of your papa."

"I'm going farther, but maybe your papa will put my trunk onto the ship."

Anthony's eyes lit up, and he grinned, showing a gap where his front teeth should be, "I bet he would."

SIXTEEN

Life on a ranch in the middle of America was no preparation for the sights and sounds of San Francisco. Even Denver, with its reputation of new money, new gamblers, and the world's oldest profession, could not compare with the City by the Bay.

With its nearly 300,000 people, San Francisco was ripe with graft and corruption. Although more civilized than it was thirty years ago, there was still enough greed and gruesome crime to shame city officials. If only it had. They, however, seemed to think it was the price of doing business.

San Francisco. Port city. Commerce. Trade. It made the world go around. And if a bit of theft and bribery made everything run smoother, so be it.

People filled the depot, coming and going, meeting and greeting. Pickpockets, con men, and ladies of the evening plied their trades. Rachel Ruth's head swirled this way and that. She clamped her gaping mouth shut and tried to absorb the worldly hustle and bustle.

John arranged for their trunks to be taken directly to the shipping company. Their suitcases and valises contained everything they needed for their short stay in the city. He hired a horse-drawn cab for the ride to the hotel.

The carriage driver's horses looked tired and worn. Rachel Ruth wished they could know the West's freedom. As they pulled away from the station, she leaned out the window. She wanted to say goodbye to little Anthony and his mother but had lost sight of them.

A few seconds later, she heard a spate of rapid Italian. Anthony shouted, "Papa. Papa!" She leaned farther and turned toward the sound.

"My son, my son!" tears streamed down the man's face. He gathered Anthony into his arms, twirled him around, kissed his face over and over, "I have waited for the day I could hold you."

Rachel Ruth waved and hollered, but the little family didn't hear. She settled back in the carriage and hoped meeting her father would be as joyful, although he would have to explain himself first. Images of that meeting kept her occupied until they reached the hotel.

Rachel Ruth's eyes gazed upward; the hotel was gaudy with its ornate trim and multiple stories. Its many employees saw to the guests every need with silent efficiency. The tranquil elegance and serene ambiance had Rachel Ruth tip-toeing toward the registration desk. Her eyes darted around the lobby. Giant potted palms, ornate overstuffed chairs, and velvet settees dotted the room. Embossed wallpaper covered the walls, and Oriental rugs spread across the floors. The simple young woman from Texas looked at her calico dress and cowboy boots and sighed.

She followed her grandfather to their suite of rooms. Grandpa John inspected the bedrooms; Rachel Ruth chose the one overlooking the street.

He spent the next fifteen hours asleep, which allowed Rachel Ruth to roam the grounds.

She especially enjoyed the formal gardens and the aviary. She finished her exploration and relaxed by reading in the enclosed butterfly garden.

"Oh! Oh! Oh!"

Rachel Ruth looked up from her book and watched as a girl in her early-teens paced back-and-forth. It disturbed the butterflies, and one caught in the girl's hair, she sank down on the bench and cried for help.

Rachel Ruth freed the butterfly and asked the distraught girl, "Are you alright, Miss?"

"I am so angry. She had no right." The girl then looked at Rachel Ruth and sighed. "I guess it's not seemly for one to tell one's troubles to a stranger."

Rachel Ruth smiled and said, "Sometimes that's the best thing to do. My name is Rachel Ruth Merritt."

"I'm Louise Larson, and my sister, Luella, thinks she is such a lady. She thinks she has the right to every eligible man around."

"Aren't you a little young to be thinking about eligible men?"

Louise wiped her eyes with a handkerchief she pulled from the reticule dangling from her wrist, chattering all the while, "I was practicing, she came along and interrupted me, said I was a silly schoolgirl playing games. Then she batted her eyes, and the gentleman in question turned all his attention to her."

"I'm confused. What were you practicing?"

"How to talk to men, of course. Mama's having our house on Nob Hill redecorated. She said we might as well stay here and be social. This is where all the eligible men have their smoking rooms, card games, and dinners. Mama wants to snag a suitable man for Luella."

Rachel Ruth thought of conversations she had with Jed, the wranglers, and even Thomas. "I didn't know there was a special way to talk to men."

"Of course, there is. It is ever so much fun, especially for me."

"Why?"

"Because I like to say nasty things about my sister, in the nicest way, of course."

"Why would you do that?"

Louise rolled her eyes and said, "Wait until you meet Luella. But enough about me, are you a cowboy, if I may be so bold as to ask?" The girl looked away from Rachel Ruth and murmured, "Mama says I mustn't... be bold, I mean. But are you?"

Rachel Ruth wondered why everybody thought she was a cowboy. Then she saw her western boot sticking out from below her faded calico dress. "You could say that. I live on a ranch, but I'm on my way to Alaska to find my father."

"All by yourself?"

"I'm with my grandfather, who's resting, but he'll be down for dinner."

"You must have dinner with us. I'll have Mama send an invitation."

The dining room with the whitest table linens and dinnerware imported from China was exquisite. Most of the decor had that Oriental touch so popular nowadays, not that Rachel Ruth was aware of that fact.

Mrs. Larson, a widow, small, round, and motherly, charmed both John and Rachel Ruth. She told John that she would be happy to include Rachel Ruth in all her daughters' activities.

"Just until our ship sails," Rachel Ruth said.

Luella frowned, Louise smiled, and Grandfather nodded.

With Rachel Ruth occupied, he could rest and prepare for the next leg of their journey.

Luella, looking askance at Rachel Ruth's dress. "Miss Merritt, wherever did you get such an original dress? I've never seen anything like it."

Louise jumped in, saying, "It's such a pretty shade of blue. It makes me think of a pale prairie sky."

Luella continued as if her sister had not spoken, "And your hair, my, isn't it something?"

"It's so long and has a nice wave." Louise rolled her eyes at her sister's comments, which might have been considered compliments had they not been uttered in such condescending tones.

John glanced at his forty-year-old suit, the only one he had. Fortunately, men's clothing did not change much. He saw Mrs. Larson's daughters, elegantly and beautifully gowned. No calico to be seen, faded or otherwise.

What kind of grandfather was he? Back on the ranch Rachel Ruth was usually dressed like the wranglers. He'd never thought about her wardrobe, although Elvira had nagged him a time or two, and Maureen had mentioned it. He vowed to take Louise aside and enlist her help. Luella's comments, on the other hand, he would leave alone.

The next afternoon, the ladies enjoyed a High Tea done in the English fashion. Mrs. Larson looked fondly at her eldest daughter. "Luella will be our hostess. She has had a season in London and knows how to hostess a High Tea."

Rachel Ruth, not prepared for Luella's delight in constantly correcting her, frowned as Luella commented, "My dear, that may be the way you do things in Texas, but it is not considered mannerly in the city." Or "Miss Merritt, you must watch how you speak. That cowboy slang simply won't do."

After complaining to her mother repeatedly, Louise kicked her sister under the table. At least, she thought it was her sister.

Mrs. Larson yelped, then banned her errant daughter from the table. Rachel Ruth wished to accompany the younger girl but didn't know how to excuse herself without seeming rude. And she did want to learn the beautiful manners of High Tea. She already felt inadequate by her faded calico and didn't want to draw attention to herself by not knowing which fork to use.

When the tea was over, she found Louise, and they retreated to the butterfly garden. They discussed John's offer to finance a shopping spree.

Matters were taken out of their hands once Mrs. Larson discovered their plan. Early the following day, Rachel Ruth was invited to the Larson's suite, and Mrs. Larson questioned her thoroughly about her clothes.

"I don't need anything fancy," she said, "I'm leaving for Alaska soon."

"Alaska? So wild." Mrs. Larson fanned herself.

"Did I forget to mention she's on her way to Alaska?" Louise said.

"You're sure you're leaving soon?" Luella asked.

"As soon as my wardrobe's finished."

Luella smiled, "Let's go shopping!"

Louise leaned close to Rachel Ruth. "She'll be extremely nice now that she knows you won't be around long. But I'll miss you. We would've been great friends."

"We are great friends, and I will write to you."

"It could be amusing to turn this rustic hayseed, this cow person into a princess, especially since she won't be around long," Luella said to herself as she crossed the room to Rachel Ruth. "Stand up. Turn around. Chin up."

She walked around Rachel Ruth three times. "Oh, Miss Merritt, what am I to do with you? Skin darkened by the sun, such a shame. Hmmm. Dark hair with tawny streaks and green eyes, I can work with that. Stay away from pastel colors, and for goodness sake, get rid of this faded calico."

Rachel Ruth bit her lip, "I don't need much."

Luella slipped her arm through Rachel Ruth's as if they were the best of friends. "Miss Merritt, you are surely going to test my fortitude."

"I am not a doll to be dressed."

Luella looked down her nose and tapped Rachel Ruth on the arm with her fan, "You're not a woman, either. At least, not one who knows how to dress properly or how to act in polite society."

Rachel Ruth felt the warmth in her face. She turned to Mrs. Larson, "I don't think this shopping trip is a good idea. We should cancel."

"Don't be childish, my dear. Luella is the epitome of good manners and elegance. She's trying to help you. A little gratitude would not go amiss."

Louise rushed in, "You're right, Mama, and you too, dear sister. Rachel Ruth hasn't had her breakfast. You know growing girls get cantankerous on an empty stomach. We'll meet you in the lobby after breakfast." She squeezed Rachel Ruth's arm and hustled her out the door.

Her mother protested, "But Louise, you've already had your breakfast." She spoke to Rachel Ruth, "Room service is such a wonderful thing. I'm surprised you haven't taken advantage of it."

"I can eat again," Louise called over her shoulder.

"Why did you hustle me out of there so fast." Rachel Ruth asked.

"You will never win an argument with either Luella or Mama; even a slight difference of opinion is not tolerated."

"But that's awful. How do you cope?"

The other girl smiled and patted her curls, "It's easy. I shut my ears, smile, and nod."

"That doesn't seem very honest."

"It keeps the peace."

"But—"

"I think what I want and do what I want. Circumspectly, of course, so they won't find out."

Rachel Ruth shook her head as the two girls entered the hotel's dining room. Life was much simpler on the ranch.

John met the four ladies at the hotel's entrance. He handed Mrs. Larson a bundle of banknotes and encouraged them to have fun.

Rachel Ruth turned to him and whispered, "Everything I get will be practical and warm, suitable for Alaska."

Mrs. Larson heard, "Practical can be pretty and warm doesn't have to be ugly. It will take a week to ten days to outfit your granddaughter. Will that fit in with your plans, Mr. Merritt?"

John started to answer but turned away to cough. Rachel Ruth saw the lines of fatigue in his face and the slight stoop to his shoulders. Once again, she saw how the journey had aged him. It hurt her heart to see him this way.

"Yes, that will be fine, Mrs. Larson." She forced herself to smile brightly even as the light in her heart dimmed. "Please, Grandpa, can we stay?"

John, grateful, nodded.

"We will see you at dinner." Mrs. Larson waved.

San Francisco: large, ribald, and in many areas, depraved, looked like a foreign country to the simple ranch girl.

None of the city's attributes fazed Luella as she guided her sister and Rachel Ruth on and off the cable cars on their way to the city's more high-class shopping area. Mrs. Larson would meet them there. She was not inclined to travel by public transport, especially noisy cable cars, which her girls thought exciting.

Rachel Ruth spent most of her time asking the gripman about the mechanics of this modern mode of transportation. He tried to answer but was soon distracted. "Please, Miss, no more questions. If I don't lower the cable at the proper time, we will careen down the hill and crash."

"Really, Miss Merritt, must you know everything about everything? It simply isn't done to waste your time talking to lowly working men." Luella did not lower her voice.

Rachel Ruth threw the gripman a look of apology that he didn't notice as he fed the cable through the car's floor and into the slot in the street.

Once again, Louise grabbed Rachel Ruth by the arm, "You know my sister is being condescending when she calls you Miss Merritt. Like I said, just close your ears."

Rachel Ruth let the younger girl direct her attention away from Luella. "See, how easy it is," Louise whispered, "just don't let her words get into your ears."

"It's not easy." Rachel Ruth said with a clenched jaw.

"Peace at any price is worth it."

Once Luella entered the expensive shops, she turned out to be very pleasant. No snide or condescending remarks colored her conversation. All business now, she determined the styles and fabrics that suited Rachel Ruth. No one else was allowed to voice an opinion unless it was to compliment Luella's choices.

She instructed and commanded the saleswomen and clerks with a firm and only slightly patronizing tone.

Rachel Ruth wished she were back on the Bar M in her ranch clothes. These underthings and corsets were so constricting, the layers and yards of fabric confining. She did admit the image in the mirror was lovely, nothing like she imagined she would ever look.

Luella insisted Rachel Ruth have a beautiful gown just in case, although Rachel Ruth didn't see the need.

At the next shop, a lovely dress hung in the window. It had been ordered earlier that year and never picked up.

Rachel Ruth twisted and turned in front of the mirror. The gown only needed a few alterations and could be ready in three days.

"The dress suits you, Miss," the shop's owner said, "That deep nutmeg color with the gold thread running through it mimics the amber strands in your hair."

"I said as much," Luella circled Rachel Ruth while giving directions to the shopkeeper, "Let down the hem several inches. Our Miss Merritt is shockingly tall. Take it in here and here." She tugged and pulled at the dress.

Rachel Ruth stood silent and pictured herself in the hayloft writing this scene while the saleswoman tucked and pinned at Luella's command. "There now, take a look, Miss."

"I do feel pretty." Rachel Ruth turned to look in the full-length mirror. She never thought about her looks while roping calves or plucking chickens, and the wranglers never commented on them. The women at church all wore calico. Life on the ranch was full, busy. It left her little time to wonder about clothes and such.

She turned toward Luella and said, "I want to thank you, Luella, for all you have done for me. I never realized how clothes could make you feel. I don't feel like myself at all."

Luella smiled and dipped her head and gave a half-smile, "That is a very good thing, Miss Merritt."

Rachel Ruth tried not to frown. She didn't like Luella and wondered if it was a sin.

Mrs. Larson said, "You are a beautiful young woman, Miss Merritt, and a kind one."

Rachel Ruth flushed, grateful Mrs. Larson couldn't read her mind.

Louise clapped her hands. "The belle of the ball, pretty as a picture."

"It's time to accessorize. Hats, gloves, a fan, some jewelry." Luella turned their attention back to the shopping.

"I've never needed a fan or worn jewelry."

"We have gloves to match the dress," the salesgirl said.

"Good, we need to cover those calloused hands," Luella took the gloves.

"Luella!" Louise cried.

"I'm only speaking the truth, little sister, so hush." She turned to Rachel Ruth, "I told Mr. Merritt I was going to find an elegant dress worthy of his granddaughter, and it required jewelry. He gave Mama extra money for that purpose." Luella fingered her cameo brooch. "Lovely man. He agreed when I suggested pearls."

Rachel Ruth blinked back tears.

"You look lovely."

Rachel Ruth twirled, and the nutmeg dress fanned out; the gold threads caught the light and glistened.

Grandpa John laughed and pointed, "I see you're still wearing your cowboy boots."

"We couldn't find any shoes or even velvet slippers for my big feet. Mrs. Larson says no one will notice."

"Are you having a good time?"

Rachel Ruth patted her newly fashioned Gibson Girl hairstyle, "Yes and no."

Grandpa John raised an eyebrow.

"I enjoyed the company of the Larson sisters, and shopping in a big city was interesting. These fine clothes make me feel pretty and elegant. A real lady. It's exciting and fun, but I feel guilty. Is it shallow to enjoy such things?"

He started to answer but coughed instead. Rachel Ruth poured him a glass of water. "Are you okay, Grandpa?"

"I just can't seem to get the dust out of my lungs. Nothing to worry about. Now, what were you saying?"

"I want to be in Alaska with my father. Everything else is a distraction, a delay, or detour."

"The three Ds, eh?"

"Yes, and I don't like any of them. I want us to be on our way. At the same time, all the glitter and glamour of this hotel and these clothes are intoxicating."

"Intoxication is dangerous, be careful."

"It's hard."

"Yes, but now it's time for your dinner."

"Aren't you coming?"

"The staff is bringing my dinner here. I'll have an early night. We sail on the next tide."

Rachel Ruth's squeal echoed through the hallway and down the grand staircase.

Mrs. Larson had arranged a dinner party in one of the hotel's private dining rooms but had asked Rachel Ruth to come to her suite first.

"Come in, my dear," she said, answering the door, "The girls have gone down, but I wanted to talk to you alone." They sat on the small brocade divan, and Mrs. Larson took her hand. "I've taken you under my wing, my dear, since I'm sure you've had no motherly influence."

Rachel Ruth thought of Aunt Elvira, not soft or cuddly but practical, persevering, and caring. She started to protest. Mrs. Larson held up her hand, "No need to thank me. I've done my best in the short time we've had together. I hope your mysterious sojourn to Alaska is over quickly, and you can return to civilization."

Once again, Rachel Ruth opened her mouth to explain but couldn't get a word in. It was as if Mrs. Larson had been practicing this speech and was determined to get through it as quickly as possible.

"In the future, I hope you will have many opportunities to meet suitable and elegant gentlemen. Tonight will be an occasion for you to watch and learn."

"Thank you, Mrs. Larson."

"One more thing, dear, no stories of hunting, roping, branding calves, or wringing chicken's heads off their necks," she shuddered.

Rachel Ruth nodded and stood. Mrs. Larson reached out and placed a hand on Rachel Ruth's shoulders.

"No ranch stories of any kind and don't mention Texas. You do not look like a cow person anymore." Her eyes softened, and she looked at Rachel Ruth. "Keep those gloves on. Your hands are rough. But you do look lovely. That dress's golden nutmeg color picks up the shine in your hair, and the pearl necklace is enchanting. Luella has such good taste." She shook herself, opened her fan, snapped it shut, and said, "Where was I? Oh yes, nothing about ranches or cattle drives. If a gentleman asks you where you are from, tilt your head, lower your eyes, wave your hand like this," she bent her elbow and gave a dismissive wave, "and say, *The East*, then quickly ask him a question. Men like to hear themselves talk."

"But Mrs. Larson," Rachel Ruth protested.

"My dear girl," Mrs. Larson tittered, "it's not a lie. Your ranch is east of here. Everything is. Come along now," she said, pulling on her satin, elbow-length gloves.

As they descended the hotel's grand staircase, Mrs. Larson whispered in the girl's ear. "Smile much, talk little, watch, and learn. Keep your eye on Luella. And in a few days, I'll arrange another little party, and you can practice again."

Rachel Ruth gulped, squared her shoulders, and followed Mrs. Larson into a room filled with San Francisco's most eligible bachelors. Suddenly, she was glad they were sailing soon.

The dining room glittered with newly installed electric lights. Rachel Ruth couldn't stop staring. It was as if thousands of candles lit the room. She remembered which fork to use, placed her napkin in her lap, and dabbed daintily at her lips after every second bite. She remembered to tilt her head and look up through her lashes, heavy with the henna Luella had applied.

Each time a gentleman asked her a question, Rachel Ruth felt Mrs. Larson's eyes on her. The motherly woman's smile made her nervous. Rachel Ruth sipped her water, nibbled the bread, and waved her hand dismissively. The gentlemen turned their attention elsewhere.

She watched as Luella fluttered her eyelashes, tipped her head, touched a man's arm with the edge of her fan, and said things that would have had Jed and Orly bursting with laughter.

City men. Elegant. A different breed from the men of Texas. These gentlemen fell over themselves for Luella's attention. She seemed to play one against the other. Rachel Ruth watched, fascinated.

Louise, too, practiced. Eyelashes fluttered; she opened her eyes wide and made her rosebud mouth form a perfect circle as she uttered a breathy, "Oh." Men seemed to think her enchanting.

The drama and production at the table reminded Rachel Ruth of the one time a traveling Shakespearean troupe had performed in town. She felt like an actress without a script and no time to rehearse.

"I say, are you ill? You've not touched your meal," the gentleman on her left said.

She turned and batted her eyes as fast as she could.

"Have you a cinder in your eye?"

She shook her head and reached for her water glass. It was empty. The gentleman on her right asked if he could refill it. She nodded and tilted her head.

"Do you have a crick in your neck, perhaps a headache?"

She waved her hand dismissively. He turned away. The water glass remained unfilled.

Rachel Ruth could shoot a bull's-eye at twenty paces, deliver and brand calves, field dress a deer, and shoe a horse. Why was this so difficult?

She stared at Luella again. The elegant Miss Larson arched an eyebrow, smiled sweetly, and raised her glass as if to say Rachel Ruth was not doing justice to the nutmeg dress.

Rachel Ruth's chin rose just a fraction of an inch. She was Rachel Ruth Merritt of the Bar M Ranch, the largest in the state of Texas. She could do anything. She could do this.

PART THREE

SEVENTEEN

John and Rachel Ruth had an early but hearty breakfast and checked out of the hotel. The day promised to be fair and sunny, not an inkling of the fog San Francisco was famous for.

John was quiet on the way to the waterfront.

"Are you well, Grandpa?"

"I'm uneasy, but I don't know why."

"Are you sick?"

"Nothing like that," he stifled a cough and closed his eyes, "I'll pray the rest of the way."

John's agitation grew the closer the carriage came to the docks. He stared at the tickets he held in his hand, then entered the shipping office. "Captain, may I have a word?"

"As soon as I sign the ship's manifest and get my papers in order."

Rachel Ruth waited on the dock. She wondered if one of the stevedores was little Anthony's papa. She saw the last of the cargo and passengers loaded onto their schooner. The Northern Star; what a fitting name. That star would guide her to her father; she was sure of it.

The Star's captain strode out of the office, brows furrowed, face marbled with anger, "Board or not, I don't care, but this ship is sailing!"

"Grandpa, what's wrong?" she rushed to his side.

"We can't go." His ashen face alarmed her.

"But why?" Rachel Ruth saw several members of the crew untying the mooring lines, "Hurry, Grandpa!"

"Rachel Ruth!" The scream echoed across the dock, and the crowd turned to look. "You will not escape me! I will have you and the ranch!"

"Grandpa! It's Thomas. Hurry!" She pulled him toward the gangplank that two crewmen began to raise.

"Stop!" Thomas pulled out a small pistol and brandished it over his head, "Stop."

"Wait. Wait for us!" She yelled. The sailors paused.

"Yes, wait," Thomas fired a shot into the air. The crowd dispersed, looking to escape this crazed young man. The sailors dragged the girl and her grandfather aboard the ship and pulled up the gangplank as Thomas ran toward them.

"I'll follow you. No matter how long it takes, I'll find you and make you pay."

A stevedore, several feet behind Thomas, picked up a small casket of rum and heaved it. The pistol flew out of Thomas' hand as he screamed and fell. Blood seeped from the lump on the back of his head.

The captain of the Northern Star ignored the drama on the dock and made the final preparations to set sail. This was San Francisco, after all, and he had seen worse.

When he saw John, he smirked, "So, you decided to sail with me after all. Don't cause me any trouble."

John tightened his lips and did not answer. As he and Rachel Ruth entered their tiny quarters, he said, "We need to talk."

"Did you see Thomas' face? So evil. But we're safe now," Rachel Ruth couldn't stop shaking. She repeated the words. *We're safe* until she calmed down. "He won't follow us, will he?" She started to shake again.

John reassured her, but his thoughts were heavy. Had he misunderstood? Did he get it wrong? Had the Lord really spoken? He needed time alone and asked his granddaughter to go topside for a while. Lines of worry crossed her face, but she did what he asked.

Standing at the rail and watching the schooner sail out of San Francisco Bay calmed her, and she pushed away the image of a raging Thomas. The pitch and roll of the ship were as comforting as riding her favorite horse. The light wind whipping through the multitude of white sails contrasted with the glorious blue of the sky and thrilled her. Soon all thoughts of her grandfather's worries turned away just like the gulls turned toward shore.

She wandered around topside, smiled, and tried to engage the other passengers in conversation. They frowned and turned away. Belatedly, she realized they had witnessed the scene on the dock. She hurried back to the cabin and hoped she had given her grandfather enough time alone.

Rachel Ruth choked back tears when he told her about the Lord's warning.

"What are we to do, Grandpa?"

"I must speak to the captain again, although I do not think he will listen."

"If he doesn't?"

"We must leave this ship or perish."

Rachel Ruth looked out the tiny porthole, "The land is so far away, I can barely see it."

John put his face in his hands.

The cabin was compact and paneled in a beautiful golden wood that might have come from Java. Several portholes allowed the midday sun to stream in and glisten off the wood.

The young woman lay in his bunk, pale, ashen. Her shallow breaths came slowly. Captain Walker watched her for more than two days, only leaving her side to check on the elderly man they had rescued with her. He spun in and out of consciousness, often mumbling incoherently.

Old Skookum had spotted the lone lifeboat. The aged sailor, still the China Doll's best lookout, loved nothing better than to spend his days in the crow's nest.

Skookum swore the apple cider vinegar he added to his tea every morning gave him his keen eyesight. Whatever the cause, Captain Harlan Walker was grateful. He remembered how Skookum scrambled down the rigging to get a close look at her when they hauled the battered lifeboat aboard.

The girl's delicate, almost ethereal features drew the Captain. She was tall, nearly filling the length of his bed, which he'd had custom-made to fit his six-foot-two frame.

The third dawn found him still perched near her. He held his breath and willed her to wake up. Her eyelids, almost translucent, fluttered, "Green, I bet her eyes are as green as the Western Ocean in the early morning," he murmured.

She opened her eyes slowly and groaned. Captain Walker stared, disappointed when they closed before he could determine their color.

Fair winds and weather and a competent first mate allowed Captain Walker to stay below deck. He clasped her, long slender fingers, surprised by their calluses.

He was by her side the following day when she whimpered and stirred in her sleep. "Grandpa?"

Captain Walker rushed to the first mate's cabin, where Mr. Ruth slept. The first mate now bunked with the Cook; neither were happy. The old man woke quickly.

"Mr. Ruth, I believe the girl is waking up."

John Merritt looked up sharply, puzzled, and said, "Thank you, Captain?"

"Harlan Walker, sir."

"Thank you, Captain Walker. Where is she?"

"Next door in my cabin."

John's eyebrows shot up.

"I've been bunking in here, Mr. Ruth, not that you've noticed."

"Thank you, Captain. She's my granddaughter, and I'm very protective."

"As you should be, sir."

"I'd like to see her."

Captain Walker helped the old man to his feet. "This way."

John sat on the stool and took Rachel Ruth's hand. "I'm here, Missy. You can wake up now."

Rachel Ruth heard him through a fog of pain. Her eyebrows drew together. He hadn't called her Missy since she was a little girl trying to act grown up.

"Grandpa?"

"How do you feel, Missy?"

"Like a bale of hay that's been thrown out of the loft, but why are you calling me...?" He pressed her hand firmly, and she mumbled, "What happened?"

Captain Walker wanted to hear every detail. He frowned when he heard Mr. Ruth say, "You need your rest, Missy. We can talk later."

She grinned, then grimaced and touched the lump on the back of her head. "You know I won't stop bothering you until you've told me everything."

"What do you remember, my dear?"

"That fancy hotel in San Francisco. I had orange juice for the first time. It was like drinking sunshine." She stared at the ceiling.

"Is that all?"

"The rest is fuzzy, bits and pieces, like a dream that doesn't make any sense." She tried to sit but groaned and lay back on the pillows.

John closed his eyes then said, "We boarded the schooner after that altercation on the wharf."

"What altercation?"

"It's not important."

John glanced at Captain Walker, who sat at his desk with no expression on his face. John cleared his throat and turned to Rachel Ruth.

"You and I shared a tiny cabin. I hung a blanket so you would have some privacy. You unpacked, but I couldn't get the Lord's warning out of my mind," The old man coughed. He pulled his handkerchief out of his pocket and covered his mouth as the spasm shook his body.

"Are you all right, Grandpa?"

"Yes, Missy, just a chill." He coughed again.

"Take your time." The Captain handed John a mug of water.

Rachel Ruth looked past her grandfather and noticed the handsome seaman. She smiled. He stared. Her smile grew wider, then faltered when he continued to stare. Finally, she shivered and turned her attention back to her grandfather.

"What then, Grandpa?"

"I warned the captain again if he did not return to port, his ship would sink, and all life would be lost. He laughed and said no landlocked cowman could tell him anything about the sea. I said he was right, but God could."

Rachel Ruth put her hand to her mouth and gasped as Captain Walker stood before John and growled, "You told him that if he didn't do what you said, your God would sink his ship."

"No, sir," John replied gently, "I merely gave him the warning the Lord had given me, but he motioned to a couple of his crew, they forced me back to the cabin and locked it. Later, when the cabin boy brought us some food, I slipped him a gold coin to take a note to the first mate."

Rachel Ruth rubbed her forehead. "I remember the first mate led us to a lifeboat. I begged him to come with us, but after that, it's all a blank."

John rubbed his hands over his eyes, then held his granddaughter's. "He said even though the wind and waves had increased, his captain said it was just a squall. I implored him to come with us, but he told me he'd rather trust the captain he knew than a God he didn't."

Rachel Ruth sniffed, wiped her eyes and said, "He helped us into the lifeboat, and when he lowered it, one of the cables broke."

"He quickly cut the other, so it splashed into the water instead of dangling vertically. You fell back and hit your head. I was thrown into the sea."

Grateful for years on the cattle drives that had hardened his muscles and given him a strength that belied his age, John clawed his way to the lifeboat as he struggled to see in the dark. *Thank you, Lord*; his heart almost smiled as a wave pushed something into his face. He grabbed his beloved Stetson.

John pulled himself into the lifeboat and lay gasping for breath, then felt for his granddaughter. There was a large lump on the back of her head, and he could not rouse her.

The rain pelted him as he fumbled for the oars but only found one. The wind shoved the small boat to the crest of a wave, then into its trough. He tried to paddle with one oar but soon gave up and bailed water with his hat.

They were utterly alone. No food or water. He nestled Rachel Ruth in his arms, sang all her favorite hymns, and recited long Scripture passages and the Shakespearean sonnets that she loved.

Although the wind abated, the clouds remained low and the fog thick. John didn't know if hours or days had passed. He could not stay awake and sank deep into troubled dreams.

When John awoke, the sun had almost finished its journey across the buttermilk sky. A sky filled with white puffy clouds that held no threat. His head swiveled from side to side; there was no sign of rescue. And still, Rachel Ruth did not awaken.

Many times, during that night, John was racked with fits of coughing. He couldn't seem to clear his lungs.

John forced the memory away and gave Rachel Ruth an abbreviated account of their time at sea. The captain and first mate, professional mariners, called it a squall.

John, a range-loving cowman, saw every wave, a mountain, and each trough, death's canyon. "Then Captain Walker fetched us into his ship." John coughed again and sat back, "God kept our little boat on top of the waves."

"It was probably the sea anchor that saved you," Captain Walker said.

"There were two in the lifeboat. The first mate said to throw them over the bow. One had a 300 ft line, and the other was longer, I think."

"You were fortunate and very foolish. If we hadn't found you when we did..." Captain Walker frowned.

"Those poor people on the Northern Star." Rachel Ruth burst into tears.

Captain Walker could tell they both believed their ship had sunk, although there would be no way to verify that fact for weeks, maybe months. He rose from his desk.

"Don't blame yourself," he said, placing his hand on John's shoulder, "I don't know of a sailor alive, myself included, that would heed a warning from a landlubber."

"But there was a captain who believed, and his men were saved because of it." Rachel Ruth's valise was next to the bunk. She reached for it, then lay back and moaned. John pulled her Bible out and turned the still damp pages to Acts 27, Paul's voyage to Rome by way of Crete.

John recited the story, "Paul told the captain he'd lose the ship unless they ran it aground on a certain island. If he did, God would save all lives. The captain obeyed Paul, and all the men survived."

Captain Walker paced the small cabin while John told the story.

"I never heard of such a thing. Never!"

"You've never read the Bible, Captain?"

"Never saw the need, Miss Ruth."

She opened her mouth at his incorrect use of her name, then read the message in Grandpa John's eyes. *Honestly, Grandpa, you and I need to have a conversation.*

She looked at Captain Walker and said softly, "Everyone has the need."

Captain Walker refused to reply.

EIGHTEEN

John coughed, sighed, and coughed again. He slipped to his knees beside the bunk and prayed for the crew and passengers of the Northern Star. He prayed they had cried out to the Lord in their last moments.

Captain Walker paced the small cabin and glanced at the older man.

"Do you never relax, Captain?" Rachel Ruth asked, "Captain," she said louder.

He stopped and nodded toward her grandfather.

"It's all right. Grandpa isn't aware of us. He's in the heavenlies. Tell me everything about our rescue." She patted the edge of the bunk, tilted her head down then looked at him through her lashes. "Don't be embarrassed that I'm in your bed. My grandfather is a proper chaperone."

Heat crawled up Captain Walker's neck. He turned his back on her. *If I were ten years younger, I'd respond to her flirting. Better make that fifteen.*

He turned back to the girl, "I thought you said he wasn't here."

She tilted her head, "There is that." Then she pulled the covers up to her chin and said, "What if I promise to be good?" She patted the edge of the bunk again.

He shook his head.

Rachel Ruth was sure if Luella were here, the Captain would

already be sitting on the edge of the bed, regaling her with tales of the sea.

"Come, Captain, you are a man of honor. There is no problem." She tried to form her lips into the perfect rosebud pout that Louise had shown her.

Captain Walker remained where he was on the far side of the room. He closed his eyes and filled his lungs, "Miss Ruth, the world is full of unsuitable men, and I may be one of them. You don't know whether I am honorable or not."

"That's right, Captain, but only a man of integrity would point that out," she patted the covers again and batted her lashes, "Come. I've had a word from the Lord about you."

His head jerked up, and his eyes locked with hers. The blood drained from his face. "What?"

Her eyes sparkled, and she grinned. She didn't often get a word like Grandpa, but she was learning to listen. Grandpa John had advised her to be discreet about sharing those words, but this handsome man of the sea unsettled her. No, it was something else, excitement, perhaps. She sighed and coaxed him, "Come over here, and I will tell you."

The older man still droned, and Captain Walker found himself putting one foot in front of the other until he stood next to the bunk. He bunched his fists and shoved them in his pockets. He cleared his throat, then cleared it again. "What's the word then?"

She patted the covers and smiled, then laughed and hoped it sounded like Luella's sophisticated titter, "We're going to have a grand adventure together, Captain."

He raised his eyebrows but didn't move, "That's the word you received from your God?"

"That's my own thought," a pink stain tinted her cheeks.

He gazed into her eyes and revised his opinion of her. He saw neither guile nor coquettishness in her. If she was flirting, she wasn't aware of its potential outcome. Not yet, anyway. He felt a little better. And when she reached for his hand, he let her take it.

She pressed it to her cheek. He thought about pulling his hand away, but she let go before he could do so. That slight feeling of ease disappeared, and his discomfort increased when she looked deep into his eyes and said, "He is neither what he was nor what he will yet be. This one is marked, mine."

Captain Walker lost all the color in his face. His heart thudded in his ears. He backed up and bumped into his desk. He mumbled something about duty calling and staggered out the door.

"Missy, I am disappointed in you."

Startled, Rachel Ruth turned her attention to him and frowned as he suffered another coughing attack. "Grandpa, are you alright?"

He sighed and looked at her sternly, "Do not try to change the subject, Missy."

She folded her arms and looked at him, "You haven't called me Missy since I was five years old."

"I must've mumbled it when unconscious. When I awoke, Captain Walker called me Mr. Ruth. I opened my mouth to correct him but didn't."

"But why, Grandpa?"

The old man took a deep breath and held it. He willed himself not to cough as he let it out slowly. He told her about Thomas' threats on the docks of San Francisco. Fear flooded her face as she remembered. She clutched her stomach and moaned. He reminded her how Maureen cautioned them about the lawlessness in Alaska and that she could be in danger as the heir to a gold mine.

Rachel Ruth had dismissed the fiery redhead's words as blarney, now they unsettled her. "But Grandpa, if we are hiding our identities, how is that trusting God?"

He patted her hand. "Remember Braxton, Maureen's Pinkerton man? He told us to know our enemies. We're not sure who is friend or foe. For now, we will take advantage of Captain Walker's mistake. I will be Mr. John Ruth, and you will be Miss Ruth."

"You mean Miss Missy Ruth?" she almost smiled.

"We need to talk about you and Captain Walker."

She hung her head and pulled the covers past her chin and over her eyes.

John sat silent for a moment. He heard her muffled voice come from under the covers. "He kept looking at me. Besides, it was the Lord who said it."

Grandpa John sighed and pulled the covers away from the girl's face. She opened one eye, looked at him cautiously, and quickly squeezed it shut. She clenched her fists and then put her hands on her hot cheeks.

"I can see all the excuses in the world run across your face. It's no good trying to justify yourself."

She remained silent.

"Now, banish those excuses."

She gave a slight nod. Eyes still squeezed shut, shoulders hunched, knees pulled up, head resting on them. John reached over and raised her chin. He looked into her eyes and said, "No condemnation, my dear."

She nodded again, and a single tear threatened to escape.

John felt old. What had he and Elvira known about raising a girl into womanhood? Elvira had never had a beau, never wanted one. She was content with her chickens, her quilts, and running the household. In her own rough way, she had mothered the wranglers and the calves, and of course, Rachel Ruth. It had been enough for her, and now she had Jed and his family.

John rubbed his hand over his eyes. He had taught Rachel Ruth all he knew about cattle and ranching as well as hunting and fishing. She learned to rope steers and mend fences. He tried to model for her the principles of godly living and taught her the Scriptures. But it had never occurred to him to teach her about men, or women for that matter. Maureen had breezed into their lives and taught Rachel Ruth so much in their short time together. He wished she were with them now.

"Grandpa, I know telling Captain Walker what the Lord said was not wise. And the rest of it..." she shrugged her shoulders. "I shouldn't have baited him like that. I'm so confused." She lay her head on her knees again and sighed.

"How did it make you feel?"

"I don't know. Powerful. Excited, a little frightened. Thrilled. My stomach fluttered and flopped."

"And his response?"

Rachel Ruth laughed out loud, "Did you see him? His face was a sun-ripened tomato."

Grandpa John frowned and left that remark alone. "Tell me, my dear, would you have ever acted that way with Jed or Orly or any of the wranglers?"

"Certainly not. Why would I?"

"Think."

Rachel Ruth closed her eyes and thought about growing up on the ranch. Jed and the wranglers were her brothers, uncles, and cousins and had watched her grow up. She opened her eyes and giggled. "Jed would've told me I sounded like a hussy, and old Orly would've put me over his knee and given me what for."

"And Thomas?"

"Disgusting!" Rachel Ruth shuddered, "I would never act like that around him."

"Why?"

"Because, well, because I wouldn't want to attract him."

John sat back and waited for the truth to wash over his granddaughter. And it did. Now she was the one with the tomato face. She patted her cheeks and moaned, "What must he think of me?"

"You have just discovered the power and control all women possess."

Rachel Ruth, eyes solemn, voice low, said, "It's dangerous!"

"Use it wisely."

"I'd rather not use it at all."

"My dear, this power is as old as Eve."

"How can I ever face Captain Walker? How shall I apologize?"

"Apologies might embarrass him further. Consider the Captain in this situation, not yourself."

"Life was a lot easier back on the ranch."

"You're growing up, my dear."

A knock on the door interrupted them, much to Rachel Ruth's relief. Abel, the cabin boy, entered, followed by Cook, "Captain had me kill a chicken. Soup. Eat." He set the tureen on the Captain's desk and left. Abel set two bowls, two spoons, and two mugs of tea alongside the tureen.

Rachel Ruth had a sleepless night. She remembered how she had watched Luella flutter her eyelashes, tilt her head, touch a gentleman's arm with the tip of her fan, and say things that would've had Orly blushing.

Rachel Ruth knew she would have to make a full confession to her grandfather. So, the following day, she told him about Mrs. Larson's dinner party, then admitted she was practicing on Captain Walker.

"Practicing?" John squirmed in his chair and wondered if it had been wise to leave his granddaughter alone with the Larson women.

"We left San Francisco before Mrs. Larson could give me the rest of the lessons."

John choked and nearly spewed his tea across the room. "Lessons? Practice?"

"Mrs. Larson was kind Grandpa. She really was."

"Hmm. I will ask you a question, and I want you to think for a few days before you answer. Twenty years from now, do you want to be like Maureen or Mrs. Larson?"

Several days later, they strolled the deck. Rachel Ruth took her grandfather's arm and said, "I'm ready to answer your question."

He leaned against the ship's rail, his back to the sea. He watched the wind fill the sails, then turned to his granddaughter, "What have you learned?"

"Mrs. Larson is a woman with impeccable manners. I believe she felt motherly toward me. But I think her goal in life is to see her daughters married to wealthy men of high social standing." She fell silent, leaned over the rail, and watched the dolphins alongside the boat.

"And?" John prodded.

"Maureen's manners are just as good, but they don't rule her. She will pick up a chicken leg with her fingers while on a picnic. She's enthusiastic about life with lots of common sense. I can't imagine her doing any of the things Mrs. Larson tried to teach me."

"And your answer is?"

"I want to be like Maureen."

"Now about this practice?"

"No need to worry. Never again," Rachel Ruth shuddered, then tilted her head, gave her grandfather a pouty, half-smile, fluttered her lashes, and said, "Although, if I put my mind to it, I know I could become an expert."

NINETEEN

Captain Walker watched the sun climb above the horizon, glistening and golding the water. This particular morning, he looked heavenward through the sails of his three-masted clipper, the China Doll.

The Doll, how he loved her! Her wood-clad iron hull was strong. Her teak planking and paneling, beautiful. She wasn't as large as some of the Australian clippers. There were no staterooms or salons for passengers.

Many years ago, his grandfather won her in a card game from a very drunk British captain and had reconfigured the Doll to carry more freight. It suited Captain Walker. He'd rather carry cargo than passengers. Less drama. Less trouble.

There was a dining room for the crew where they ate, played cards, and Skookum, that old whaler, worked on his scrimshaw. There was another, larger dining salon for himself and the officers.

Like his grandfather, he had made changes to his Doll. He had installed patent steering gear, patent topsails, and several pumps. Nothing fancy or decorative, but it made her faster, more competitive.

Steam, quick and reliable, was replacing these graceful ladies of the sea, but as long as he could take care of his crew and make a decent living, he would keep the China Doll. With each voyage, his profits lessened, and his love for his ship increased.

He ran his hand over the smooth teak rail of his lady. Finely grained. Beautiful. The old girl had been good to him, and he would be faithful to her as long as possible.

Josiah, the first mate, shared his sentiments, although he thought they should install a steam engine. They could use it when the trade winds becalmed the ship.

"I'll not do it." Captain Walker sighed and wished he had been born many decades earlier. The purity and beauty of wind and sail graced his soul. Modern steam engines would eat away at it.

Captain Walker squinted towards the crow's nest, his hand to his forehead. Old Skookum saluted and shouted, "All's well."

Absently, the Captain returned the salute and continued his musings. They say the sea is a cruel mistress, and she had been, but he loved her. He even forgave her for taking his father and, before that, his grandfather. The love of the sea flowed from their veins to his.

He had lost count of the times he sailed from Alaska to San Francisco, then to Hawaii and Hong Kong. First, as a cabin boy with his grandfather until his mother restricted him to the West Coast, then as the first mate with his father. He was the Captain now, but he had no wife to come home to nor son to leave a legacy.

He sighed and continued pacing. Old Skookum had declared all was well. Captain Walker wondered if that was so.

It broke Rachel Ruth's heart when the days warmed, and the sea turned a brighter blue. They should be sailing north, not south. Abel told her the sea would become more vivid and warmer the closer they got to the Hawaiian Islands. It did not cheer her.

She peeked at the nautical charts on Captain Walker's desk. Alaska was at the top of the Pacific Ocean. Hawaii was thousands of miles in the other direction. She wanted to rip those charts to pieces.

How could this be happening? Her heart screamed, and her head ached. *Why were they rescued by a ship going in the wrong direction? It wasn't right. It wasn't fair. Why, God, why?*

She paced the cabin. In her mind, she presented several arguments to Captain Walker, reasons why he should turn the China Doll around and head north. Even to her, they sounded silly and childish. She threw herself on the bunk and gave herself a stern talking to.

She slowed her breathing and forced herself to feel a calmness that was anything but peaceful. She repeated one of Grandpa John's favorite sayings; *Time is one of the enemy's favorite weapons and one of the Lord's greatest tools.* She said it aloud several times. It didn't help.

Every morning Rachel Ruth lectured herself in the sternest way possible. *You can stand here and let the devil's weapon hit its target, or you can duck.* Sometimes she ducked, but the weapon often hit its mark. Her eyes, shadowed and sad, revealed a longing for the north.

Perhaps the warmer weather would benefit Grandpa John. Unfortunately, his cough had gotten worse, and he often had trouble breathing. The rattle in his chest worried her. Now, a raging fever forced him to remain in bed. She couldn't remember when he first became ill. In San Francisco, perhaps?

Even as Rachel Ruth cared for the old man, thoughts of Alaska filled her mind and her heart. Patience? She feared she would never learn it. Peace? She feared she would never have it.

"Just another spoonful, please."

"Yes, Missy," he whispered.

She smiled at his insistence on using her childhood pet name, even when they were alone.

"I want you to go on deck, get some fresh air," he said.

"I'd rather stay with you,"

"When you take the dishes back to the galley, ask Cook if Abel can visit."

"Such a sweet boy, only twelve, and already he's been at sea for two years," she smiled.

"At least, he has his uncle to watch out for him, a bit of family. So many cabin boys don't have that kind of support or protection," John sighed.

"He seems eager to visit you."

John stifled a cough, then said, "I tell him stories of the ranch, and he tells me stories of the sea. I use your Bible to help him with his reading."

She kissed his cheek, picked up the tray, and said, "I think stories of the sea are fascinating."

John's eyes twinkled, "Captain Walker tells you his adventures?"

"Actually, I haven't had the opportunity to talk to him."

She saw Grandpa John frown.

"I will speak to him today, but I will not mention my lessons about talking to men, it would only embarrass him."

It would shame her as well. She set the tray down, settled the blankets around her grandfather, kissed his forehead, and picked it up again. "You don't have to say anything, Grandpa. I will make it a point to speak to him soon."

"Cook?" She entered the galley, "I want to thank you for the meals you've prepared for us."

"It's nothing, Miss Ruth." The man wiped his hands on his apron and took the tray from her, beaming. "Abel says he's a grand old man, don't eat much, though."

"I worry about his lack of an appetite," Rachel Ruth said. "Would you allow me into your domain? I'd like to make him an egg custard."

Cook squinted, then frowned, "Ain't never had a woman in my galley before, makes me a mite nervous, Miss Ruth."

"The galley is your kingdom, and you are its sovereign."

He gave a slight nod.

"I'll make a deal with you. You spend the afternoon with Abel and Grandpa, and when you return, your kingdom will be as it is now."

"I couldn't do that, Miss Ruth. What about supper? I don't think the Captain would like it."

"I'll take care of supper." Rachel Ruth maneuvered him toward the door. "I'll take care of the Captain, too," she said with more confidence than she felt. This was just the distraction she needed. Keep busy. Don't think.

"Miss Ruth, tomorrow I'll show you how to make fish chowder. I first had it while sailing around Madagascar many years ago," Cook said one evening.

Rachel Ruth replied, "I'll write down exactly what you do. And then I'll always know how to make it. Tonight, I'll show you how to make an Apple Brown Betty. Aunt Elvira taught me when I was ten."

There were certain galley chores, scrubbing pots and such, that Cook did not relish. Rachel Ruth offered to do them if he would visit her grandfather. It was a fair trade, and Cook was more than happy to oblige.

Today, she finished early and went to check on her grandfather before going topside. She rounded the corner of the ship's narrow hallway and saw Old Skookum outside the cabin. Tears streamed down his face.

"Silas, go in," she whispered. She heard Grandpa telling a Bible story to Abel and Cook.

"No, Miss Ruth. I've lived a hard life, wicked."

Rachel Ruth looked deep into his eyes. "Everyone has, Silas, in thought, if not in deed."

He closed his eyes, leaned against the wall, and sighed. Rachel Ruth watched him silently.

He opened those world-weary eyes, "Just the same I'll stay out here."

She squeezed his arm and whispered, "Promise me you'll come back tomorrow and listen again."

He looked away.

"Silas? If you promise, I will believe you."

"I promise, Miss Ruth," His voice was flat, and his eyes dull.

"Good." She surprised him by kissing his cheek. She took a few steps, turned, laughed, and said, "It's not like I couldn't check up on you, dear Silas."

The old sailor watched her leave. He leaned his ear towards the door, listened to Abel read, and to John, who explained what it meant.

As she climbed the stairs to the deck and the sunlight hit her face, Rachel Ruth decided tomorrow Grandpa John must tell the story of the thief on the cross. *Silas, you are going to get an earful.*

Rachel Ruth stood at the rail and watched the sea. She was thousands of miles, and who knew how many weeks from where she wanted to be. Grandpa was not well; her father was somewhere in the wilds of Alaska. She sighed and leaned over the rail. Grandpa said God had a plan, and His plans were always good. She would believe it even though she didn't feel it.

Captain Walker saw Miss Ruth emerge from below deck. He wondered if she had been avoiding him, although he couldn't say if it was deliberate. It was just that, wherever he was, she wasn't. If he went to the galley, she was with her grandfather. If he went to check on John, she was topside. If he was topside, she was in his cabin; if he went to record in the ship's log, she wasn't there.

He shook his head and chuckled. Perhaps, she was afraid he'd respond to her flirtation. He wished again he was ten years younger. Fifteen, he chided himself, at least fifteen.

She leaned too far over the rail. Captain Walker expected to hear 'Man overboard!' any minute. He took a few steps towards her, then stopped. He clenched his fists behind his back and willed himself not to approach her. He continued to watch as she sang to the dolphins escorting his ship. She appeared to think they sang back.

His first mate came up behind him, "Beggin' your pardon, Captain."

"Yes?"

The first mate was silent, watching the girl.

"What is it, Josiah?"

The first mate nodded in the girl's direction, "Sir, there've been some complaints."

"About her?" Captain Walker stiffened. He would give the worst of the ship's duties to whoever had criticized the girl.

"I don't rightly know how to say this, Captain, but a few," he scratched his head and counted on his fingers. "No, more like, a dozen of the—"

"A dozen? What could she have possibly done to a dozen of the crew?"

Josiah had been his first mate for decades, and Captain Walker knew the man always fingered the gold hoop in his right ear when nervous. "Captain, she took all their money." His ear, red and swollen from the tugs, looked painful.

The Captain spoke through clenched teeth and kept his voice low, "She's a thief? What proof do you have?"

"I don't mean she stole it," Josiah's voice fell to a whisper, "What I mean is, she relieved them of their markers."

Captain Walker glanced at Miss Ruth, who still leaned over the side and sang to the dolphins. He rubbed his hand across his forehead and looked his first mate in the eye. "Explain."

"You see, sir, they was playing cards."

"Serves them right, trying to take advantage of an innocent girl. What were they thinking, enticing her to gamble?"

"Beggin' your pardon, Captain. It weren't like that. No, sir, it weren't like that at all." He glared at the girl.

Captain Walker forced himself to remain calm, "Perhaps, you better tell me what it was like."

"She seemed like a gentle miss, but nosy, always asking the men about their lives. What they was like as wee boys, where they was from, writing everything down in her little book." His voice drifted away.

"Go on."

"None of us minded the questions, leastwise not so much, except Old Skookum. He said she were a *fair miss,* but his life was his own business, said she knew too much already, even his name which he don't tell nobody. Then, all innocent as you please, Miss Ruth takes his cards and says all sweet like, 'Mr. Skookum, I bet you'll tell me all about your life before the evening's over.'" The first mate sighed, leaned on the rail, and stared at the horizon.

Captain Walker groaned. He couldn't imagine Old Skookum passing up a bet. Skookum, always bet and usually lost. "Tell me the rest."

"She dealt the cards and told Skookum he'd have to answer one question for every hand she won."

"What would Miss Ruth have to do if she lost?"

"Don't know, Captain. Skookum won't say. Don't matter, though. She won every hand."

Captain Walker swallowed his laughter and wished he could picture it. He wondered what questions Miss Ruth asked and how the keen-eyed old sailor, who'd been a member of his crew for years, had answered. "If she didn't lose, how did the rest of the crew come to play with her?"

"She said they was a feared to play a girl, and Old Skookum jeered at 'em. Said he let her win, just to be friendly-like."

Captain Walker's gaze drifted to the front of the ship, where this female card shark enjoyed the sunshine. He might have to challenge her to a game. "Cards, you say?"

"Poker, Captain!"

"Surely not!"

"Yes, sir, not a game for a female, I know, but she were a wily one. She won just enough to make it interesting, if you know what I mean. She let 'em win a hand now and then. The men jostled one another for a chance; all of them thought they could take her down. Then she turned on us, er, them."

"What do you mean, turned on you?"

"Each of the crew lost enough to be painful, see? They insisted she keep playing so's they could win their money back." The first mate slammed his fist into the palm of his other hand. "She's evil, that one. She won all our money and lectured us on the evils of gambling while she done it. Took our markers since we don't get paid until we reach the islands."

Captain Walker couldn't help himself. He laughed at his first mate and continued to smile even though Josiah scowled at him and fingered his gold ring.

"And I suppose you want me to—" the Captain paused, "—to do what exactly?"

The first mate couldn't meet his eyes. "Don't rightly know, sir, but you bein' the Captain, we thought you could fix her, like."

"Very well." He tried to sound stern and failed. Josiah tipped his cap and returned to his duties, giving Miss Ruth a wide berth.

Rachel Ruth watched the Captain stride across the deck. She greeted him with her arms thrown wide as she spun around, "Captain Walker, aren't you thrilled with your life on the sea? Your days filled with sunshine and dolphins. I love them so! And I saw a fish jump so high out of the water, he practically flew!"

He stood next to her, and they watched the sea together. He found himself telling her about his life on the sea, days of sunshine, but also days of darkness and storm. Whenever he paused, she prodded him with another question. His first mate walked past them twice and scowled each time. The third time he approached, Captain Walker stepped toward him.

Rachel Ruth put a restraining hand on his arm. "I think I know what this is about, may I?"

Captain Walker, back to the rail, watched.

"Josiah, may I call you Josiah?" her voice soft as a young seabird.

Josiah glared over her shoulder at the Captain, then snatched his cap off and muttered, "Yes, ma'am."

"You know, Josiah, from what I've seen on this ship, I believe I've done you and your men a good turn."

He jammed his cap back on his head and scowled. She took him by the arm and strolled the deck with him, leaving Captain Walker staring. Three times around the entire length of his ship, up the port side, down the starboard, and back again.

Josiah set his face like flint, and each time they passed a member of the crew, he flinched and glanced away. Rachel Ruth appeared not to notice as she smiled and chatted. They strolled around the

China Doll a fourth time. As they returned, Josiah's face had softened, and he was all smiles.

"You truly are a dear man, Josiah. Thank you," Rachel Ruth said.

The first mate blushed, fingered his gold hoop, and said, "No, Ma'am, you're the dear one, I mean, yes, ma'am. Thank you. I'll do everything you said." He scuttled off without meeting the Captain's eyes.

"What was that all about?" Captain Walker stared after his first mate.

"I have a few more details to work out, and then I'll tell you everything. Can I count on you to help?"

The Captain nodded, then said, "You seem different today, fetching. I mean, you look lovely every day...." He stammered and clamped his lips together.

"It's the clothes," she said, twirling.

He took a second look and blanched. Miss Ruth wore his only dress shirt. The softest Egyptian cotton, made in Hong Kong by one of the city's finest tailors. He only wore it when trying to impress prospective merchants who needed their goods moved from one side of the Pacific to the other.

It was apparent she had tailored it to fit her slender figure. And, if he was not mistaken, she had made the skirt out of his linen tablecloth. Last night, when he asked Cook why they were dining on a bare table, the man had shrugged, retreated to the galley, and slammed his pots and pans around, everyone's clue to leave well enough alone.

"Thank you so much, Captain. I know Cook said you preferred I not mention your kindness, but I'm grateful, especially since all that survived were the few things in my valise and Grandpa's small satchel."

Cook certainly deserved a dressing down, usurping his authority like that. On the other hand, he should have realized they'd lost everything. She was a vision in white. He was not above taking credit for it. He gave a slight bow, quirked his eyebrow, and said, "Consider my ship your private shopping emporium, Miss Ruth."

"Look," she raised her skirt a little. "Silas made me these out of a bit of sail and oilcloth. Can you imagine canvas slippers? He's working on my boots too, the seawater damaged the leather, but he thinks he can restore them."

He gave a brief nod toward the slippers, then muttered almost to himself, "Silas? There's no one aboard named Silas."

She threw back her head and laughed. The delicate arch of her neck distracted him more than the shape of her ankles had. "Captain, surely, you don't think any mother in the world would name her baby boy Skookum?"

"I can't imagine that old salt even having a mother."

Rachel Ruth turned and waved toward the crow's nest. She pointed to her shoes. Old Skookum waved. She blew him a kiss. He saluted.

"Now, about this situation with my crew."

"I'll tell you when we get to Honolulu, that is if you will give me an entire day."

"I will."

She went to check on her grandfather, and the Captain returned to his duties. Miss Ruth now treated him the same way she treated Josiah and Skookum. She chatted with him in the same direct and friendly manner. He didn't like it.

Did he want her to think he was eligible and interested? He pushed his pilot aside and grabbed the ship's wheel. The sea and the sky were his world, and he didn't need any distractions.

Whatever anomaly caused her flirtatious attitude when she came out of her coma was gone. She was more interesting now—but not interested in him. Still, there was something about her.

He gazed at the variegated blue-greens of the sea and felt the wind on his face. He had never considered any other kind of life until he pulled Miss Ruth from that lonely lifeboat. Today the clacking chatter of the dolphins disturbed rather than delighted him.

TWENTY

They sailed over smooth waters for several more days. Grandpa John wasn't any better no matter how hard Rachel Ruth prayed or how enticing Cook's offerings were.

She was on deck early, as usual, and watched Captain Walker take a turn piloting the ship. His hands, large and weathered, were firm on the wheel.

"Captain," she said as she approached, "You know I hold the crew's markers. I will need to cash them in when we arrive in the islands."

"I was shocked to learn you were gambling with my crew." He said half-seriously, "Where did you learn?"

"You forget, I grew up on a ranch in the middle of Texas. We didn't even have a town or a church nearby until the railroad came. By then, I was nearly grown." She shook her head and sunlight danced on her hair.

It distracted him. "You didn't go to school?"

"My aunt taught me."

"So, you were raised in the middle of nowhere. I ask again, how did you learn to play cards?"

"The wranglers, of course. I practically grew up in the bunkhouse. My poker skills are excellent. I'm not bragging, just stating facts. However, I disapprove of gambling."

"You are an expert poker player who disapproves of gambling?" He threw back his head and laughed.

"Makes perfect sense to me."

"Uh-huh."

"Jed, our foreman, never let me play for money. I could build a house with all the toothpicks I won."

"I see."

"Captain Walker, about those markers?"

"I can settle with you now if you like."

"When we reach the islands is fine," she said, "I was unaware most sailors are broke after a few days ashore. They either spend it on drink, gambling, or things I'm not supposed to know about."

"I'm afraid it's a common problem among mariners. I offer to hold back some of their wages every voyage, but it's their money. I mean, your winnings. What are you planning?"

"We're going to have a hoe-down!"

"What?"

"A shindig!"

"Excuse me?"

"A barbecue!"

He wondered if they were speaking the same language, "Could you be more precise?"

"You know, eat outside, and have a real Hawaiian picnic."

"You mean a luau?"

She clapped her hands, eyes dancing, "That's what Cook called it. I couldn't remember. It's for the crew. I wanted them to know how much Grandpa and I appreciate them. I have a very long shopping list."

"Shopping?" He paled.

"Yes, Captain, remember you said you would give me an entire day."

"What kind of shopping?"

"Food for the luau, and Silas has always wanted to buy a length of silk for his granddaughter. Blue to match her eyes. Unfortunately, he usually gambles away his wages before he accomplishes that task. And poor Abel, all of his clothes are too small, even his shoes. He wants to send his mother a teak or koa wood keepsake box with something special in it. I thought if we could find a photographer, we could have his picture taken. And then there's Josiah, did you know he is a fan of Shakespeare?"

Captain Walker shook his head. He didn't, nor did he know Skookum had a granddaughter.

"Cook wants some special spices for the galley."

"I'll buy those and Abel's clothes."

She grinned and reached into her pocket, "In that case, Captain, I've made a list of things that will make life at sea a little more convenient and comfortable for your crew and yourself."

He scanned the list. Most were things he should've thought of himself. He smiled and tucked it inside his jacket.

"I think there will be a considerable amount of money left. I would like you to send half of it home to the crew's families. After I'm gone, give the rest to the men with my blessing."

"You amaze me, Miss Ruth."

"Nothing amazing about me. I'm just an ordinary girl from Texas."

"I doubt that very much." He paused and cleared his throat. "I feel I must warn you, but I'm not sure how to put it into words."

"Warn me about what?"

"The crew, sailors, men in general, we're not often gentlemen. Be careful when you leave this ship."

She held up her hand to stop him. "Your crew reminds me of a lot of our wranglers. They were a rough bunch that sometimes forgot to censor themselves. I was the owner's granddaughter, and that protected me."

"Now you are under my protection, Miss Ruth," Captain Walker said, "but once you're off my ship, I will no longer be able to offer that protection, and you're a long way away from your ranch."

"I'll be fine."

She was too innocent, beautiful. She would not be fine.

"Hawaii is a crossroads of commerce and cultures, Miss Ruth. Ships from all over the world trade here. Sailors of every type, most are unsavory. They are eager to ah, fulfill their fleshly desires once ashore. I cannot bear to see you unprotected."

"Have no fear, Captain Walker. I have protection you cannot see. God's voice in my heart, angels ready to do battle."

Captain Walker frowned and paced.

"If it will make you feel better, Captain, I will tell you a secret. My boots have a hidden loop that holds a small derringer. I'm an excellent shot, although the gun is gone. I'll replace it eventually. And Silas is making progress on those boots."

The derringer, that's the first item on our shopping list, he thought. "Thank you, Miss Ruth. I do feel better, and I will not ask if you've ever used the gun."

"Then, I'll not tell you." Miss Ruth smiled. No need to tell him the small gun had never been fired.

Captain Walker threw back his head and laughed. He seemed to do that frequently when in conversation with her. "As I said, Miss Ruth, you are an amazing woman. And I pray if there is a God, that He has half a dozen angels watching you."

TWENTY-ONE

John rallied for a few days, then fell ill again. Even so, his small gatherings grew. Different members of the crew visited whenever their duties allowed. Cook hoped to entice John with savory treats. The others happily consumed the leftovers.

"It's too much, Grandpa. I'm going to tell everyone to let you rest."

"Let them come. I look forward to having visitors."

Silas, however, remained outside the door.

"Please, Silas, you would be welcomed." Miss Ruth urged.

"No, Miss Ruth, I'm not worthy. You don't know what I've done."

There was no point in arguing with the old sailor. He could not unload the guilt he carried. It broke her heart. Still, she was thankful he continued to hover outside the door.

"Remember your promise."

"Yes, Miss Ruth, but I don't like it."

"It's a wonderful idea, Silas, and I'm looking forward to it."

"I'm afraid for you, Miss. Don't make me do this."

"You agreed, and you'll not go back on your word." She patted his cheek.

He watched her retreating figure and knew the Captain's wrath would fall on him.

Rachel Ruth was up before dawn. Last night she had rifled through Captain Walker's wardrobe. She found a pair of breeches, a tad too long, but she rolled them to just below her knees. The other day Abel brought her a bit of rope. Bless him. He had not asked why she wanted it. She pulled it through the loops of the Captain's trousers and secured the waist. One of his everyday shirts, sleeves rolled to the elbows, completed her outfit.

She left Grandpa a note saying she would check on him around noon. She left another message for Cook telling him she could not help in the galley this morning.

Josiah asked Cook where Miss Ruth was. Cook slammed a pot onto the stove, grumbled, and told him to mind his business if he wanted any breakfast.

Captain Walker looked for her after breakfast. When he did not find her, he assumed she was with her Grandfather. She was not. His hands fisted, and his knuckles went white when John showed him the note.

"I'm worried, John. It's like she's disappeared, and according to this note, on purpose." Fear knotted the Captain's stomach, "You don't think she's gone overboard, do you? I know she's not happy we're sailing south."

It was apparent the Captain was not thinking clearly. "I do not think anything of the kind," John said. "She's come to terms with this little detour in our journey."

"I think I need to do a thorough search of the ship."

John took a deep breath, and his eyes twinkled. "Didn't you say the islands would come into view today?"

"Yes, but..."

"I think you should check your cabin, sir."

"I knocked earlier; there was no answer."

"Check again. You might find a clue."

Captain Walker banged on the cabin door repeatedly. "I'm coming in," he yelled. His dress shirt and the white skirt lay on the bunk, his wardrobe door was ajar, but there was no sign of Miss Ruth. Bile rose in his throat, and his heart drummed in his chest. He rushed back to John.

John climbed out of the bunk and stretched, "It's a beautiful day, Captain. I believe I'm strong enough to go on deck for a bit."

"This is a dire situation. You are not taking it seriously."

"I'm giving it all the attention it deserves."

"But John...."

"I'm sure Josiah could fashion some kind of cot or hammock for me."

"But sir, your granddaughter—"

"I would be grateful if you would arrange it right away." John insisted.

The drumming in Captain Walker's heart still pounded. "Fine. But then I'm searching the ship."

"You do that."

Captain Walker hurried out, the door slammed, and John heard him bellow orders before he was even topside.

John settled in the hammock mid-ships, near the waist. Swayed by the tropical breeze, he breathed deeply. The fresh air and the sun on his face let him breathe easier.

Captain Harlan Walker searched every nook and cranny of his

ship. Nothing made any sense. He leaned against the boxes of farm tools in the hold and put his head in his hands.

Captain Walker, face full of fear, stood before John. Before he could say anything, the older man looked through the sails and waved.

Captain Walker followed his gaze. He saw Skookum in the crow's nest. He shaded his eyes and looked again. His stomach dropped. "She's up there?"

"Yes."

"And you allowed it?" The Captain had a hard time keeping his voice calm.

"She didn't ask my permission,"

The Captain walked to where the sails did not interfere with his view. He lifted his head and cupped his hands around his mouth. "Miss Ruth!"

"Aye, Aye, Captain," she yelled back and saluted.

The crew jerked their heads up, all eyes on the crow's nest, then the Captain, then back to the crow's nest. Miss Ruth was with Old Skookum!

"Come down!" Captain Walker thundered.

She leaned over and yelled. "I can't."

"Don't be afraid. I'll fetch you." He was already taking his shoes off.

"Not afraid." She hollered back. "I have a bet with Silas."

Captain Walker stared. Miss Ruth's hair blew about wildly, the color of tortoise shells. Lovely. He shook his head to clear it. "Skookum, bring her down."

The wily old sailor held his hand up to his ear, indicating he could not hear. Captain Walker paced, swore under his breath, and paced again.

"John, this is dangerous. She must come down."

"She will."

"Now! The wind is rising," he bellowed.

The crew scuttled back to their duties but kept one eye on the crow's nest. No one wanted to draw the Captain's attention.

"Sir, I have seen my granddaughter scale the side of a cliff to rescue a baby mountain goat trapped on a narrow ledge after the mother had fallen to her death. Missy will come down when she's ready."

Captain Walker put his hand on the ratlines and shook them with all the anger he had in him. They barely moved. "Miss Ruth. I am in command of this ship, and I'm ordering you. COME DOWN NOW."

The crew turned away to hide their smiles. No one defied the Captain. Not ever!

"Very well." Her hair blew across her face, and she pushed it away. "As soon as I've won the bet!"

Heads snapped upward once again, and there was silent laughter from the crew. Miss Ruth had bested them at poker, and now she had challenged their Captain.

Harlan Walker stood by John's hammock and growled. "How do you control that girl?"

John raised his eyebrows, then shrugged. "I give her advice when she asks, and I pray. I do try to intervene when she behaves unwisely."

"This is unwise, John. Very unwise."

"Only because you do not know her strengths. She was raised

on a ranch and can do most things as well as any of my wranglers." He reached over and patted the Captain's arm. "She'll be fine."

The China Doll's master stared at the crow's nest. He wouldn't breathe easy until that contrary female had both her feet on the deck.

Rachel Ruth borrowed Silas's neckerchief and tied her hair up. "That's better. Thank you, Silas."

"Captain's awful mad, Miss." He pulled on his drooping mustache; his wrinkled weathered face had gone sallow.

"We'll not let him spoil this for us." She said sternly, "Just look! The sea and all that's in it, the sky and the sun. Oh, God, you are glorious! Your creation is wonderful!" She yelled into the trade winds.

"Yes, Miss Ruth, it surely is." He saw it through her eyes.

"Silas, how deep is the sea?"

"Nobody knows."

"My suitcases and my trunk are at the bottom of the sea."

"I'm sorry, Miss, your things are gone forever."

"But what if we knew where they went down? Could we salvage them?"

"No, Miss Ruth, it's impossible."

"Silas, the Lord says if you give him all your wrong thoughts and evil desires, He'll forgive you and bury them in the deepest sea.

"Really, Miss Ruth, all?"

"He makes Himself forget where those bad things are so He can never retrieve them."

The old mariner circled himself in the crow's nest and scanned the sea. "He would do that for me?"

"Absolutely."

"I will think on it, Miss Ruth. I surely will." She saw a spark of hope in his eyes.

The haze in the distance dissipated. The duo in the crow's nest yelled "Land Ho!" at the same time. They threw their arms around each other in joy-filled excitement. In a few minutes, Rachel Ruth scampered down the rigging.

Relieved she was safe but still angry for what she put him through, the Captain's heart pounded. He could not tear his eyes away from the girl. He removed his cap and dragged his hand through his hair, "Breeches! You're wearing my breeches!"

John grinned and said, "She often wore trousers while doing a man's work on the ranch; it's practical."

"But... my... breeches!" He moaned, not knowing if he felt embarrassed, relieved, angry, or bemused. He had never seen a woman in trousers before, much less ones rolled up to the knees. He was not the only one staring.

She let go of the rigging and jumped the last few feet to the deck. "We're here! We're here!" She squealed. She whipped the neckerchief off her head, shook her hair out, and bowed.

The crew admired her courage and daring. She had defied the Captain and survived. So, despite her holding their markers, they cheered, clapped, and stomped their feet.

Captain Walker stretched his six-foot, two-inch frame until, to the crew, he looked nine feet tall. They quietly shuffled away to their various duties. However, they kept one eye on him and one on the girl.

Rachel Ruth hugged her grandfather. "It was glorious, Grandpa. How I wish you were able to climb up there with me."

"Describe it to me, Missy. Let me see it."

After several minutes she turned to Captain Walker. "Why haven't I seen you up there, Captain? The sky, so close, the sea, endless and full of life. Sails below, sun above. The water glistens as if made of diamonds."

"Miss Ruth…"

"Thank you so much, Captain. It was heavenly."

"But, Miss Ruth…"

"I'm filled with the joy of it, ready to explode. The islands in the distance, lush and surrounded by a ring of blue-green water." She turned toward the hammock, "It truly looks like paradise, Grandpa. I know you'll get better there."

Captain Walker frowned and opened his mouth, determined to speak. He had no trouble giving commands and orders to his crew. Why was he hesitant and tongue-tied around this young woman?

"Abel, Abel, come here." Rachel Ruth looked around the deck for the boy.

"Yes, Miss Ruth."

She grabbed his hand. "Let's show them the jig you taught me."

The boy glanced at the Captain and stuttered, "Now, Miss?"

"Right now," she said,

Josiah produced his harmonica, and the crew clapped in rhythm. John winked at Captain Walker, who shrugged, defeated. He watched her dancing a jig with Abel and clapped along with the others. John was right; it seemed she no longer pined for the north. or if she did, she kept it to herself.

TWENTY-TWO

Early the following day, Rachel Ruth came to the galley to help Cook as she had for the past few weeks. He handed her the large wooden spoon used to stir the oatmeal. She heard him chuckle as he fetched the kettle and poured the men's tea.

The crew dribbled into the tiny dining room off the galley, eager for their vittles.

"It ain't natural, I tell you."

"I bet she's going up," another deckhand answered, "ain't no other reason for her to be wearing Cap's breeches again."

"I dunno," the pilot said, "I kinda like the looks of them. Maybe she does, too."

"That's enough!" Cook growled. "No more talk like that. Besides, I wager the Captain will stop her."

"I'll take that bet," the words echoed across the dining room to where Old Skookum ate his porridge. He heard the words 'wager' and 'bet.' He pushed the oatmeal away and rushed across the room, "No one's betting on anything without me."

Old Skookum's oatmeal jumped in his belly, and his brain shifted this way and that. He favored the Captain, who ran a tight ship and would have his way, but he only had to think of her sea-green eyes, and he couldn't bet against her. Skookum pressed his hand on his stomach. Several moments passed before he conquered his rebellious oatmeal.

He looked around, glad Miss Ruth had gone topside. She would not be pleased to see the crew gambling over her. That thought added to his resolve. He raised his hand and said, "I've changed my mind. I'll not bet, but I'll hold your markers."

This reminded the crew that Miss Ruth had their markers, and they would be betting wages earned on their next voyage. It turned the odds against her.

The old mariner worried the Captain would blame him. Cook decided Skookum should stay out of sight. The Captain couldn't blame him if he wasn't there. Skookum frowned, unsure if it was right to let her face the Captain's wrath alone.

If questioned, he was to say he had come down with a dread disease. "Perhaps the oatmeal affected his innards," one of the crew yelled.

Cook objected to that but was shouted down by several crew members who rubbed their stomachs and scowled.

Skookum took the markers and went to his hammock. If anyone approached, he was to writhe and moan. Abel would bring him news of any action topside. But under no circumstances was he to show himself.

Unaware that she was the cause of massive speculation and serious wagering, Rachel Ruth lifted her face to the sun as she came on deck. She breathed deeply and gazed at the empty crow's nest. She wondered where Silas was.

"Good morning, Miss Ruth." Captain Walker said. He saw her wild tortoiseshell hair, unbound and rippling in the breeze. Highlights of amber and honey streaked through her dark tresses.

"Good morning, Captain." She twirled, her hair a halo of fire that mesmerized Captain Walker. Then he saw that she was wearing his breeches again.

He frowned, "Miss Ruth?"

"Captain, I want to thank you for the concern you showed me yesterday."

He made a slight adjustment to the ship's wheel. He usually enjoyed guiding the China Doll in the early morning, but now he wished the pilot was back from breakfast. He would enjoy strolling the deck with Miss Ruth even if she did look like a tall cabin boy. It would be better for him if she were attired in proper female clothes. "You're welcome, Miss Ruth," he said and wondered if he should ask about the breeches.

"I appreciate that you have my best interests at heart, and you want to keep me safe."

He gave a slight nod.

"You are constantly watching out for your crew, are you not? Teaching and training them in the ways of the sea."

"Of course, any leader worth his salt does."

"I have a solution for your angst."

"I have no angst."

"Captain Harlan Walker, it's dripping off your face!" Her eyes glistened like the sun on the sea.

He shook his head, and his hands tightened on the ship's wheel.

"I know you have forbidden the crow's nest to me."

He nodded without meeting her eyes; instead, he kept his gaze on her wondrous hair.

"I will not disobey you, Captain."

"Good."

"I will not disobey you, as long as I am on your ship. But wouldn't it be better if you taught me the proper way to scale the rigging. Yesterday, I just crawled up, holding onto whatever I could grasp."

"No!" The word shot out of Captain Walker's mouth, "That's not the way to do it."

"Will you teach me?" She asked with a grin. "You do want me safe on other ships, do you not?"

He clenched his jaw and frowned at the thought of her on another ship.

She pointed skyward, "The crow's nest is empty. It's a perfect time for a lesson."

He jerked his head up, peering through the sails.

"Skookum!" He bellowed, "Where are you?"

"Not here," Josiah said.

"I can see that!" The Captain's eyes flashed.

"Writhing," Abel said.

"Writhing?"

"It's a new word I just learned. It means rolling around," Abel tried not to smile.

"In his hammock," Cook added.

"Must've been something he et," Josiah said.

Cook glared at him, but Josiah kept smiling. There were several titters from the crew.

Captain Walker noticed they seemed more interested in him and Miss Ruth than in their duties. Their eyes darted from the crow's nest to them and back again. He knew he'd been outmaneuvered.

"Back to your duties, men." He ordered mildly. He couldn't blame them. He had trouble keeping his mind on his duties with her around. As they scattered, he turned to Miss Ruth. "You win, Missy." He said, rubbing his hand over his eyes.

The pilot stepped forward, took the wheel, and beamed to Josiah, "I knew Miss Ruth was a sure thing."

"What's so amusing, Pilot?" A scowling Captain Walker asked.

Pilot tore his gaze away from Miss Ruth. "Nothing, sir, that is, dolphins on the port side. Amusing."

Rachel Ruth ran to look. Captain Walker followed slowly.

"As you say, Captain Walker, I have won, but when we are up there," she pointed skyward, "you will realize that you have also won."

"I expect you to obey every order and instruction instantly, understood?"

"Aye, aye, Sir," she saluted. The breeze blew a few strands of hair across her face. She reached up and pushed them out of the way. "May I borrow your neckerchief to tie up my hair? It flies about so."

He pulled the scarf from around his neck. He hated to see her tresses bound in those awful bun things. "Perhaps you could make a braid?"

Her eyes questioned him.

"My mother always had a braid hanging halfway down her back," he said wistfully, "Your hair's color is similar to hers."

"I'd be delighted." Rachel Ruth deftly plaited her hair and tied it with his neckerchief.

The sun, soft as warm butterscotch, the breeze, fresh as spring rain. Captain Walker smiled to himself as he gazed at his men from the crow's nest. There was many a glance upward as they performed their duties.

The other occupant of this lookout post concentrated on sea and sky, unaware of his lingering gaze. Grateful she had invited him aloft, he chuckled then corrected himself; it wasn't an invitation. She had outmaneuvered him, pure and simple. The image of her on another ship with another captain still irritated him.

"How long since you've been up on this wonderful perch?" she asked.

The wind ruffled his hair. The smile lines crinkled around his eyes. "Much too long, Miss Ruth."

She laughed out loud, "If only we could be here for the whole voyage."

The roll and pitch of the ship did not faze her in the least. She was an incredible sailor. She swept her gaze from horizon to horizon and pointed to the not too distant islands.

"Sky, sea, and shore, it's creation's trinity, isn't it?"

"If you say so. Look there, a whale breaching, see the calf?"

Rachel Ruth leaned over the bucket of the crow's nest as the ship passed the whales. After a few moments of thoughtful silence, she said: "This must be how God sees the world, from His throne in heaven. And yet, He can look into the deepest recesses of our souls just as easily."

Captain Walker groaned inwardly. One could not have a conversation with this young woman without her bringing God into it. At first, it had surprised him, now it annoyed him. To be fair, she did not preach or lecture. She certainly wasn't judgmental or condemning. "Your God seems very real to you, Miss Ruth."

"He is more wondrous and glorious than all of this." She spread her arms wide despite the confined space.

Captain Walker did not want to argue with her; neither did he want to continue this conversation. He remained quiet for several moments. Despite his intentions, he looked deep into his own soul. "You almost convince me."

The light in her eyes became even brighter, and she said, "It's not me that does the convincing."

The hairs on the back of his neck stood at attention. An indication he was on edge. He clamped his lips together and refused to speak.

The young woman seemed comfortable in the silence and ignored his discomfort.

Captain Walker leaned over, grabbed the rigging, and pulled himself out of the nest. "Time to go."

"Right behind you, sir." She scampered down the ratlines after him.

Captain Walker sat at the small desk and flipped the pages of the ship's log. He threw his pen down and looked toward the light streaming in from the porthole. Unfortunately, all he could see were images from last night's dream.

Miss Ruth had fallen from the rigging. He reached for her, but she slipped through his arms. *God save her!* Miss Ruth landed safely as if invisible arms caught her and set her gently on the deck. Then he fell. As much as he tried, he couldn't release the words *God save me.* He clawed at his throat, but they wouldn't form. He drowned in stormy seas with no hope of rescue. He woke drenched in sweat, full of fear.

Captain Walker brushed his hand over his eyes. He rubbed his chest, trying to dislodge the hard knot that encased his heart. He fished around in the bottom drawer for the bottle that rarely saw the light of day.

There was a soft knock at the door.

"Enter." He shoved the drawer closed with his foot. He stood and gathered his papers as he saw Miss Ruth.

"Sit, please. It's you I've come to see, but I can come back when you're finished." She nodded toward the open logbook.

"What can I do for you, Miss Ruth?" He was glad for the diversion. As long as she didn't start any God-talk.

"I've come on official business."

She sat at attention, her hands folded in her lap. Seriousness flooded her eyes.

"More ideas for the luau?"

"I've come to pay our debt."

"Debt?" He raised his eyebrows. "I don't understand."

"We are merely passengers on your vessel."

"Not by choice." He muttered, almost to himself.

"Yours or mine?"

His eyes widened, "I would've rescued whoever I found adrift. I was happy I was there."

"Others you might have rescued would not have been as much trouble."

"You mean they wouldn't have stripped my men of their wages, frightened me to death by scaling the ratlines, worn my breaches, preached to my crew, improved Cook's disposition, given Abel some much-needed mothering or written letters home for the men? Shall I go on?"

She blushed. "That is not necessary, Captain, but you must admit, we have depleted your medical supplies, not to mention your table linens." She smoothed the white skirt, "The cages that held Cook's chickens are empty. There have been expenses, Captain, not to mention the inconvenience."

He started to protest, but she held her palm upright, "I'm not here to negotiate, Captain."

"You've won so much from the crew then. You're able to afford the luau, your large shopping list, and pay for your passage?"

"I'll spend my gambling money on the men and no one else. It would be dishonorable to do otherwise." She crossed to the corner of the room and fumbled with the latch on her valise. It had rusted from being drenched in seawater. "I'll pay with this." Dangling from her fingers was a long strand of pearls, pale and milky. She reached into the pocket of her skirt. "I've made a list of everything Grandpa and I will need when we arrive in Hawaii. First, we will pay our debt to you, then a doctor for Grandpa. I believe the value of the pearls will cover everything."

"First, I'll go for the doctor."

"Thank you, Captain; you are very kind."

He shook his head and held out his hand, "May I see the list?" He tucked it into his vest pocket, then said, "That is a fascinating necklace. May I ask where you got it?"

"I went on a shopping extravaganza with two sisters I met in San Francisco." She felt a pang when she thought of her new wardrobe at the bottom of the sea, especially the nutmeg dress. For a moment, she pictured herself in that lovely gown with the sweetheart neckline and dainty puff sleeves set slightly off her shoulders. She loved how the dress moved when she walked. The way it made her waist look so tiny. Though not significant, the bustle tried her patience—the thin doeskin gloves in that delicious nutmeg color, ridiculous but, at the same time, lovely.

In her mind, she saw herself curtsy deeply to a handsome sea captain. He bowed and held out his arms. She entered them, and he twirled and spun her around the deck from aft to stern. She hummed the music only she could hear.

"Miss Ruth...?"

"Wha...?" She blinked.

"The necklace?"

Her fingers touched her throat, where the necklace had once felt warm and soft against her skin.

"The necklace?" he said again.

She cleared her throat. "Yes, Luella had a gentleman friend who knew a man on the waterfront with a shop full of treasures from around the world. It looked rather seedy on the outside, but it was like entering Aladdin's cave."

He ran the pearls through his fingers. He held them up to the light. He squinted, then bit gently on one of them. "Hmm." They were not real, a decent imitation, to be sure, but fake.

"Aren't they lovely? It's the first jewelry I've ever had. I know it will fetch a good price."

"Are you sure you want to part with them? I can advance you and John enough money to get by and provide passage to Alaska."

"I appreciate your offer Captain Walker, but as my Aunt Elvira would say, that necklace is just a material thing. Our debt to you is more important. We are honor-bound to pay it."

"All right then. Will you trust me with these, Miss Ruth? I, too, know a man on the waterfront."

"Does he have an Aladdin's cave? May I come with you, just to look?"

"When we dock, I will send for a doctor. You'll want to be here when he arrives."

She looked down at her hands, clasped tightly together. "I hope the doctor has a medicine that will allow Grandpa to travel right away. He seems so weak. I don't want to delay our journey any longer, and grandfather doesn't either."

"Wait and see what the doctor says." He wanted to ask why they were heading North, but both she and her grandfather had been vague when questioned about their personal business.

She rose and held out her hand. "Thank you, Captain."

He stood, giving a slight bow as he took her hand. "You are welcome, Miss Ruth. I am at your service."

Captain Walker's gaze lingered on her as she left the cabin. Staring at her was getting to be a habit, one he didn't like. Maybe if he went ashore and experienced every kind of pleasure the port offered, as he had done in years past, this ache would be soothed.

He shook his head. This was a different, unusual kind of yearning. There was something about this woman; compassionate, kind, joyful, and so much more. What was it about Miss Ruth?

"*Me.*" Came a whisper from deep inside. Captain Walker jumped to his feet. He was a man of action, a man of the sea. He'd rather be in the middle of a typhoon with treacherous waves and wind than do battle with a force he didn't understand and couldn't see.

He opened the drawer again and took out the bottle. He stared at it, took a long drink, regretted it, then opened the porthole and threw the bottle into the sea.

He pocketed the pearls, convinced he would not make a profit from this voyage. Perhaps it would be better for him when she departed the China Doll, and he never saw her again. Easier on his mind, not his heart. He gazed out of the porthole and wanted to retrieve the sunken bottle.

He patted his pocket. Thank God for the pearls and the luau. *Thank God? Where did that thought originate?*

John and Rachel Ruth stood in the bow of the China Doll as the Hawaiian Islands grew larger with each passing minute.

"I'm glad you're feeling better, Grandpa."

John, weak and still very ill, leaned heavily on the rail. He nodded but did not trust himself to speak. He had made an effort to stand and watch as they approached Honolulu, but he didn't feel any better. The pressure in his lungs seemed to increase by the day.

Rachel Ruth plunged into the middle of an ongoing conversation, "Here we are in the South Seas, and all I want to do is throw my arms around my father and cry, *Daddy, I love you.* I also want to cross my arms, stomp my foot, look him in the eye, and berate him for abandoning my mother and me. I almost hate him at times, but then my heart leans toward him with a love I don't understand. It's confusing! I try not to think about it. Is that wrong?"

"It's very human, my dear."

Rachel Ruth nodded, gazed at the horizon, then turned toward her grandfather with pleading eyes, "But is it wrong?"

"Things tend to fester when one doesn't deal with them. Look at your situation with Thomas."

Rachel Ruth covered her face with her hands, "What a mess that was."

He brushed her cheek with his knuckles, "And so?"

She shook her head, "Sometimes I'm just so furious."

"What emotion is causing your anger?"

"I don't know."

"Anger always sits on something. Hurt. Loss. Sadness. Most people are more comfortable with vexation and rage than deep pain."

The lemon drop sun and cotton candy clouds seemed an incongruous setting to talk about anger. The scent of the island's flowers, sweet and pure, seemed to mock her.

"What do you do, Grandpa? You're so calm."

John inhaled the sweet breeze and thought for a moment. He laid his hands on the rail. Rachel Ruth covered them with her own, "Grandpa?"

"He was always more his mother's child. As he got older, he competed with me, needed to best me in whatever we were doing." John shook his head and gazed over the water. "He wasn't able to recognize my love or receive it."

Rachel Ruth squeezed his hand, and sadness filled her voice, "How could he not?"

They gazed at the buildings of Honolulu as they came into focus. The old man rubbed his eyes and blinked away the moisture. "When he abandoned you and your mother, I lost what little respect I had for him. I knew I had not been the father he needed."

"But he sent for you, Grandpa. He wanted you to take care of things. I try to remember that when I'm so mad, I could spit."

John kissed her cheek, "Thank God he telegraphed me. I shudder to think what would have happened if...." John closed his eyes and sent a brief thank-you upward, "Just before she died, your mother begged me to forgive him. With God's help, I did."

Rachel Ruth hung her head and whispered, "I can't even pray."

"I couldn't either, and I told the Lord that," John chuckled and kissed Rachel Ruth's hand, "He answered most strangely."

"How?"

"He gave this crusty old cowboy a poem. I laugh when I think about it."

"But Grandpa, you read a lot, all kinds of things."

"I don't usually read poetry. But when I don't know what to pray, I recite this one. Let's see, how did it go?"

Like Elisha's servant captured by fear,
Show me angel armies hovering near.
Give me spiritual eyes to know what's real
Beyond what I see, beyond what I feel.

Like Elijah standing in the mouth of the cave
When I run away, not feeling brave.
Give me spiritual ears so I can hear
Your still small voice, loud and clear.

Like two men walking the Emmaus road,
Walk beside me now and lighten my load.
Give me a spiritual mind to understand
Your marvelous, timeless, grace-filled plan.

You offer me a Spirit-filled soul
Where guilt and shame have no control.
And when I falter and when I fail,
The hands that lift me bear the print of a nail.

They stood at the rail and watched the sailors scramble to obey Captain Walker's orders, anchoring the ship and mooring it securely to the dock.

John doubled over and clutched his chest, unable to control his coughing. The air in his lungs seemed as thick as jam, and he couldn't clear them. He wheezed and coughed. Josiah and Abel ran to support him and half-carried him to his bunk below. Rachel Ruth followed and tried to remember the words to his poem.

"Go topside, Missy. I don't want you to miss anything. I'm going to have a little sleep."

She kissed his cheek. Abel met her outside the cabin door, "Will he be alright, Miss Ruth?"

She pushed the worry from her voice and said, "Of course he will, Abel. Now explain everything that's happening in the harbor."

They stood in the stern, out of the way of the crew's hustle and bustle—shouts from the Captain and the first mate, sailors scrambling to obey.

Abel pointed out the different types of ships; inter-island schooners, aging clippers, and their ugly stepsisters, the steamships that belched black smoke. There were fishing boats, an out-of-date whaler, and several outrigger canoes. The unfamiliar noise and hodge-podge of movement confused the rancher's granddaughter.

After completing the necessary paperwork for the cargo's offloading, Captain Walker left the shipping company's dockside office. He was off to find a doctor and see a man about some pearls. Josiah could see to the remaining chores. He didn't see his cabin boy and the lovely Miss Ruth waving to him.

"Miss Ruth?"

"Yes, Abel." She smiled down at him.

"Have you ever eaten a pineapple?"

"I've never even heard of a pineapple."

"You would love it. It's yellow, like sunshine."

"I'm sure I would." She wondered if they tasted like the oranges she ate in San Francisco. "Have you ever eaten a crabapple?"

"No, never heard of it. Have you ever eaten mango?"

"Can't say that I have. What about huckleberries?"

"Nope," Abel said.

They continued this conversation for several minutes, then Abel pointed to an elderly man boarding the ship. "That's Doctor Browning."

"Good afternoon, young man. How's that leg of yours?"

Abel danced a bit of a jig and grinned at the doctor. "Stronger than ever, you'd never know it was busted."

"Good boy." Doctor Browning patted him on the shoulder and glanced toward her, "Captain Walker sent me, I assume you are Miss Ruth. Now, where's my patient?"

She stepped forward and introduced herself, "That would be my grandfather. This way, Doctor."

She stood outside the door and waited while Doctor Browning examined the old man. Rachel Ruth forced herself to remain calm, but her stomach quivered just the same.

Doctor Browning beckoned, and she crossed the tiny cabin, knelt next to the bunk, took her grandfather's hand, and pressed it to her cheek.

"It's all right, Missy," John sighed and smiled at her.

"Being exposed to the elements during a terrible storm did him no good, Doctor Browning. Several times since, he seemed to rally and get a bit better, but it never lasted," Rachel Ruth said.

"Yes, to be expected, and each time left him weaker?"

"That's right."

"Can I travel? We were on our way to Alaska, and...." John's voice faded as he saw the Doctor frown.

Rachel Ruth squeezed her grandfather's hand. "The important thing is for you to get better, Grandpa." She turned to Doctor Browning and pleaded, "Please, I'll do anything."

"I would like to put him in the hospital."

"No hospital," John objected as a round of coughing and wheezing assailed him. His eyes pleaded with his granddaughter.

"You rest while I escort the Doctor to the deck. He'll give me instructions for your care."

As they left, Doctor Browning told the young woman, "His cough is an attempt to release the fluid building up in his lungs. Unfortunately, it's not an effective means in his weakened state. He must not travel."

"Not at all?"

"Not until he's much stronger."

She saw the lie in the doctor's eyes and heard the deceit in his tone. She pushed away the thought that Grandpa would never leave these islands.

She squared her shoulders and took a deep breath, "I'll have to find a place to live and a way to support us. Frankly, Doctor Browning, I have very few skills that would translate to this tropical city. I can herd cattle, rope and brand calves, kill, and pluck chickens. I can shoot and hunt."

He smiled sadly. "The next few months will be difficult. Could you teach children? There is a mission school just outside of town."

"Our foreman has a little boy and a girl who I love, but I've never taught them." She remembered Ellie's school and how the teacher said she was a natural.

Doctor Browning brushed her lack of experience aside. "Sister Agnes has been in Hawaii for nearly forty years. She's never married, and her brothers and sister in New England are anxious for her to visit. Lots of nieces and nephews to meet, some even grown with children of their own."

"Is she a good teacher?"

"I sent my children to the mission school so that they could learn from her, and now they send theirs."

Rachel Ruth took a deep breath and stretched down to her toes, "If she's willing to teach me to teach, I will be a good student."

He scribbled the name on a scrap of paper and handed it to her, "I wish there was more I could do for you, Miss Ruth."

"Thank you, Doctor Browning," she held out her hand. "About the hospital, does he have to go?"

"I've written my name and office address on that paper. Let me know where you'll be living. In any case, I want to see your grandfather again next week. If he takes a turn for the worse, I will definitely put him in the hospital." Chin tucked into his shoulders, the medical man turned away.

Rachel Ruth stood on deck and watched the waves crashing against Diamond Head's rocky base. Tears streamed down her cheeks, unchecked.

I'm a long way from Texas, Lord, and even farther from Alaska. And now the only father I have ever known, my own dear Grandpa John—

Captain Walker mentally reviewed his list. Cargo manifest, check. Doctor Browning, check. Bank, check. Now he needed to see a man about some pearls.

"You right, Captain Walker," the aged Chinese trader behind the counter said. "These pearls, fake. Many be fooled. I take them off your hands, you like?"

Captain Walker shook his head, "That won't be necessary, Chen, sentimental value only. But I would like to see some real pearls, and don't try to fool me, you old cheater."

"Never you, Captain Walker, you too clever." Chen cackled as he brought a tray of pearls from the backroom of his crowded establishment and set them on the counter. They were all lovely. The luster shone even in the dim light of the windowless cubbyhole the old man called a shop. One pearl stood out above all the others, three times as large, creamier, smoother, and more lustrous. Captain Walker picked it up.

"Very good. You choose Pearl of Great Price."

"All your pearls have a great price, I'm sure." Captain Walker snorted.

"But this pearl, a man sell all to buy, Sister Agnes say. You know, missionary teacher lady?"

"I've heard of her, but what does she have to do with these pearls?"

Chen shook his head, "Sister Agnes, tell of pearl so perfect, you must give all to possess, I ask where to buy. She say, not talking pearls. Very confusing. Bible talk, I think."

Captain Walker thought Miss Ruth probably knew, "I want it, and I'll pay a fair, not a great price."

Chen bobbed his head up and down. Captain Walker had purchased many things over the years but never gems or jewelry. "You have woman now, maybe wife?"

"Mind your own business, Chen, and put this on a gold chain. I'll pick it up tomorrow."

"Excellent, Captain."

His last errand took more time than he liked. Captain Walker stopped at the newspaper office to check on the Northern Star, then hired a carriage to take him back to the waterfront and what he anticipated was going to be an intriguing and informative conversation. There was no mention of the Ruths on the Northern

Star's passenger list, which the newspaper had printed when the ship was presumed lost at sea.

Who were they, really? And why did he feel such a great responsibility toward them?

"I'm afraid I have bad news, Miss Ruth; the Northern Star never made it to Alaska and is presumed lost at sea."

"My heart hurts to hear you say it."

Now was the time to tell her there was no record of a John or Missy Ruth on board. He couldn't get the words out. "I have stops at several other islands, and then I sail to Cartagena and finally San Francisco. Your family has probably been notified that you perished at sea, but I can send a telegram from Frisco saying you are alive and well in Hawaii."

Rachel Ruth thought briefly of Aunt Ellie, then shook her head. "Thank you, Captain Walker, but no."

"No?" He frowned and picked his spyglass off his desk.

"I'll wait until Grandfather, that is...." She shuddered.

"Is that kind? They think you died." He put the glass down and opened the ship's log. What was she hiding?

"But what happens if Grandpa doesn't get better? They would have to go through that horrible grief all over again."

"But surely..."

"I know my Aunt Ellie. She'd overcome every obstacle to come here. She's older than Grandpa and such a homebody. Besides, there's Jed and Mary and all the babies. I won't take her away from them."

"You know best, Miss Ruth." Captain Walker snapped his log-book closed.

Rachel Ruth bit her lip, "I don't. You should ask Grandpa."

"Will you agree to whatever he thinks is best?"

"I will."

Alone in his cabin, Captain Walker pulled the fake pearls from his pocket and slid them into the bottom drawer of his desk. He thought about how dearly he had paid for Chen's Pearl of Great Price. How would he present the necklace so she would accept it and what had possessed him to spend such a fortune on it?

He leaned back in his chair and closed his eyes, and thought about all he needed to do before his next voyage. Fortunately, he had several weeks before he sailed. At the top of the list was Cook's name. He just might be the solution to all of Miss Ruth's problems.

TWENTY-THREE

A day made of diamonds, every facet expertly cut, sharp, and clear. It was a time of accomplishing tasks for Rachel Ruth as Captain Walker escorted her from shop to shop.

"Isn't this blue silk lovely? Silas will be pleased, and his granddaughter will be thrilled."

"This green one matches your eyes." He said, lifting a bolt from the pile on the table.

"It's pretty, maybe someday."

"I'll buy it for you."

"You will do no such thing! You've wanted to buy me something in every shop we've entered. Please, let's focus on the crew." She waved her list at him.

"Truly?"

"Truly." Seeing the disappointment in his eyes, she quickly added, "There is something you can treat me to if you are willing."

"Anything, Miss Ruth." The Captain returned her smile.

"Can we stop at that quaint little tea shop we passed? I never realized how thirsty shopping makes one."

The smell of plumeria and tuberose blossoms filled the air as they walked to the dainty shop. He opened the door and bowed, "Your wish is my command."

Rachel Ruth noticed how large the Captain looked in the too-small chair; he squirmed, trying to get comfortable, but he did not complain. She admired him even more. As the only male in the place, he suffered several feminine stares.

The miniature pineapple and macadamia nut scones were perfect. Rachel Ruth matched him scone for scone, and he reordered twice. The Chinese green tea was light and thirst-quenching. Captain Walker told her a steaming mug of Kona coffee would give her more satisfaction.

Rachel Ruth touched her napkin to the corners of her mouth then picked up her list. "I'm almost done. I've made purchases to send to the men's families. That was great fun. But you bought Abel way too many clothes."

"I bought several sizes, and the boy will grow."

"Thank you for that suggestion, Captain. I wouldn't have thought of that."

She was quiet for a moment then said, "I want to buy the men pocketknives and neckerchiefs, candy and tobacco, little things."

"We'll stop at the Island Mercantile on the way back to the ship."

"Thank you, Captain."

As they left the shop, Rachel Ruth remembered she needed to replace her stationery. "I've written farewell letters to the crew. Will you give them to the men after you have sailed?"

He nodded and hoped that she had written to him, as well.

Rachel Ruth stopped midway up the gangplank and looked at all the ships in the harbor. The fragrances of the island's flora and fauna had streamed all the way to the docks. It mixed with the heady smells of cinnamon and nutmeg from the Spice Islands being off-loaded from a nearby ship. She breathed deeply and smiled as she saw the crew doing their chores, anxious to be ashore. They had become as dear to her as the wranglers on the ranch.

"Are you sure the luau is taken care of, Captain? I know you said to leave it to you."

"I gave the money to Cook, and he will procure the provisions and do all the cooking."

"But I wanted him to enjoy himself."

He took her elbow and led her up the gangplank. "Believe me, he will. His wife, Iolana, is Kanaka Maoli, what we call Hawaiian, and comes from a large family. They will provide the labor, and he will be the boss. Cook will expand his menu beyond plain ship's fare. You will taste things you can't even imagine."

"I look forward to it."

"I've taken the liberty to talk to Cook about other things."

"Other things?"

"I heard you have an appointment with Sister Agnes at the mission school. I'm sure she will take you on."

"I hope so."

"You and John will need a place to live."

"I'm going to ask Sister Agnes for a recommendation."

"Cook's place is half of a mile this side of the mission school. It's nothing more than a village. Most of Iolana's relatives live there."

"Would there be a place for us?"

"Cook says you would be welcome, that is if you would not object..." he sputtered.

"Object to what?"

"You would be the only white person."

"Does anyone speak English?"

"Iolana, plus the children who learned from Sister Agnes."

"Do you think she would teach me some Hawaiian words?" Rachel Ruth thought for a minute and looked at the Captain, "Are you sure they would accept me?" Doubt flickered in her eyes.

"Cook says they are looking forward to meeting the white woman who helped him in the galley and defied the captain."

"Defied?"

"Wore his breeches, climbed into the crow's nest. You're practically a legend."

Rachel Ruth joined in his laughter. "This will be better for Grandpa than a hospital, and I am not a city girl."

Captain Walker, relieved, although it was the response he had expected, said, "Are you sure about this, Miss Ruth? You're not offended?"

"Captain, I've slept under stormy skies during cattle drives and campouts. I don't need luxury."

Captain Walker tugged at his neckerchief, "I meant, are you okay with being the only white in the village?"

"Remember when I told you the wranglers were my playmates, practically family?"

"Yes?"

"What you don't know is those men included a freed slave, a Choctaw, a Mexican, and a sweet little old Chinaman who had run away from the railroad."

"A Chinaman?"

"I was ten when Grandpa found him half dead on the plains. We nursed him back to health, and when he recovered, Grandpa offered to stake him and take him wherever he wanted to go."

"Of course, he chose to stay."

Rachel Ruth laughed, pointed her toes toward each other, pressed her palms together as if in prayer, and said – "Ling Si bowed to Grandpa and said, 'Mr. John, you belly good cowboy,' then he pointed to himself and said, 'Ling Si belly good cowboy.' He was terrified of horses and cattle, but he planted a garden out behind the chicken coops." She shuddered, "He made the foulest smelling and worst tasting concoctions from herbs and such. He kept us healthy over the years, the animals, too."

Captain Walker's eyes lit up, and he snapped his fingers, "That's an idea!"

"What?"

"There are many Chinese working on the sugar plantations. There must be an herbalist or two among them. They might know something about John's condition."

"Oh, I hope so. Did you know there's a verse in the Bible that says God has given us every leaf for medicine?"

"Of course, there is," he sighed.

The village, perched on a little knoll with a view of Diamond Head, exuded a tropical lushness vastly different from Texas. Rachel Ruth's head swiveled back and forth, each flowering bush and tree more delightful and fragrant than the last.

Captain Walker ignored the villagers' greetings as he strode through the cluster of small houses. He gave a quick nod when it couldn't be avoided.

"I don't want you to meet anyone until after you've seen the hut. If it's not suitable, we'll slip away and pretend we were never here."

Rachel Ruth's eyebrows drew together, and she wanted to protest. Instead, she lengthened her stride to match his. The path angled around a giant banyan tree.

"There it is," he said.

She drew in her breath. "You said this was nothing more than a hut."

"That's all it is."

She peeked in the front window, "I've never seen a hut with such lovely wooden floors or beautiful white shutters."

"The floor is koa, a wood native to these islands."

There was no lock on the door, and Captain Walker entered without knocking. Rachel Ruth opened the inner doors revealing two small bedrooms. A tiny cooking area, a sitting room, and a huge covered porch in the back completed her inspection. "It's lovely, Captain, and the back porch is almost as big as the whole cottage." She looked at him and added, "I refuse to call it a hut."

"Lanai."

"What?"

"In Hawaii, the outdoor living space is called a lanai. You will spend a lot of time there."

"Grandpa, too, there's a hammock strung between those two palm trees."

She pointed toward a small building behind a large bush.

"The necessary." He said, his face the color of a nearby hibiscus.

"At home, we called it the outhouse."

They heard giggling from the overgrown garden surrounding the lanai. Rachel Ruth saw several brown faces peeking through the foliage. Excited whispers and giggles filled the air.

Captain Walker stood at attention and took a whistle from his jacket pocket. He tweeted twice, "Ahoy, you scalawags. Come forward and give Miss Ruth a proper Hawaiian greeting, or I'll make you all walk the plank."

A gaggle of laughing children burst forth and surrounded Captain Walker. He bent down, and they placed leis of pikake and orchids around his neck and kissed his cheek, chattering in a mixture of Hawaiian and English that Rachel Ruth did not understand.

Captain Walker reached out and pulled her to her knees. The children turned their attention to her. Soon she was up to her eyebrows in the fragrant leis. Her cheeks, still sticky from the children's sweet kisses, dampened with happy tears. She plopped down on the grass, and two toddlers tumbled into her lap. She laughed and kissed them on the top of their heads.

The first of your many children, the unexpected whisper rose from her heart. She closed her eyes in confused wonder then pushed the thought aside.

Captain Walker stared at Miss Ruth and cleared his throat. Neither she nor the children paid attention until he blew his whistle again. He raised his eyebrows and nodded toward the cottage.

She scampered to her feet as the Captain announced Miss Ruth and her grandfather would stay in the village. They hugged his knees and nodded their heads as he charged them to take care of their guests.

"No worries, Captain, we take good care of your lady," one of the boys said.

Both Rachel Ruth and Captain Walker blushed. He blew his whistle and shooed the children away. "The luau will be on the other side of that banyan tree, Cook's front lawn. We can hang a hammock so John can be a part of the festivities."

"You thought of everything Captain Walker. I am in your debt once again."

He smiled to himself. *If only she knew.* "Miss Ruth, I have thought of something else. Whenever you're ready to sail to Alaska, that is, —" He paused to find the right words.

"Have you been talking to my grandfather, Captain Walker?"

"What?"

"Grandpa and I have discussed that very thing. If I need to travel to Alaska alone," her voice broke, and she took a deep breath, "I know it's a lot to ask, probably terribly impractical, not to mention horribly expensive for you. Never mind, it's impossible."

"Haven't you told me nothing is impossible with your God?" He teased.

"Yes, but...some things are highly improbable."

"And aren't you always saying faith can move mountains?"

"Yes, but..."

"Don't you think your faith can move the China Doll from Hawaii to Alaska?"

"But it's such a huge imposition."

"Miss Ruth, you usually don't dither."

"Truth be told, Captain, I'm feeling too prideful to be direct."

"Then let me be direct for you. I would like your word that you'll not sail to Alaska with any other captain."

She let out a sigh of relief yet continued with a myriad of objections.

"I have several connections in Alaska, Miss Ruth. When my grandfather took me on as a cabin boy, my mother put her foot down on long sea voyages. So, we sailed from San Francisco to Alaska with foodstuffs and tools and brought back furs and huge ice blocks from Swan Lake in Sitka. I've even brought ice from that lake here to Honolulu. I won't have any trouble getting cargo to take to and from Alaska."

"Grandfather will be so relieved. I promised him I wouldn't sail with anyone but you."

"Now, promise me."

"But we've already talked about it. It's decided."

"Miss Ruth, I may be away when John passes." He cleared his throat and forced himself to go on, "it may be months before I put into port here. Promise me you'll wait."

Her tears had a mind of their own. They would not obey her command to stay where they belonged. Captain Walker had said when, not if.

"The thought of Grandpa's death tears at my heart."

Captain Walker held her as she grieved for the man who was both father and grandfather, friend and mentor, the man who might soon leave her terribly alone.

The donkey's bray told Rachel Ruth, Kamalei, Cook's son, had arrived to take her to town. She kissed her grandfather. "I'll return soon."

"Give my best to Captain Walker and the crew. Tell them I will pray for calm seas and fair winds."

"I will."

"Miss Ruth, wait." Iolana, Cook's wife, ran across the lawn. She clutched a ridiculously frilly pink parasol. The Hawaiian woman's face exploded into a huge smile, "For you. All the fancy ladies in

Honolulu have them. Hawaiian sun is strong. White ladies are weak. Excuse me, I didn't mean—"

"Thank you, Iolana. You are most kind." Rachel Ruth's smile was almost as big as Iolana's. She looked at the woman's brown face and then down at her own tanned hands, clutching the parasol. There were just a few shades of difference in their skin tones. Nevertheless, it was a kind gesture.

"Hurry, Miss Ruth," Kamalei called as he brought the donkey and cart to the front of the little cottage. "Papa says they sail on the tide."

"Just a moment Kamalei." Rachel Ruth ran inside to fetch the basket containing her gift for Captain Walker and the ginger cake she had made for the crew.

The donkey clip-clopped along at a good pace. "Miss Ruth, why do you use the parasol? You're almost as brown as me."

She laughed as she stowed the parasol next to her in the seat. "It does seem silly, doesn't it? Growing up under the hot Texas sun, not to mention weeks on the sea, have darkened my skin." She put her bare arm next to his, "I'm almost as pretty as you."

"I never met a white lady like you. Most white people do not like us, except Papa and Captain Walker, and Sister Agnes, of course. But the white ladies in town hide behind their parasols, afraid of the sun, afraid of us."

"But, it's glorious," Rachel Ruth protested as she raised her face to the sun.

"You're not like a white person at all."

"And what about you, Kamalei? Your father is white. That makes you half white."

"It is difficult," the young man said with pain in his eyes, "to my father's people, I am not white. To my mother's people, I am not

235

Kanaka Maoli."

"I'm so sorry," Rachel Ruth put her arm around his shoulders.

"Maybe God should make all the white people marry all the dark people, and then we would all be the same color."

"I think He delights in all the different colors He made."

"Still, it is difficult." He shrugged his shoulders and slapped the reins, "Do you want me to sample that ginger cake?"

"Only if you tell me it's good enough to give to the crew."

"I'm sure it's not. I better eat it all."

"You'll have one piece and no more, young man." She reached for the basket housing the cake, then asked, "Will you be a sailor when you're older?"

"I will be a cook, but in a fancy hotel. Did you know my papa visits fine restaurants in every port to try their food? When he's between voyages, he practices on us. I like it so much when he's home."

"I was amazed by what he made for the luau."

They crested a small hill and saw the harbor. As noisy and busy as it was when Rachel Ruth first arrived. It didn't take long to spot the China Doll.

Kamalei slapped the reins, the donkey picked up the pace, and they soon arrived at the dock. He tied the sweaty animal to a mooring cable, gave him half a guava, and raced up the gangplank and into the galley. The crew noticed their arrival.

"Ahoy, Miss Ruth."

"Thanks for the luau, Miss Ruth."

"What's in the basket, Miss Ruth?" Abel asked.

"A little something for Captain Walker."

She saw disappointment run across Abel's face, "And a little something for the rest of you." He brightened as she handed him the basket and gave him instructions to hand out the golden-brown cake.

The Captain, who'd been giving orders to his first mate, turned to her and tipped his cap. "Miss Ruth."

"Captain Walker."

"This is it, then."

"Yes, it is. I brought you something." She held out the packet of letters for the crew. He beckoned Abel and gave him instructions to put them in his cabin.

Rachel Ruth gave him a package wrapped in brown paper. "This is for you, my Bible."

Captain Walker thought about his long conversation with John, who told him they had left the ranch in Texas, visited a silver mine in Denver, escaped Miss Ruth's deranged suitor on the pier in San Francisco, and then endured the ordeal at sea before Old Skookum spotted their lifeboat.

He ran his thumb over the embossed name on the cover, RR Merritt. 'Rachel Ruth Merritt,' John had told him her name. "I will treasure it and accept it on one condition."

"What is that, Captain?"

"That you accept this." He took a small box from his pocket and handed it to her.

"My gift also comes with a condition, Captain."

"And that is?" He smiled at her.

"I want you to read it."

"I want you to wear it."

She opened the box and gasped. He saw the refusal in her eyes.

"I was told it was a Pearl of Great Price," he said softly.

Her gaze shifted from the necklace to him. "In that case, I will wear it next to my heart." She slipped the chain over her head and beneath her blouse. Her eyes glistened with tears as she thanked him.

He did not need all the arguments he had prepared to convince her to accept the expensive gift. Once again, Miss Ruth had surprised him.

"It will remind me to pray you find the true Pearl of Great Price," she whispered.

He looked at her, puzzled. She laid her hand on the Bible. "You will find it in here. I could have purchased a new Bible for you, Captain. But I thought it more meaningful for you to have mine. It's underlined and scribbled in. I even drenched it in seawater."

"It will remind me of you."

"It will point you to Him."

He nodded as the ship's whistle blew.

"Goodbye, Captain Harlan Walker. I will miss you." Rachel Ruth held out her hand.

He looked deep into her eyes. "Goodbye, Rachel Ruth Merritt. I will see you on my return."

TWENTY-FOUR

Rachel Ruth fluttered about the little cottage. She checked her hair in the gilded mirror above the credenza that housed the ornate Victorian dishes. "I can't believe this cottage belongs to Captain Walker. Why would he lead me to believe it was guest quarters used by Cook's extended family?"

"Perhaps he thought you would be uncomfortable living in his house."

"It was kind of him, but I feel badly he had to stay aboard his ship these past weeks."

"Hmmm." It was clear to John the girl had no idea the handsome, older seaman loved her. But was he in love with her? And what were her feelings for the attractive sea-faring man?

John watched his granddaughter as she fiddled with her socks and boots, then discarded them in favor of the thin sandals Iolana had provided.

"He has some wonderful things from his world travels, doesn't he, Grandpa?"

"And your favorite would be the massive bookcase in his bedroom, right?"

"I want to read every volume before he returns." She sliced a pineapple as she talked and took two bananas from the small table's wooden bowl. "He's a good man. I'm sure the Lord sent him to rescue us."

John agreed and wondered if absence would cause the Captain's heart to grow fonder or if he would be satisfied with a deep friendship?

"Iolana's Aunties will be over soon. I can't pronounce their names. Hawaiian is such a lyrical language, don't you think?" She took her hair down, brushed it out, and put it back up into a tighter bun this time.

"Missy, you'll be fine." Violent coughing interrupted him. He waved away her concern. "I agree the language is beautiful. You get your love of words from your father."

"Don't you wonder why we ended up here? What is God doing? Why you're so sick?" She came and knelt before him. He saw the doubt and worry etched on her face.

He took a deep breath and fought the urge to cough. The rattle in his chest was more pronounced, and his ability to clear the fluid in his lungs, weaker. He looked into his granddaughter's face, grateful he was there at her birth. He reached out and touched her cheek. "When you have lived as long as I have, my dear, curiosity often fades, and it is enough to know that God is working."

"I hope so."

"Only hope so?"

She kissed his cheek, "My curiosity and anxiety about what, when, how, and why He's doing what He's doing would kill several cats."

She hugged him and frowned. He could tell she wondered where the robust and well-muscled pioneer of the American West had gone. His heart hurt to have his dear granddaughter see him so weak.

She found the pink parasol, set it by the front door, and then brought her grandfather the sliced pineapple and bananas. She patted him on the shoulder. "Now, where's that silly parasol?"

He pointed to the dainty thing leaning against the door. "Missy, do not be nervous. You will be fine."

"I'd feel better if I had already met Sister Agnes. Unfortunately, my interview with the superintendent, Mr. Lewis, did not go well. He seemed stiff and less than impressed with my lack of experience. I get the impression he wanted to tell me not to come, but there were no other applicants."

"From what I've heard, 'stiff' is a word no one would ever use to describe this Sister Agnes."

"I need her approval if I'm to have the job," She looked in the mirror again, raised her hand to her hair, sighed, "I'll be back this afternoon."

The screen door banged, and he heard Cook's children greet her. All eight of them were students at the Mission School. He settled back with his bowl of fruit and bowed his head.

I sense you are cocooning Rachel Ruth in this lush green land. Sister Agnes will give her a way to support herself. Cook's family will comfort her as she grieves. And, of course, Captain Walker will be her protector on the next leg of her journey. Thank you. He fell asleep before his final amen.

Mid-morning, the whispers of Iolana and her Aunties woke him. They made short work of tidying the cottage. They squeezed oranges for juice, boiled eggs, baked coconut muffins. The Aunties did not speak English but chattered, laughed, and fluttered about like colorful birds of paradise.

After settling him in the hammock, they begged for cowboy stories, and Iolana interpreted. John wanted to hear about the sea-going adventures of their ancestors.

After lunch, Iolana read from the Psalms. First a line in English, then Hawaiian. He breathed more naturally as the melodic sound of her voice washed over him.

He asked her why all the Aunties came every day. She laughed and said each one wanted the privilege of caring for him, but no one wanted to take turns, so they all came. It was only fair.

Yesterday, Doctor Browning frowned through his entire examination and shook his head. The Aunties looked suitably solemn and nodded as he gave them detailed instructions, which they didn't understand and promptly ignored. They much preferred giving John the concoctions from the Chinese herbalist.

John thought the tinctures were as foul-tasting as anything Ling Si had prepared back home. He drank everything he was given, more to placate them than from any hope of improvement. They giggled at the awful faces he made, then smiled and patted him when he finished. He felt about six years old.

He drifted off to sleep, a fitful nap interrupted by bouts of uncontrolled coughing. It was getting harder and harder to breathe.

Iolana's four Aunties sat on the lanai and made leis, crocheted, or shelled macadamia nuts. They shook their heads as they watched over the old man. This cowboy, a friend of Iolana's husband, was ohana, family.

Cook's two oldest boys walked on either side of Rachel Ruth. The others skipped ahead or trailed behind.

"I see you still carry the parasol," Kamalei said.

"It is to remind me of your mother's kindness."

"But it remains unopened." Kamalei laughed.

Rachel Ruth brandished the parasol like a sword. "It will come in handy if we encounter pirates."

"No pirates here, just Sister Agnes, and she is a sweetie cake." He scratched his head and said, "a sweet cookie?"

"Sweetie pie."

As they approached the mission compound, the children ran ahead. They surrounded their beloved teacher, and all talked at once. Several fingers pointed in Miss Ruth's direction. The small plump schoolteacher looked over the heads of the young ones.

"It's very nice to meet you, Sister Agnes. I've heard so much about you." Rachel Ruth extended her hand.

Sister Agnes ignored it, "I don't have time for you right now, Miss Ruth. Sit on that bench. I will attend to you when I can."

"Yes, ma'am." Rachel Ruth felt her cheeks flame. *Had she done something wrong?*

Rachel Ruth felt the children's young eyes follow her as she made her way to the bench. She gave them a wave and a huge smile to erase the worry in their eyes or perhaps to relieve the concern in her own.

"Come, children," Sister Agnes said, "We will begin where we left off yesterday."

The mission school's main building was a solid wooden structure with a tile roof. But Sister Agnes held her classes under a thatched roof held up by four stout poles. The children sat on bamboo mats that covered the bare ground.

Sister Agnes, wearing a brightly colored muumuu, looked native. She wore flowers in her grey hair, and her feet were bare. Rachel Ruth smiled and nodded whenever the teacher glanced in her direction.

Twice during the day, Kamalei started in her direction with a jug of water. Sister Agnes stopped him. He frowned, looked at Miss Ruth, shrugged, and went back to his studies.

At the end of their lessons, Sister Agnes dismissed the children. They gathered their things and left, throwing confused glances toward Miss Ruth.

Sister Agnes disappeared for about twenty minutes. When she returned, she handed Miss Ruth the jug of water and a plate of fruit and fried fish. Rachel Ruth whispered a soft thank you, took a long drink of water, and ate a mango.

Sister Agnes circled the bench, then sat on a mat next to Miss Ruth. "You'll do."

"How can you know that? You haven't talked to me. You don't know if I have the skills." Her eyebrows drew down, and so did the corners of her mouth.

"I watched you on the road. You talked with the children, laughed, they chased you, you chased them, you are adept at engaging them. The only thing that puzzled me was the parasol flaying about."

The young woman hung her head and mumbled, "A sword."

"I beg your pardon, speak up, and don't ever be ashamed of the words you say."

She cleared her throat, straightened her shoulders, looked the elderly teacher in the eye, and said, "It was a sword. Protection from pirates."

Sister Agnes gave her a long solemn look. Rachel Ruth squirmed, then relaxed as the Sister said, "There are a lot of those in these islands. It was a good thing you were armed."

They laughed, then Rachel Ruth took another piece of fruit and asked, "What else do you know about me, Sister?"

"I see your lovely hair is fighting its restraining bun. The streaks of gold tell me you've spent a lot of time outdoors. Your calloused hands and tanned skin show me you work hard. I was short with you this morning, perhaps even rude, and you did not respond in kind but displayed good manners throughout the day. That tells me you have a measure of self-control.

"I ordered you to sit on this bench until I had time for you, and here you are six hours later, so I know you are either patient, persevering, or stubborn. Perhaps all three." Her eyes twinkled as she picked a strawberry off the fruit plate. "You are capable of following directions, but I have learned from a certain old salt that you managed to bend those directions to your will when you chose."

Rachel Ruth blushed and opened her mouth but didn't know what to say.

Sister Agnes patted her knee and said, "Silas is an old and dear friend of mine, but I could never interest him in spiritual things. I'm in your debt, Miss Ruth."

"I love him so."

"He was a bo'sun on the ship I traveled on decades ago. Someday I'll tell you how we sailed around the Horn."

"Yes, please."

"Back to business," Sister Agnes said, "I assume those are your notes." She looked at the papers on the bench.

Rachel Ruth gathered them together and handed them to Sister Agnes. "I confess I started taking them to keep from falling asleep. It was so muggy when the breeze died."

Sister Agnes gestured to the building next to their open-air pavilion. "It's even worse in there. I've taught my classes out here for the last thirty years. Don't let Mr. Lewis take this class inside." She looked at the papers in her hand and read:

> *Sister Agnes makes eye contact whenever she speaks with a child. Often, she gets down on her knees to look them in the eye. When Sister Agnes asked the children, "Is it okay to lie?"*
>
> *They all cried, "No!"*
>
> *Sister Agnes said, "But why is it wrong to lie?"*
>
> *Kamalei raised his hand and said, "Because the Bible said so."*
>
> *Sister Agnes told him that it was a perfect answer and then asked why the Bible says that? Silence. Sister Agnes leaned close to them and whispered, "Because, children, God is truth."*
>
> *The children clapped their hands and said: "We do not lie because God is the truth!" Sister Agnes is a genius!*

The good Sister looked up and said, "I'm no genius, but I do try to bring everything back to the character of God."

She continued reading:

> *I love how she sprinkles her lessons with Hawaiian words and even asks the children to help with pronunciation. She joins in the laughter when she butchers a word and lets the children gleefully correct her. I suspect she sometimes does it on purpose.*

Sister Agnes winked at Miss Ruth, poured herself a glass of water, took a long drink, then looked back down at the paper:

> *Sister Agnes asked about a little girl's mother who had been sick. Helped Iolana's daughter, Lani, get the tangles out of her hair. She seemed to know all about each child's family's joys and sorrows. She spent time with each one; a gentle touch here, a nod there, a wink and a grin for this one, a slight shake of*

her head to that one. Reading, writing, and arithmetic seemed to come second. These are lovely children who come from a strong and beautiful people. I like the way Sister Agnes references their history with dignity and respect.

The old missionary folded the paper, breathed a sigh of relief, and gave it back to Miss Ruth. "You'll do, Miss Ruth. Yes, indeed. You'll do."

It was the beginning of a beautiful friendship. Day after day, week after week, the older woman taught, the younger woman learned. Finally, Sister Agnes said she could leave her beloved students in Miss Ruth's hands.

The class had a good-bye party for their teacher with much laughter and a few tears.

Even though Alaska occupied Rachel Ruth's thoughts and her longing for her father did not abate, she gave her heart to these children of the Pacific. She aimed to become a teacher, mentor, and friend to these beautiful young ones.

The weeks melted into each other. Often Rachel Ruth stood on the knoll's crest at the edge of the village and looked beyond the bustle of the city, beyond Diamond Head, beyond the clippers and steamers. North, always, north. She prayed daily for her grandfather, who continued to weaken, and her father in far-off Alaska. She thought of Aunt Elvira and Jed's family back on the ranch and Maureen and Sean in Ireland and hoped they would all meet again.

She prayed for Captain Walker on the high seas. She checked her calendar daily but had no idea when the China Doll would sail into the harbor. It was difficult to believe she had been in this tropical haven for over a year. She was glad Sister Agnes was due to return in two months.

Rachel Ruth still worried her grandfather was not fit to travel. The journey across the West and their ordeal at sea had taken a toll on him. *Would he still be strong and vigorous if they had stayed on the ranch? If only he were more robust, they could plan their journey to Alaska.*

TWENTY-FIVE

Rachel Ruth and the children ignored the rain that had fallen steadily since the first class of the morning. However, its intensity had increased during the last two hours, and the wind shook the poles holding up the thatched roof.

Kamalei stood close to her and whispered, "The air is too warm, the sky too dark."

"Are we safe here, or should we go into the school building?"

He went to the edge of the mats and looked to the sky. "The children must go home to their families, get behind strong walls. There is time if we go now. But we must run."

"I'll go with the village children. You take the children of the sugar workers to the plantation. Mr. Townsend must shelter them in the big house."

She looked into his face. There was a history there. Centuries of sea-going people who knew how to read the sky and the winds. She gave him a quick hug. "Be safe, Kamalei, and hurry home."

"You also, Miss Ruth."

She gathered the village children and waved as Kamalei and his small group of students quickly left.

Mr. Lewis strode out of his classroom. "Surely, Miss Ruth, you are not taking the children out in this weather. Come into the building."

"I've been told it's going to get much worse, sir. I think it best to return them to their parents."

"Nonsense. It's this thatched abomination that's unsafe." He hurried back to the building but looked over his shoulder and barked, "I expect you to obey."

Did she believe Kamalei, whose heritage and knowledge of these islands went back centuries? Should she obey Mr. Lewis? She peered down the lane leading to the sugar plantation. Kamalei and his little group were already out of sight.

The others had scurried back to their mats when Mr. Lewis arrived. Rachel Ruth gathered them around her once more and said, "It's an adventure, dear ones. We're going to pretend pirates are after us and run to the village as fast as we can."

"Real pirates?" Lani's lip quivered.

Just Mr. Lewis, Rachel Ruth thought, then admonished herself. *He's probably doing the best he can, but he would do better if he trusted the Islanders.*

Rachel Ruth hoisted the little girl onto her back, "Certainly not. I would never let real pirates in my class, but it's exciting to pretend."

Lani held on to Miss Ruth's neck. "I'm not afraid."

"Of course not. You are courageous."

"Me too!"

"I'm brave."

"So am I."

"Yes, you are. We're going to get wet, but we won't mind. The biggest of you take the hands of the smallest. Quick march!" She held the parasol high like a banner, "Forward!"

Mr. Lewis yelled from an open window, "Miss Ruth, what are you doing?"

"What?" she hollered above the wind.

"Stop! I say," he bellowed, banged his head on the sill, and swore.

"Run, children. Pirates!" She pointed the pink parasol toward the village. They laughed and ran.

Mr. Lewis raged at the storm as he secured the shutters. "That Miss Ruth is as incorrigible as Sister Agnes. If only most of the donations weren't directed to the Sister. Now I'm saddled with her undesirable substitute."

"Did you say something, Mr. Lewis?" one of his students asked

"No," he growled while picturing Miss Ruth, who smiled politely and offered him a lemon drop whenever he gave her advice or directions. *Impertinent chit!* As soon as his back was turned, she followed all of Sister Agnes' dictates.

He secured the windows and the interior shutters and muttered about that feckless Miss Ruth.

The rain fell, warm and heavy. The wind groaned then howled, but it did not unleash its fury until the children were near the village. Mamas and papas snatched their precious ones, hurriedly thanked Miss Ruth, and ran for shelter.

She heard the words *cyclone* and *typhoon*. "I thought Hawaii was out of the path of severe tropical storms," Rachel Ruth said as she put Lani into her mother's arms.

"I'm not afraid of pirates, Mama. I'm brave."

Iolana spoke over the little girl's head, "We only get a storm like this once in a generation."

They heard a loud crack; a thick branch broke off the banyan tree and fell across the lane. Shingles, barrels, and small branches were pushed before it.

"Best get home, Miss Ruth. Fasten the shutters and get the lanai furniture in the house if you can. Stay inside."

"Yes, ma'am." The wind's increased strength forced her to double over as the rain slammed into her face. She had been in some fierce storms on the ranch, but nothing like this.

As she neared Captain Walker's cottage, she saw the front door had blown open, and the shutters flapped. She fastened them even as she called for her grandfather. The mango tree had snapped off at its base and fallen across the lanai, partially collapsing the corner of the roof. The kukui trees had been uprooted and tossed about, the palms nearly doubled over, and the hammock had blown away.

Heart pounding, the roaring in her ears louder than the wind, she searched for the old man. A few minutes later, almost miraculously, she was in a sea of calm. The wind died. The air steamed, muggy and oppressive. The rain had blinded her eyes; now, it was tears.

"Oh, Grandpa." It was apparent he had fallen from the hammock. She knelt and felt his legs, no broken bones. She moved the brush and the first of the small branches, then used a larger one as leverage to push the others out of the way. All the years of hard work on the ranch had developed her strength. She needed it now.

John moaned and opened glazed, unfocused eyes.

"Is the baby all right?" He held out his arms, "Born this Easter morning."

"Grandpa, it's me, Rachel Ruth." She felt his forehead, hot as lava.

He tried to rise but fell back.

"Don't try to move."

She looked around the lanai and saw the wind had torn the door off the Necessary and wedged it between two thick bushes. There was no sign of the outhouse except for the sizeable odorous hole in the ground. She rolled Grandpa onto the door and pulled it through the lanai. She had to stop several times and catch her breath before she had him in the house.

He opened his eyes. "I'm okay, Missy. I have been more uncomfortable on cattle drives," then winced as the pain in his chest let him know he had a couple of cracked ribs, or worse, broken ones.

"We've slept on the ground often enough, haven't we?" she said.

He nodded, then winced again.

"Stay right there. I'll bring the bed to you."

"Not going anywhere..." he panted.

Rachel Ruth pulled the mattress off his bed. As the wind howled and swirled, she got him out of his rain-soaked clothes and under the blankets.

The wind had blown out the bedroom window. Rachel Ruth pushed the Captain's massive bookcase in front of the window with a strength she didn't know she had, then shoved the dresser and the bed next to them and hoped for the best. Exhausted and unmindful of her chattering teeth and wet clothes, she lay next to Grandpa John and slept.

The storm flattened the sugarcane fields, Mr. Townsend's mill, and most of the workers' thatched huts. The plantation's main house was damaged but remained standing. Other outbuildings had been smashed or torn off their foundations.

Coconuts and breadfruit branches and tools littered the fields. Outdoor furniture had galloped down the street. Chickens and parrots were tossed about, and several goats met their fate.

Rachel Ruth felt guilty for not helping, but Iolana wouldn't hear of it. "Dr. Browning may not be available for a few days or even longer. I worry about John." Iolana held her briefly, "I will send you my oldest Auntie, don't worry that she doesn't have any English; she can't hear anyway."

Rachel Ruth smiled despite herself. She would rather sit and hold Grandpa's hands but knew he'd want her to take care of the cottage and yard as much as she was able. She owed it to Captain Walker.

Iolana's son, Kamalei, had already repaired the torn shutters. The village men found the outhouse unscathed and lying on its side under the banyan tree. It was now back in its rightful place with the door firmly reattached.

She looked through the back door and saw the men had hauled away the large branches and portions of the collapsed roof. Tomorrow she would deal with the smaller debris and try to replant some of the uprooted bushes.

There was a knock at the door. One of the Aunties held little Lani's hand. "Miss Ruth, did the pirate blow everything away?"

"It was a wicked pirate wind, but it has blown itself away."

"Will it come back?" The little girl's lip quivered, and Rachel Ruth felt her heart melt. She took Lani in her arms and whispered in her ear, "Not until you are as old as this Auntie."

The girl squealed and looked at the ancient Hawaiian woman, "That will be forever."

John felt old and worn out. This unprecedented storm had taken what little strength he had left and given him a chill. He knew his granddaughter would journey to Alaska alone.

He no longer had the strength to grip his pen, and he couldn't seem to focus for more than a minute or two. He needed to complete these letters to Robert and Elvira, and he longed to continue his journal writing. With every breath, he felt he was drowning.

He wished he had written a long letter to Rachel Ruth but was glad he had penned several short notes over the past months and tucked them into his journal.

He paused between each breath, then forced himself to take the next one. He motioned for Lani to get Miss Ruth.

"Come, Auntie. Let's go find Miss Ruth."

He saw understanding and pity in the old woman's eyes as she took the little girl's hand. Lani pulled away and patted the old man's unshaven cheek, "You're scratchy, Grandpa John, but I still love you."

TWENTY-SIX

Rachel Ruth knelt on the floor next to her grandfather. "It wasn't supposed to be like this. We were going to find him together. That was the dream."

"Let your dream fade so your destiny can shine." John struggled to sit but failed, and his head fell back on the pillows. His eyes glazed, and there was a pause between each sentence he spoke.

"Finding my father is a good thing. Losing you is horrible. Surely God agrees?"

John closed his eyes, "Trust Him always."

"I'm trying, Grandpa," She struggled but couldn't hold back her tears.

"He holds your destiny."

"And my dream?"

"Destiny...more important." He gasped the words one at a time. The sweat plastered his hair to his forehead. His face, tinged with grey, turned toward her.

She placed her fingers on his lips. "It's okay, Grandpa, don't try to talk."

Her eyes glistened, and her tears dropped. He tried to grasp her hand, but it fell back. She held it with both of hers.

"I will always picture you in the saddle, your big Stetson shading your eyes. The cattle before you, your horse underneath you. Oh, Grandpa, I'm going to miss you so."

"Your destiny…" Tears gathered in the corners of his eyes.

She wiped them away with her thumb. "Just think, you'll be with Mama and my sister and brothers. Will you tell them stories about the ranch, Grandpa? Stories about me?"

His eyes told her he would carry out her request. He took a deep breath and let it out slowly. Its fragrance came from beyond, sweeter than any Texas wildflowers.

Sometime later, Kamalei crossed the lanai with a pitcher of pineapple juice. Rachel Ruth met him near the hammock, "He's gone, Kamalei."

The pitcher slipped from his hands, and he lost all color. He took a step toward her, arms outstretched, then stopped. His awkward attempt to comfort broke her. She threw herself into his arms and wept. Once her weeping subsided, Kamalei said, "I will get my mother."

"Don't leave me. Not yet." The red-blotchy face beseeched him.

"Are you all right?"

"No."

He took her hand. "I've heard him pray that God's Great Son would be close to you always. It is your destiny."

At the word destiny, she drew her handkerchief out of the vast pocket of her Hawaiian muumuu and scrubbed her face.

"Thank you. I treasure you."

"And I treasured Grandpa John. So many times, he talked of my destiny."

"Destiny?"

"To walk in the ways of the great King. My dream is to be a great chef, but if it is my destiny, I do not know."

She squeezed his hand and said, "Get your mother, please."

Rachel Ruth, restless after the funeral, walked past the school and beyond the Townsend sugar plantation. Only when she felt like collapsing did she turn back.

Kamalei approached in his cart, "I thought you would walk all the way to the mountains."

"Were you following me?"

He handed her a jug of mango juice, dipped a pail into the small barrel of water in the back of the cart, and gave his little donkey a drink. "Mama sent me."

As they headed back to town, Kamalei said, "Tell me about Grandpa John's heaven."

She put her arm around his shoulder and hugged him tightly. "Did anyone ever tell you how wise you are, Kamalei?"

"Me? What did I say?"

"Your question caused me to focus on the glories of heaven where Grandpa is. I grieve for myself." She could not control her tears.

He pulled on the reins to slow the animal, "Tell me."

Rachel Ruth waved to Kamalei, then entered the quiet cottage and wandered from room to room. She sat on the lanai and stared at the hammock, too restless to pray.

She started toward Iolana's house, then stopped and leaned

against the banyan tree. The large gash from the broken branch mirrored the wound in her heart.

She slid to her knees, her back up against the tree, and spoke aloud, "I know how hard it has been on him these past few months, and I'm glad he's breathing heaven's pure air, but I can't bear it. I'm so alone."

Rachel Ruth scrunched her handkerchief in her hand. "Oh, Grandpa, I want my Daddy!" She burst into tears again.

She sat under the banyan tree throughout the day. Mid-afternoon, Iolana brought her a pot of tea, a jug of pineapple juice, and the macadamia scones she loved. The Hawaiian woman quietly spread a bright-colored cloth on the ground next to the grieving young woman and left her offering. Rachel Ruth didn't notice, and the offering remained untouched.

The children crept close, one by one, throughout the day. Some left a flower or a drawing. Some patted her cheek or held her hand for a moment. Two ate the scones then ran away. Again, the desolate young woman remained unaware.

As the sun fell below the horizon, Lani climbed into the grieving woman's lap. Absently, her's arms circled the child. After a time, she glanced and saw silent tears, zigzag down plump, brown cheeks. It caused Rachel Ruth's tears to fall afresh.

Through her pain, Rachel Ruth whispered, "I remember when I was a little girl just like you. Grandpa John rode up to the ranch house on his big horse, leading the sweetest little pinto pony. I named him Roger."

The sky darkened, the stars came out. Kamalei brought several torches and stuck them in the ground forming a circle around the pair. The light glowed on the young woman and the little girl.

Kamalei settled near the edge of the torch's light and kept watch. The people of the village came by ones and twos. They sat in the darkness and gazed at the grieving young woman. Some stayed a few moments; others stayed hours. All kept a silent vigil.

The sun crept over the mountains, and Rachel Ruth realized it was morning. She yawned, then smiled at Kamalei, who told her how John helped him understand scripture and helped him with his confusing algebra.

Iolana said, "My husband watched your grandfather on the ship. He noticed John's kindness, from the top officers down to the lowliest deckhands. He treated everyone with dignity and respect."

Several of the villagers shared their views of John. The Aunties jabbered and wiped their eyes. Iolana translated.

When Mr. Lewis, the minister, as well as teacher and principal, had officiated at the funeral, he said all the right things, but there was no life in his words. Rachel Ruth had blocked his voice as he droned on during the service.

However, with these people, she was comforted, although it did not lessen her pain. The Aunties cried and sang John's favorite Hawaiian lullaby.

Lani wriggled in Rachel Ruth's lap and woke up, "Why are you in my bedroom, Miss Ruth? Where's my breakfast? And why do the Aunties sing when I wake up?"

Iolana scooped up the little girl, "Come, we will make pineapple pancakes." She looked at Miss Ruth and said, "You have not slept well for two days, my dear."

"I didn't think I would ever sleep again, Iolana, but now…." She looked at the villagers drifting off to begin their day, touched Lani's hair, and tried to express her gratitude but interrupted herself with a huge yawn.

Iolana hugged her and said, "Sleep now."

Rachel Ruth sighed and strolled to Captain Walker's cottage. The following weeks were troublesome. Mr. Lewis came to offer his condolences and announced he was folding her class into his own. There was no need for her to teach at such a difficult time.

Rachel Ruth nearly dropped the teapot, "I will continue teaching until Sister Agnes returns. She is the one to decide about her class."

"Now listen to me, Miss Ruth. You are in no fit state."

"Nevertheless—"

"I will order the children into the building."

"I will be at the school on time. If my students are in the building, I will come and get them. I am duty-bound to fulfill my obligations to Sister Agnes." Rachel Ruth stood tall and stiff, although she quaked inside. She stared at Mr. Lewis as if he were a rattlesnake about to strike.

"Fine. Just fine. But don't blame me if you fall to pieces. Women!" He stalked out.

Rachel Ruth forced herself to be cordial and pleasant in front of the children. She kept her grief contained and covered until she was alone. After school, Kamalei asked for stories about Grandpa John as they walked home. His brothers and sisters begged for them, too. Little by little, day after day, her stories became more animated, and she told them from the heart and not by rote.

One day, she waved goodbye and turned toward the cottage. She blinked, then blinked again; Sister Agnes sat on a white wicker chair on the porch. The old woman held out her arms, and Rachel Ruth sank into them. They sat together in silence until the girl gave a slight snore.

Sister Agnes smiled, shook the young woman, and pushed the young woman to her feet. "Let's get you to bed for a proper sleep."

Rachel Ruth awoke to the smell of strong coffee and cinnamon rolls. She stumbled into the kitchen and saw Sister Agnes pulling a pan out of the oven. "I'm sorry. I haven't slept well since – "

"I've put my things in the small bedroom. I'm here until you tell me to go."

"Thank you. I'm sorry I couldn't keep my eyes open."

Sister Agnes piled the rolls onto a plate. She said, "Grief has its own timetable, but eventually, your body and your mind will return to a normal rhythm."

The younger woman nodded and turned her attention to the table. "For a moment, those smelled like my Aunt Elvira's cinnamon rolls."

"She gave me her recipe." The Sister answered calmly.

There was a thudding in the vicinity of Rachel Ruth's heart. "What?" She fell into the nearest chair, "What?"

Sister Agnes poured a cup of hot Kona coffee into Grandpa John's favorite mug and put a large roll on a small china plate. She placed them before Miss Ruth. "As long as you keep eating and drinking, I'll keep talking."

Rachel Ruth cupped the mug with her hands.

"Drink."

"Yes, ma'am." She raised the mug to her lips and took a tiny sip.

"I now consider Ellie one of my dearest friends."

Rachel Ruth's eyes bulged as Sister Agnes laughed out loud, "I can see you want me to begin with the middle of the story rather than the beginning."

"Yes. Hurry."

"Remember all those Sundays I came for dinner? While you bustled about the kitchen, John and I talked. Soon, I had your whole life story. I disagreed with him about keeping your aunt in the dark. Before I left, he had a change of heart. When I arrived in San Francisco, I wrote Ellie a letter on the mission's stationery. I'm familiar with small towns. There was no need to arouse anyone's curiosity. In the letter, I asked if I might speak at the church on my way back to Hawaii. That would be my official reason for coming— to raise funds for my work. I wrote that I had information about the Easter baby."

"Easter baby?" Rachel Ruth asked, remembering Grandpa murmuring something about an Easter baby on the day of the storm.

"You were born on Easter Sunday. John said Ellie would understand, and he left it to my discretion of what exactly to tell his sister. He was so afraid she would leave everything to come and comfort you."

Rachel Ruth nodded as she took another bite of the roll. "How is she? What did you tell her? How are Mary and Jed? What about the children and new babies? And my wranglers?" She set her coffee cup down and covered her face with her hands, "Oh, Sister Agnes, we have to tell her Grandpa's gone."

"No, dear," Sister Agnes came around the table and put her arms around the young woman, "Ellie knows her brother is no longer on this earth."

Sister Agnes pulled a hanky out of her apron pocket and handed it to the girl. "John knew how sick he was, but he refused to let the doctor tell you how little time he had left.   I knew John would be gone by the time I was to return. I spoke at your church and spent three days with Ellie. Mary has not regained her strength, and the three babies are already walking. Ellie is devoted to nursing Mary and teaching the older children. Ling Si has moved into one of the smaller bedrooms and has become chief cook and bottle washer."

"Did she mention Thomas?"

Sister Agnes snorted, "Ellie told me about your so-called fiancé. She sent him on the trail of the daughter of a British aristocrat who bought a lot of land in Wyoming. She hadn't seen him since."

Rachel Ruth nodded but didn't mention the episode with Thomas in San Francisco. Some things were better forgotten; besides, he must have heard that the Northern Star was lost at sea.

"I miss them all so much." Rachel Ruth put the hanky to good use.

"Wait here." Sister Agnes soon returned, her arms full. She laid a pile of newspapers, letters, and several small parcels on the table, "These are from Ellie and your ranch family. And these are envelopes with my mission's return address embossed on them. It's probably against some rule, but use them when you write home, at least while in Hawaii. That way, no one...."

"But you said Thomas was gone, and everyone thinks that we died at sea."

"The truth has a way of coming out, my dear, no matter how careful and secretive one tries to be."

Rachel Ruth shivered and reached for the stack of letters. Sister Agnes poured her another cup of coffee. "I'll give you some time to yourself, my dear. I'll take a little walk and let Mr. Lewis know I have returned."

"He's tried to take over your class several times just like you said he would. I stood my ground. He accused me of being rude and obnoxious."

"That's what he says to everyone who disagrees with him. Thanks for protecting my students."

"You'll be wanting your class back."

"I thought we could teach together until it's time for you to head north."

"I'd like that, but Mr. Lewis won't."

"You leave him to me."

TWENTY-SEVEN

Several weeks passed with the speed of a snail, and Rachel Ruth struggled to contain her sorrow. Some days the grief overcame her like a typhoon. Other days it was a deep pool she walked around and tried to avoid.

She carried that grief constantly, and when the day of her departure approached, her heart had the added burden of leaving the islanders she loved.

The whole village accompanied her to the docks of Honolulu.

"Here's your parasol, Iolana. I'm sure I won't need it in Alaska."

"You keep it to remember me."

"Me, too." Lani held her arms out, and Rachel Ruth scooped her up.

"I love you all."

"You are ohana, family." Kamalei blinked back tears.

Rachel Ruth gave him an extra hug, "You are the brother of my heart, and I will never forget you. I will send you my address as soon as I am settled, and we will be great letter friends."

He shuffled his feet and bit his lip, "It won't be the same."

"No, it won't, but it will be good. I promise."

Iolana handed her a basket of fruit. Her grandfather's journal nestled among the bananas and pineapples.

Rachel Ruth stood in the bow of the Aloha, Captain Walker's new steamship. It approached the coast of Baranof Island in the Alexander Archipelago of Southeast Alaska.

"Are you alright, Miss Rachel Ruth Merritt? You look rather melancholy."

She lifted sad eyes to him, "Grandpa thought it best I remain 'Miss Ruth' even in Alaska."

He clicked his heels together and gave her a courtly bow, "I stand corrected."

Her sea-green eyes darkened, "I'm serious, Captain." She explained the warning from Sister Agnes that Thomas may yet learn the truth about her and seek vengeance.

"I thought you said Elvira sent him after that British heiress."

Rachel Ruth sighed, "She did, and I still don't know how I feel about that. Poor girl. There is little chance of seeing Thomas again, but I am still the heiress to my father's share of the Con-Mer gold mine."

"Yes, you must be careful. Fortunately, there haven't been any big strikes in Alaska like the one in California in '49." He clicked his heels again, "Henceforth, you shall be Miss Ruth."

She leaned against the ship's rail as they approached Sitka Sound. "I have always thought of myself as Rachel Ruth, granddaughter of John Merritt, Texan," she choked.

He took a step closer to pull her into his arms; instead, he lay his hand over hers. The cold steel of the rail had chilled her fingers.

"From now on, I shall only think of myself as Miss Ruth." The word *orphan* hovered on her lips, but she did not utter it. *I am still the granddaughter of John Merritt, and more important, I am the daughter of the High King of Heaven.*

The ship rounded Japonski Island, and she saw the village of Sitka clinging to that small piece of land between the mountains and the water. Her eyes misted, and she blinked away the moisture. "I am Miss Ruth, Alaskan." She lifted her eyes to his then turned her gaze to the forested mountains that populated the island. "Look! There's a cross on that mountain."

"It's the way the cleft in the rock is configured. The snow doesn't often have a chance to melt. Some say when the Russians saw it, they carried a huge cross up there. Anyway, it's called Cross Mountain."

"The Lord is reminding me I'm not alone."

He rubbed the back of his neck and frowned. He wanted to be her consolation, her companion, but no, he had given up any thought of romance; her destiny was here, and he had cargo to deliver. He knew he would leave a piece of his heart with her. "Are you sure you won't come to Juneau? From what you've told me about the Connors, I'm sure they would love to have you."

Sunlight danced on her untamed hair as she shook her head. "I'd love to see them, but I must earn my keep and find my father."

"Perhaps they've heard from him."

"Maureen said his last known contact was with Reverend Jackson. I'll start there."

He patted his jacket pocket. "I'll give the Connors your letters.

"You've been a good friend to me, Captain. I treasure you."

"And I, you."

Captain Walker signaled his first mate, who returned with fresh cups of Kona coffee. She inhaled the steam rising from the dark liquid. "I can't believe the whole world doesn't drink this."

"It's good. But right now, the money's in sugar. I'm sure some planters will diversify in the future. Be glad I have a friend with a small coffee plantation."

"The other thing I can't believe is that you sold the China Doll."

He leaned against the rail and said, "The clippers are almost all gone now, replaced by these modern steamers."

"The Aloha seems like a high society matron compared to the Doll."

He drew his brows together, "What do you mean?"

"This steamship has a lounge with that glittering chandelier, embossed wallpaper, and velvet curtains. The staterooms are carpeted and outfitted with elegant furniture. I can't imagine the Doll dressed in such an ostentatious way."

"You might have to," he replied, "When Cook and Josiah bought the old girl, they told me they were going to rip out everything below decks and turn her into a luxury yacht."

"Oh, my goodness."

Captain Walker shuddered. "The Doll will be an exclusive fine dining establishment and available for inter-island charter."

"Are you talking about starched white linens and crystal goblets?"

The Captain nodded.

Miss Ruth shook her head. "The China Doll is entering the world of high and mighty society matrons, indeed."

She was silent for a moment, thinking of her time on the clipper and how she came to love the crew. "I miss them all, especially Silas."

"I wanted Old Skookum to come with me," the Captain said softly.

"I'm surprised he didn't."

"He said his old bones were more suited to the warmth of islands."

"What will he do? He's only ever known the sea."

Captain Walker threw back his head and laughed. "Cook had a Commodore's uniform made for the old sea dog. Everyone now refers to him as Commodore Silas. He lives on the Doll and regales the passengers with tales of the sea."

"I'm so happy for him."

"Me too. In fact, I almost envy him."

She saw his sadness at the end of an era. "I imagine Cook is looking forward to delighting the palates of all those tourists and rich businessmen."

"And Josiah is just as delighted to make them pay for it, especially the plantation owners when they entertain prospective investors."

"I hope his prices are outrageous. It's wrong how those beautiful islands and their lovely people are being exploited."

"It's the way of the world, I'm afraid."

"Only until the Lord returns."

The pilot cut the engines, and the Aloha glided into her berth. The drizzle stopped and the northern sun, low in the sky, burst through the gray, nearly blinding them.

Captain Walker took off his cap and shielded his eyes. "It will be like that, won't it? Dazzling? Blinding?"

"Why Captain Walker, you sound like you believe." She searched his face, hope in her eyes.

"How could I not, after knowing you and John for nearly two years."

"You mustn't believe it because we do!"

"Do not fret, Miss Ruth. I've been reading the Book every day. When I do, He whispers to me."

Tears sprang to her eyes. She laughed, spun around, and squealed with the joy of it, "Oh, Captain! If we were on the China

Doll, I believe I would scramble up the crow's nest and shout it to the world. You are now my very own brother in the Lord." She threw her arms around him and held on tight.

"Does this mean you will listen and do as I say like a good little sister?"

Her eyes crinkled at the corners, and she grinned back at him, "What do you think?"

TWENTY-EIGHT

Sitka, Alaska, known as the Paris of the Pacific when it was Russian America's capital, retained remnants of its past in its churches and native surnames. The culture and court of the Russians were long gone. Today Sitka was little more than a fishing village crawling with a few prospective gold-seekers and many more ne'er-do-wells.

Captain Walker escorted Miss Ruth through town, appalled at the brazen looks and coarse offers this dark-haired beauty received. His scowl deepened, and he lost his civility with each group of men they passed.

Miss Ruth, relieved she had reached her journey's end, tried to turn away from the pain of being here without her grandfather. She looked intently into every face they passed and listened intently to passers-by, hoping to hear the name Denver Dan. Some of the looks she received in return caused her to hastily lower her eyes.

She almost stumbled over a pile of cedar baskets stacked on the rough wooden sidewalk. She turned to the Captain, "Just look at the artistry and talents of these women." She knelt beside the Indian women who displayed cedar baskets and hats, carved spoons, and trinkets. As she picked up each basket and examined it, rough hands stroked her sun-drenched hair.

Captain Walker moved to intervene but stopped when Miss Ruth gave the tiniest shake of her head.

She held out her arms to a young mother. Miss Ruth hummed a lullaby as a raven-haired toddler was placed in her arms. The little one pulled a fist from his mouth and grabbed the errant strands cascading over Miss Ruth's shoulder; they all laughed as he tried to stuff them into his mouth.

Captain Walker drew in his breath. She looked like the Sitka Madonna, an icon he had encountered when still a cabin boy. He remembered he wanted to be a real ship's mate.

Such a long time ago, he thought. The crew had cut large blocks of ice from Swan Lake for shipment to San Francisco. He had insisted on working with them as they fitted the massive chunks into the hold. Inadvertently, he had been locked in overnight. They found him the following day, unconscious and blue.

When they could not revive him with hot rocks in his bunk, the first mate, an old Tlingit, carried him to St. Michael, the Archangel, Russian Orthodox church. Harlan's father, drowning his despair in a bottle, staggered behind.

They laid the boy on the polished wooden floor and wrapped him in furs. Above him, the Sitka Madonna, a precious icon sent from Russia, gazed down on him. The lay priest swung his incense pot and murmured healing prayers.

They couldn't control his shivering, so they carried him to the Bishop's house, further down Lincoln Street.

The house, built in the Russian style, had double walls insulated with tons of sand from nearby Crescent Bay. It was the best constructed and warmest building in Sitka.

Log after log went into the European furnace. There was a water reservoir attached to the stove. The Archbishop let boiling water flow through a network of pipes under the floor by turning several levers. Soon the first mate stripped off his jacket and shirt and the Archbishop, his cassock.

They filled pots with steaming water and threw in dried leaves; their medicinal value helped the boy. After several hours the Father threw in a handful of incense. He hoped the hot vapors would warm young Harlan from the inside.

The boy whimpered in the early morning hours, then screamed as the feeling returned to his hands and feet. When he opened his eyes, he looked for the Madonna.

Captain Walker returned to the present and thought Miss Ruth's gaze at this toddler similar to the Madonna's.

When the Aloha docked in Sitka, Captain Walker had sent a message to the Sitka Industrial School for Natives and asked Rev. Jackson to meet Miss Ruth at the town's only hotel. They secured a table in the tea room and waited for him.

They placed their order. The waiter returned with tea and scones in a few minutes—Miss Ruth reached for the white china teapot.

She handed him a dainty china cup and smiled at him, then jumped at the stern voice behind her. "That will not do!"

Miss Ruth and Captain Walker turned to see a thin man in a clerical collar and a rather stout woman, dressed in black, who scowled at their linked hands and said, "Since you are the only woman here, I assume you are Miss Ruth, and I tell you again it will not do."

Miss Ruth started to pull her hand out from Captain Walker's, but he increased his grip and winked at her.

The thwack across his knuckles by the woman's walking stick shocked him. He'd thrown men in the brig for less or knocked them sideways. He swallowed his anger as he saw the twinkle in Miss Ruth's eyes.

Easy for her; she's not the one with broken fingers. Nevertheless, he remembered his manners, rose to his feet, and said, "Mrs. Jackson."

"Certainly not." She ignored his outstretched hand and summoned the waiter with a wave of her cane. She ordered tea for herself and water with lemon for the little man who hovered behind her and tried to adjust her chair.

"We have no lemons, ma'am," the waiter stuttered.

"Then bring him a glass of water with a little salt in it."

The waiter hurried to do her bidding.

"Oh, do sit down, Gordon. You make me nervous."

The tea tray was set on the table with a thud, and the waiter retreated in relieved silence. The contentious middle-aged woman picked up a sugar cube and held it between her teeth. She slurped tea through the sugar. After draining her cup, she sighed. "It's so much better when experienced the Russian way. Now down to business."

"Excuse me, but who are you?" Captain Walker addressed the minister.

"Gordon Monroe."

"The Reverend, Mr. Gordon Monroe," his wife hissed and nudged him with her elbow.

"And this is my wife," he sighed.

"It's a pleasure to meet you, Mrs. Monroe," Miss Ruth said.

"Gordon," the older woman slapped her napkin at him.

Gordon Monroe's Adam's apple bobbed, and he tugged his clerical collar. "If you don't mind, it's the Reverend, Mrs. Gordon

Monroe." He swallowed and patted his wife's arm as she preened. "After all, she is such a help to me in my work, er, our work," he corrected himself before his wife hissed again.

"We stand corrected," Captain Walker said. Miss Ruth had warned him about religious people as opposed to authentic followers of God. It seemed to him these were very religious people.

Miss Ruth leaned across the table and smiled. "I'm pleased to meet you, Mrs. Reverend Monroe. But where are the Jacksons?"

"The Reverend comes before the Mrs. It's the most important." The Reverend Mrs. Monroe glanced at the teapot, then inclined her head toward the cup. Miss Ruth poured the hot amber liquid.

"Mrs. Jackson is accompanying her husband to Washington DC. You must be aware the Secretary of the Interior has appointed him the General Agent for Education for all of Alaska. So, of course, his wife is indispensable to his work."

"I didn't know."

The Reverend Mrs. eyes' glittered, "There will be church conferences and congressional meetings, forums, dinners. Hopefully, he can secure more government money as well as church donations for my work."

Gordon Monroe nervously cleared his throat as he picked up his water.

"Our work." The Reverend Mrs. Monroe corrected herself with a dark look toward her husband. "I will…"

The Reverend Mr. Monroe cleared his throat again.

"I mean, we will be in charge while they are gone." She glared at the little man. Unnoticed, he stared into the glass he held.

"I see. According to the letter I received from Reverend Jackson, I am to teach," Miss Ruth said.

"First, I have to verify your credentials and assess your references. Most importantly, I must evaluate your moral character before I can allow you into any of my classrooms."

The older woman glared at Captain Walker, who felt himself blush. Could the old sea hag perceive his true feelings for Miss Ruth? *They're honorable, and she has no cause to judge.* He was more comfortable navigating a storm at sea. He picked up his dainty teacup and tried to hide behind it.

"Of course," Miss Ruth agreed in a soothing voice.

"Humph." The sea hag glared at both of them.

"Now, see here," Captain Walker said, "I can attest to her good character."

"I think not," the Reverend Mrs. sniffed and allowed herself two more nagoonberry scones. "After all, she traveled on your ship without an appropriate chaperone or companion."

Captain Walker clenched his fists at his side then felt the heavy pressure of Miss Ruth's cowboy boot on his foot.

Miss Ruth smiled, "You mentioned evaluations, recommendations?"

"Yes, I have received a letter from Sister Agnes." The Reverend Mrs. Monroe pulled a sheaf of papers from her reticule.

"I just love her."

The Reverend Mrs. Monroe's brow furrowed, and she sniffed. "She was two years ahead of me at the academy in St. Louis. Articulate, intelligent, but she had some nontraditional ideas about educating children." She looked down her nose at Miss Ruth. "She trained you?"

"I learned so much from her."

The Reverend Mrs. Monroe held up her hand, "The children need to be civilized before they can be educated. That is my primary concern."

"But..."

This time, it was Captain Walker's heel on Miss Ruth's foot. She pressed her lips together and said nothing.

The Reverend Mrs. shuffled her papers aside, "Let's hope Sister Agnes' training didn't do too much damage."

Captain Walker's boot still rested on Miss Ruth's foot. She glared at him. He winked and mouthed, first, get the job.

"I have a letter of recommendation from Jack Connor, although he states he's never met you. Is that correct?"

"Yes, ma'am, but I know Mrs. Connor."

The Reverend Mrs. Monroe shuddered, "Dresses like a man half the time, packs a gun, hunts, and fishes, so unfeminine. Barbaric, really."

"But Maureen is..."

"Resist the temptation to change my mind." The Reverend Mrs. Monroe flashed her eyes at Miss Ruth, sighed, stuck the papers back into her reticule, and looked down her nose at the young woman once more. "One must maintain one's standards, especially when one is living beyond the edge of civilization. However, there is much work to do, and Mr. Connor is one of our biggest supporters." She frowned and slurped another cup of tea. "I suppose there is no help for it. I will take you on."

Another clearing of the throat.

"Oh, for goodness sake, Gordon, drink your water."

The little man picked up his glass. Captain Walker scowled. No need to wonder who commanded that ship.

"Captain Walker. You are no longer needed. You may go." The Reverend Mrs. Monroe ordered.

His face reddened. Nasty old sea hag. He felt the pressure of Miss Ruth's foot on his boot. Were they taking turns stepping on each other's toes? He looked, and she gave him a slight smile.

"Captain Walker, will you see to it that my things are delivered to the hotel this afternoon?" Miss Ruth said.

The Reverend Mrs. interrupted, "We have room at the school." She reached into her bag and handed her husband a list. "Gordon, be a dear and pick up these things for me. Don't forget to go to the post office."

The silent Reverend made his escape. He nodded at both Miss Ruth and the Captain.

"Come, Miss Ruth."

"Thank you, Reverend Mrs. Monroe, but I've already paid for the hotel room. I have some letters to write, and I want to explore. "

"Explore?" the older woman's eyebrows raised to the point of no return.

"Let's just say I have one or two things to settle before I give myself to your work."

"I insist you come with me now so I can get you some proper clothing. You cannot flounce around Sitka looking like that."

"Flounce?" Miss Ruth said.

"She looks lovely."

"Precisely my point, Captain." The Reverend Mrs. Monroe looked at him as if she wondered why he was still there. "As you well know, Captain, men have a low and base nature. Therefore, it would be prudent for Miss Ruth to dress in black as I do. There is no need to tempt the male of the species. On the contrary, it is our duty as godly women to do everything in our power to avoid it."

Captain Walker opened his mouth to tell the Reverend Mrs. Monroe she had succeeded. He couldn't imagine any man being tempted by her, no matter how base his nature.

Miss Ruth picked up a plate and said, "Scone, Captain?"

He looked into her eyes and saw she was not at all put out by the pompous old matron. He took two.

"I will be happy to accompany you right now, Reverend Mrs. Monroe."

Miss Ruth held out her hand, "Goodbye, Captain. Will you have my things delivered? Four o'clock?"

He nodded, and she gave his hand an extra squeeze. He sat back and watched as Miss Ruth followed the lady in black out of the hotel's dining room.

Every man in the place followed Miss Ruth with his eyes, their interest apparent on their faces. Captain Walker slumped in the chair and stuffed both scones in his mouth.

He didn't like the way the prospectors and gold seekers had looked at her on the rough wooden sidewalk. The men in the dining room were more discrete, but he was inclined to think the old sea hag was right; all men were base.

She arrived at the hotel lobby promptly at four, covered from neck to ankles in black.

"How do I look?" She pirouetted, and her waist-length hair fanned out like angel wings. Every time she moved, her hair captured the light. It glistened and shined with a life of its own. The men in the lobby followed her every move. He groaned. The

Reverend Mrs. Monroe's plan had failed.

"Charming." He gazed at those tresses.

"Every female who works at the mission school dresses this way. I'm sure I'll get used to it, although I feel like a nun. I have orders to cover or bind up my hair."

He took her arm and led her out of the hotel. "Walk with me to the Aloha. I have something for you."

"Why didn't you bring it with you? Is it too big to carry? Oh, what can it be?"

She was as excited as a child at Christmas. He hoped she'd like it, although he wouldn't. But now, he felt somewhat sympathetic to Mrs. Monroe. The Reverend Mrs. Monroe, he corrected himself.

Two more steamships had docked and unloaded several hundred gold-seekers, and the crowded sidewalks slowed their progress.

"I'm glad you haven't become a part of this gold fever nonsense." She pulled at her jacket's collar.

"Poor fellows. Most of them have scraped together every nickel just to get here, and most of them will return home empty-handed if they can even come up with the funds to return. It's placer gold."

"What's that?"

Gold that's found in creeks and streams. Lord help us if anyone finds the motherlode, that is, the main deposit in the ground."

"I feel so sorry for these men but still, it must be tempting for you to bring them here. Ticket prices are outrageous."

"I'll return to Seattle for mining tools and food, especially things like sugar and coffee, flour, and tins of milk, but I'll not bring men running after a false hope."

"When are you leaving?" She asked.

"I'll be around for a while. Will you miss me?"

"You know I will. I thought I would be out in the wild right away. Jack advised me to keep the search quiet, not even taking the Jacksons and now, I suppose, the Monroes into my confidence. I see the wisdom in his advice, but it makes the task harder."

"I have stops in several of the islands, mining camps, as well as towns. I will make inquiries discreetly, of course."

"Thank you, Captain, you've been a true friend." She looked toward the Aloha. "She does not have the graceful lines and beautiful silhouettes of the China Doll, but she's fine in her own way. She will serve you, and I think you will grow to love her."

He gazed at her intently and murmured, "I already do."

She coughed, looked away, then said, "Now, where's my present?"

He clicked his heels together and saluted. "Close your eyes. I'll fetch it from my cabin."

She felt the breeze from the Pacific on her face, cold and brisk, so different from the fragrant flower-scented air of the islands. She lifted her head and sniffed cedar, spruce, and fish. Lots of fish.

Captain Walker came up behind her, and she felt him squash something on her head. She opened her eyes and snatched it off her tresses. "Old Skookum's hat! I love it, but how did you end up with it?"

Captain Walker used Old Skookum's voice to reply. "'Cap'n, I ain't got much to my name, but I wants to give you a token so's you don't forget Old Skookum.' I told him he was like a grandfather to me, and I would always remember him, but he shook his head and said, 'That may be so. But I don't needs it no more, sir. I got me a commodore's hat. You hang Old Skookum's hat on your bedpost, and every night when you say your prayers like Miss Ruth says we ought, you, say one for Old Skookum. He needs 'em.'"

Miss Ruth, tears in her eyes, lifted the beat-up old hat to her face and sniffed. "I can almost smell him."

"I'm not surprised." Captain Walker took the smelly old hat and squashed it back on her head. "Now, the idea is to push all your hair up underneath."

"Oh. Hold it for a minute, please." She bent from the waist, throwing her long tresses forward. She grabbed, twisted, turned, and wound, then held out her hand for the cap. "How's that?"

Captain Walker winced at the sight of her. Horrible. He was almost glad. "There's no evidence of Miss Ruth left. Not one trace for any of the Reverend Mrs.'s base men to see."

"There's a bit of Miss Ruth left," she said, sticking her toes out from under her skirt.

"You kept your cowboy boots. Good for you!"

She laughed. "I'm grateful none of those old-lady clod-hoppers they called shoes fit me. They went through all the missionary barrels and couldn't find anything for my big feet."

"I'm glad that there's a little of Miss Ruth under those skirts."

Her eyes sparkled, and she looked around. They were alone on the deck. "There's more than that, Captain."

"I'm intrigued."

"Are you now?" Her eyes twinkled.

"Tell me." He ordered.

She looked around again, then lifted her skirt a few inches. Captain Walker saw she was wearing bright red petticoats.

"There's still more," she said.

"More?"

She lifted the red petticoats a tiny bit further, and he saw under everything she had on his white breeches.

He threw back his head and laughed, "Alaska, I hope you are ready for Miss Ruth."

PART
FOUR

TWENTY-NINE

"Good night," Margret Mary called as she shrugged into her coat, "Don't stay too long. Sadsack is waiting."

Sam finished the copy for the next issue with satisfaction. Even as he shuffled and proofread the galleys, Miss Ruth lingered in the back of his mind. What about the rest of her life in Alaska? The 'letters to the editor' gave him bits and pieces. They enlightened but did not satisfy.

"Sam, Sadsack is waiting."

"You said that already," Sam growled about that darn cat, stuck his hat on his head, and fished Firy Baas's letter out of the waste-basket. After rereading it, he slapped it against his leg and swore. So many unknowns. He dropped the letter into the wastebasket once again. *At least I have these papers*; he patted his vest pocket. *Bless your leg, Conner, you wily old coot.*

Earlier that afternoon, Connor's leg slipped to the floor. Sarah rushed to set it upright. It slid again. She wrestled with it for several minutes, "Chuck, I can't make Connor behave."

Chuck picked up the leg by its straps and slammed it into the corner. "There!"

"You broke it." Sarah's cry caught Sam's attention.

He hung up the phone and said, "I'll take care of it."

"Sorry, Boss," Chuck said as he laid the wooden leg on Sam's desk. Just above the knee hinge, he noticed a slight gap.

"Chuck, you might have just discovered the secret to why Connor bequeathed me his leg."

"Huh?"

Sam pulled several gold nuggets out of the leg's secret compartment. Sarah and Chuck admired them, then left for the day. Sam slipped a packet of papers into his vest pocket. He'd share them with the two want-to-be reporters later.

The packet, heavy in his pocket, screamed to be read. Sadsack's indignant meows echoed in his mind. *How had he come to be ruled by a cat?* Disgusted with himself, Sam turned out the lights, grabbed his hat, and hurried to the Sitka Café.

Anticipation overcame disgust as he thought about what the packet might contain. Even Sitka's ever-present drizzle did not faze him. He had imagined every possible scenario the papers might hold. He hoped he wouldn't be disappointed.

Sam settled near his fireplace and reached for the unopened packet. It had lain on the table and tempted Sam all through dinner. Fear of disappointment made him hesitate.

Sammy Boy, open it. Get this story written. Don't let Miss Ruth take over your life. As usual, Sadsack paced the hearth then settled at Sam's feet to nap.

A few moments later, Sam picked up the old tabby and explained his dilemma. The cat looked at him with unblinking eyes, then arched his back, meowed, and knocked the packet off the table. With a disdainful twitch of his tail, he jumped off Sam's lap and went to his favorite spot in the front windowsill.

288

Sam reached for the packet, wrapped in brown paper and tied with twine. There was a legal document from a law firm in Juneau instructing RRM how to access funds from the Con–Mer gold mine, a hostile letter from Wyatt Earp telling Miss Ruth to stop all that God-talk with his wife, and a small notebook written in code.

Four columns: a date, then a set of initials. It took a while to figure out the third column. Sam concluded they were Bible references when he saw J. 3:16. Even he knew that verse. He set the little book aside to review later.

He must've dozed. Sometime past midnight, Sam stood and stretched, "Come on, Sad, we better turn in. I'm taking Alice to church tomorrow. Like me, she hasn't been in years."

The cat opened one eye and blinked. "Don't look at me like that, you heathen feline. It would probably do you some good as well..."

Sadsack stood, twitched his tail, and headed for the hearth. He circled himself twice and settled close to the dying embers. "Fine," Sam muttered, "doesn't matter to me where you sleep."

Some hours later, Sadsack awoke and padded to the bedroom door. Sam thrashed from side to side as he had all week. This night, however, the blankets landed on the floor, and Sam moaned. Behind closed lids, his eyes fluttered to and fro.

Sadsack sighed if cats could sigh, then jumped on the bed. He crept near Sam and licked his face. He lay on the man's chest and heard his rapidly beating heart.

Sam's arms closed around the cat, and soon his heartbeat matched the cat's purr.

Sadsack slept, knowing he had done his job. He dreamt of mice and fish and Agrefena's fry bread. Sam's dreams were altogether different.

He woke in a foul mood, threw the covers back, stepped on Sad's tail, and yelled at the cat when he screeched. "What happened to Miss Ruth once she reached Sitka? Can you tell me that you lousy cat?"

Sadsack blinked, put his nose in the air, and walked off.

Sam cut himself shaving, swore, then rinsed his face and showered. Why couldn't he be satisfied with what he already knew? Sam shook his head in disgust. He wanted more, needed more, and by golly, he would get more. He was a newspaperman, after all.

THIRTY

Skin weathered with a bronze patina and eyes like soot, the older man stood in the Sentinel's doorway. Sam tried to see the room from this stranger's point of view.

A counter in front of Sam's desk provided a practical barrier. His customers liked to lean over it to place their ads or complain about a news story. Piled with out-of-state newspapers and those from the southeast, the counter caused most Sitkans to stand on tiptoe to see the editor hunched over his typewriter.

At well over six feet, this stranger did not need to stretch. Those charcoal eyes rested on Sam briefly then surveyed the room. Sam didn't recognize his tribe, definitely not Tlinkit or Haida, not even Yupik, perhaps North Coast Salish from British Colombia or Washington state.

The almost antique but still functional press took up a sizable portion of the room. Silent today, it would rattle and clang tomorrow when Sam ran the weekly issue.

Always faithful, always diligent, Margaret Mary dumped another load of slugs into the smelter and cranked up the temperature gauge. Then she sat at her beloved linotype, opposite a row of filing cabinets that lined the wall next to the window behind Sam's desk. A large oak table filled the center of the room.

Sam's desk matched the table, but no one ever saw its surface. Stacks of unfinished articles and files, half-eaten fry bread, and several overfilled ashtrays created a disorganized mess that only Sam could decipher.

He drew comfort from the ubiquitous chaos that was the Sentinel. It didn't matter what this stranger or anybody else thought. "Can I help you?" Sam asked.

"No."

Sam ripped the paper out of his typewriter, crumpled it, and tossed it toward the wastepaper basket. He missed. "Can I help you?" he asked again, pulling the cellophane wrapper off of a fresh cigar.

"I told you, no."

Had this fellow wandered away from the Pioneers' Home? Sam lit his cigar and, after a puff or two, said, "I'm Sam Mitchell, owner, and editor of this newspaper."

"I know who you are," the gentleman took a chair from the worktable, turned it toward Sam's desk, and sat.

"If I can't help you, why are you here?"

"To help you— if I so choose," he produced a letter from his vest and held it high. Sam couldn't see the address, but Miss Ruth's name was in the upper left-hand corner. Sam reached for it, but it was pulled away.

"I am Kamalei," the old man said.

Sam scratched his head then held out his hand, "Of course, the Hawaiian boy from John Merritt's Journal."

"Hardly a boy."

Sam grinned, "How old was Miss Ruth when you two met?"

"In my day, we didn't ask a woman her age, but I think she was nearly half a dozen years older than me. I was in my early teens." Kamalei uncrossed his legs and stared through the window behind Sam, smoky eyes lost in the past.

"Mr. Kamalei?"

It took a moment for the old Hawaiian to focus, "I was thinking about Miss Ruth. We've corresponded regularly since the 1890s, some 70 years."

"Did you keep all of her letters?" Sam couldn't keep the eagerness from his voice.

"When my last letter was returned, deceased, I called the See House. Even though she'd been in Nome for a few months, I knew Sitka was her home. The secretary sent me her obituary."

"And you brought me her letters?"

Pain flashed across Kamalei's face, and Sam cursed himself. He grabbed his hat and said, "Let me show you the places she loved. We'll have dinner at the Sitka Café, and the old-timers will tell their stories about Miss Ruth."

"I'd like that, Mr. Mitchell."

Sam slapped the old Hawaiian on the back, but gently, "Call me Sam. This is going to be the beginning of a beautiful friendship," he said in his best Humphrey Bogart voice.

Kamalei turned from his perusal of Lincoln Street, "I hope so, Sam, or I will go back to Hawaii with all the letters, hundreds of them." His solemn face and earnest eyes told Sam he meant it.

Sam stopped in the middle of the sidewalk, patted his pocket, and scowled. He'd left his cigars behind.

Everyone, except Sam, was amazed Miss Ruth had set sail for Alaska but ended up in Hawaii. They begged Kamalei for the story. After that, the old-timers told their stories with great enthusiasm and embellishment. Each old sourdough tried to outdo the others.

Kamalei surprised them when he said, "This is the way Miss Ruth told that story." His knowledge of Sitka and its inhabitants seemed up close and personal.

The week passed too quickly, and Sam still didn't have the letters.

"My plane leaves in half an hour, Sam. This is goodbye."

Sam opened his mouth to ask for the letters but heard himself say, "Thank you for coming. My time with you meant a lot."

Kamalei's weathered face lit up, "It meant a lot to me as well. I miss her dreadfully, but I'm proud of the way she met her destiny."

Sam nodded, threw his pencil down, and reached for another cigar, "Was your visit everything you hoped it would be?"

"It was. You were."

They looked at each other for a moment, then Kamalei said, "It's the end of an era."

Sam pointed to the cardboard box atop his filing cabinets, "See that? It's overflowing with letters to the editor, all of them about Miss Ruth. I've read them and still can't figure her out."

"Are you saying you didn't know her at all?"

Sam shrugged and spread his fingers, "She was just an old lady in black who roamed the streets of Sitka, helping people. Like a nun or something, at least, that's what I thought when I was a kid."

"And now?"

"I want to know what motivated her. Why were people so drawn to her?" Sam sighed, reached for a cigar, and changed his mind, "I wish I'd had some kind of meaningful encounter with her."

"But you did."

Images of Miss Ruth kaleidoscoped through Sam's mind, but no matter how he twisted and turned, he could not piece them together. He did see himself having dinner with Katharine Hepburn. Strange. Sam shook his head, "If I did, I'd remember."

"It was a traumatic time for you, Sam, your injury during basic training, and subsequent infections. You nearly died of sepsis. A few short weeks later, your father's illness and fatal heart attack. Caring for your mother, taking over the paper. So many traumatic events happening in such a short period can affect one's memory."

"How did you ... what do you mean?" Sam rubbed his offending leg. It had grown stronger over the years, and sometimes, he forgot about his old army injury. He remembered how he had moved through those weeks at a glacial pace, numb, frozen. Even his heart had iced over. Sam rubbed his chest and watched the old Hawaiian.

Kamalei opened the small suitcase he held on his lap. Inside, hundreds of letters, filed by decades, stood at attention. Kamalei shuffled through them, pulled one out, and handed it to Sam. "It wasn't in Sitka, and she wasn't wearing black."

Sam's fingers tingled like never before. An encounter with Miss Ruth, where? When? He wanted to snatch the letter but restrained himself, "Thank you, Kamalei, you've piqued my curiosity."

"I'm sure her words will refresh your memory." Sam, head bent over the letter, white knuckles grasping the pages, didn't respond.

"Goodbye, Sam. I'll leave you alone with Miss Ruth."

EPILOGUE

Sam scanned the letter. A young Sam Mitchell, Jr, and an old Miss Ruth were together in a hotel in Seattle, Washington? With Katharine Hepburn? Of course! The pieces fell into place even as the cigar fell out of his mouth. Sam's grip tightened on the letter, and his eyes moved across the pages even faster. His heart raced, and his fingers tingled, "Kamalei, why didn't you—"

The chair was empty. Miss Ruth's life-long friend had gone. Sam swore, grabbed his coat, and wondered if he could make it to the dock before Kamalei's floatplane took off.

He's only taken three steps when the open suitcase, filled with Miss Ruth's letters, in the middle of the worktable stopped him.

ALASKA'S MAMA

Book Three

Seattle, Washington 1942

Dear Kamalei,

I am at the Northwest Plaza Hotel in Seattle, Washington. As I mentioned in my last letter, I'm taking my father's remains back to the ranch. Let me tell you what happened last night.

I noticed a young man in the lobby, half-hidden by an ornate potted palm. He sat and lit a cigar.

"Foul thing, how can dad stand them?" He pulled his fedora low on his forehead and stretched his leg out. He seemed to be people watching. After recognizing him, I turned away lest he see me.

I looked down at my ivory silk shirt and chocolate rayon trousers—pure Hepburn. I'd been compared with that glamorous movie star several times. Excellent posture, better bone structure, and good skin, for which I give Sitka's misty weather full credit. Other than that, I don't see the resemblance. However, I did have her dark honey-colored hair once upon a time. My western boots peeked out from my trousers. No glamour there.

"It is you."

I turned to see the young man limp across the lobby, "Sammy Mitchell. I thought you were in the Army."

He cursed, "I got booted out. Busted my leg during training."

I lay my hand on his arm until he looked me in the eye. "They wouldn't discharge you for a simple break. It was more than that, wasn't it?"

"Busted in a couple of places. Infected. Sepsis. I spent several weeks in the station hospital at Fort Lewis." He swore, rubbed his leg, and said, "Sorry, Miss Ruth. Language."

"I've heard worse." I wanted to put him at ease.

"But you!" He indicated my clothes. "You don't look like yourself."

"You found out my secret, Sam, but let's not tell anybody back home."

"But why? You look good."

"For a woman of a certain age?"

He sputtered, red-faced.

"An old spinster?" I couldn't resist.

"I don't understand why you wear all that black in Alaska."

"In 1890, I met the Rev. Mrs. Monroe. Hence the black."

"Good grief! That was 50 years ago. What's the story?"

"I'll tell you, Sam, but it's off the record." Words no newspaper journalist wants to hear, but I knew Sam would honor those words.

"Tell me over dinner, Miss Ruth."

"Lovely. But only if we pool our ration cards."

"I have a condition of my own," he said, "you must wear what you have on. I'm taking a movie star out to dinner, not Sitka's lady in black."

We agreed to meet in the lobby in an hour. I exited the elevator wearing a camel color coat tied at the waist, a ridiculous hat with two pheasant feathers that jutted from the brim. Sam whistled, and heads turned.

I stopped midstride, struck a movie star pose, and threw Sam a kiss with pouty red lips. Bellhops tipped their caps, servicemen saluted, and older gentlemen smiled behind their newspapers.

Oh, Kam, young Sam blushed but took my arm and escorted me out of the hotel. We walked a few blocks to a quiet restaurant. The longer we walked, the more pronounced his limp. He grimaced a few times, but I knew better than to comment. I decided that after dinner, I would be a tired old lady who needed a taxi.

The restaurant specialized in seafood, but Sam and I ordered pot roast, mashed potatoes with gravy, and glazed carrots. Two inhabitants from a small town who didn't really know each other, but like all small-town folk, we thought we did.

"Tell me about the lady in black," Sam said.

I explained how the Rev. Mrs. Monroe thought it a woman's duty to protect men from their base natures. Sam's jaw dropped, he closed it abruptly, then said, "Surely, there is no need to continue."

"You mean now that I'm a bit over seventy and wrinkled and unable to tempt all you base and wicked men."

Sam stammered, "Yes, er, no."

"Maybe not now, but back in the day," I teased him.

"Well, it's not back in the day, and that get-up is so..." The word ugly hung in the air.

Finally, I took pity on the poor boy. "At first, it was a job requirement, then a habit, then a convenience. Whenever anyone in Sitka needed help, they looked for the lady in black."

"I agree you were easy to find. Everybody knew you."

"Really, Sam? Do you know me?" I felt my eyes twinkle but could see he took the question seriously.

He ate several bites of his pot roast while he thought, "No, Miss Ruth. I don't know you at all. But as you say, you're noticeable. That black get-up and all. And that hideous hat you always wore."

I laughed, "Don't disparage my hat, Sam. It was given to me decades ago by an ancient mariner."

"There's so much about you I don't know. For instance, why are you in Seattle?"

"There's not much you need to know, dear boy. Although, I once had a lovely nutmeg dress." I stared into the flame of the table's single candle.

"Nutmeg dress?"

I waved my fork at him and smiled, "It's at the bottom of the Pacific Ocean somewhere between San Francisco and Honolulu."

"What?"

"We've talked about me all through dinner. What about you? What are you going to do now that you're out of the Army?"

"I'm scrounging for ink and newsprint for dad until the next semester at the University starts."

Our bread pudding with maple walnut sauce arrived, and I kept Sam talking about his future. Degrees in journalism and writing, jobs at big-city newspapers, the desire to be an international correspondent, and writing the Great American Novel. I told him those were beautiful dreams.

"I'll make them all come true."

As we took a taxi back to the hotel, I said, "A college education is important to you, isn't it?"

"Of course, it's step one in achieving my dreams."

"I'm old enough to be your grandmother, so I'm going to be frank with you, Sam. If you want to be the best newspaperman in Alaska or even the world, go home. Learn from your father."

"But..."

"I'm not telling you what to do, of course, but the apartment above the Sentinel is empty. Live there. Whenever anyone comes into the Sentinel's office, listen. See how your father interviews and crafts the story, learn how he keeps his articles objective and only offers an opinion in his editorials. See how he lives with integrity. Sit at his feet, Sam."

"But..."

"Notice how he respects people and offers those with opposing views an opportunity to express their opinions. If I were you, Sam, I'd go home."

"Yes, but..."

"Live and breathe the newspaper. Let your dad mentor you."

I could see Sam was confused and trying to digest everything I said. He didn't know how to respond to my suggestions. But I knew he was thinking.

"My train leaves in the morning," I yawned.

"Where are you going?"

"I'm tired, Sam."

"I'll meet you for breakfast," he said.

I smiled but didn't answer.

Once in my room, I made several phone calls before retiring for the night. Sam Jr. wouldn't see me at breakfast, but he would find a bus ticket to Boeing Field. I knew Sam Sr. would fuss, but he would relish the time with his son. The Doc and I were the only ones in town that knew Sam Sr. only had a few months to live.

Sam raced through the letter then reread it slowly. He leaned back in his chair, put his feet on his desk, and closed his eyes. He clasped his hands behind his head and let the memories wash over him.

After saying good night to Miss Ruth, he had put the key in the lock of his hotel room and admonished himself for being a lousy reporter. If his time with Miss Ruth had been an interview, all he could say was she looked like a movie star and had a nutmeg dress at the bottom of the Pacific Ocean. He didn't even know what nutmeg was, a color, a style, or a type of fabric? He had always thought it was a spice.

Sam's feet slammed to the floor. He reached for the coffee pot. Empty. He leaned his forehead on the window and sighed. He hadn't finished college, never worked for a big-city newspaper or been a foreign correspondent, and no, he hadn't written the Great American novel.

Sam reached for the telephone. He needed to talk to Alice. She'd help him figure this out—something Miss Ruth said about dreams and destiny.

CPSIA information can be obtained
at www.ICGtesting.com
Printed in the USA
FSHW011956101221
86862FS